A Line
To Kill

Also by Anthony Horowitz

The House of Silk
Moriarty
Trigger Mortis
Magpie Murders
The Word is Murder
Forever and a Day
The Sentence is Death
Moonflower Murders

ANTHONY HOROWITZ

A Line To Kill

PENGUIN BOOKS

PENGUIN BOOKS

UK | USA | Canada | Ireland | Australia
India | New Zealand | South Africa

Penguin Books is part of the Penguin Random House group of companies
whose addresses can be found at global.penguinrandomhouse.com

First published by Century in 2021
Published in Penguin Books 2022
001

Copyright © Anthony Horowitz, 2021

The moral right of the author has been asserted

Map © Darren Bennett at DKB Creative Ltd (www.dkbcreative.com)

Typeset in 12.77/16.15 pt Fournier MT
by Integra Software Services Pvt. Ltd, Pondicherry

Printed and bound in Great Britain by Clays Ltd, Elcograf S.p.A.

The authorised representative in the EEA is Penguin Random House Ireland,
Morrison Chambers, 32 Nassau Street, Dublin D02 YH68

A CIP catalogue record for this book is available from the British Library

ISBN: 978–1–52–915696–6
ISBN: 978–1–52–915697–3 (export)

www.greenpenguin.co.uk

MIX
Paper from
responsible sources
FSC® C018179

Penguin Random House is committed to a
sustainable future for our business, our readers
and our planet. This book is made from Forest
Stewardship Council® certified paper.

For Jill, who took me
back to Alderney.
With love.

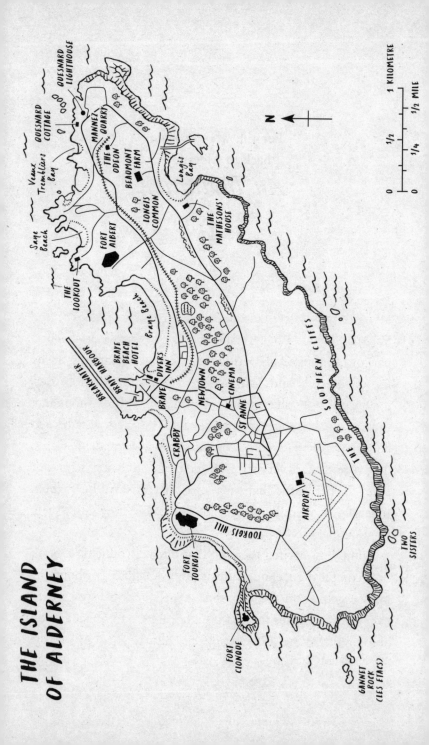

THE ISLAND OF ALDERNEY

QUESNARD LIGHTHOUSE
QUESNARD COTTAGE
Veaux Trembliers Bay
MANNEZ QUARRY
THE ODEON
BEAUMONT FARM
Saye Beach
LONGIS COMMON
Longis Bay
FORT ALBERT
THE MATHESONS' HOUSE
THE LOOKOUT
Braye Bay
BRAYE BEACH HOTEL
DIVERS INN
BREAKWATER
BRAYE HARBOUR
BRAYE
NEWTOWN
CINEMA
CRABBY
ST ANNE
THE SOUTHERN CLIFFS
TOURGIS HILL
AIRPORT
FORT TOURGIS
TWO SISTERS
FORT CLONQUE
GANNET ROCK (LES ETACS)

N

0   ¼   ½   ¾   1 MILE
0   ½   1 KILOMETRE

1

An Invitation

My publishers, Penguin Random House, have offices on the Vauxhall Bridge Road, the other side of Victoria. It's an odd part of London. Considering that the River Thames is at the top of the road and Tate Britain is just around the corner, it's surprisingly shabby and unattractive, full of shops that look as if they should have gone out of business decades ago and blocks of flats with too many windows and no views. The road itself is very straight and unusually wide, with four lanes for the traffic that rushes past like dust in the vacuum tube of a hoover. There are side streets but they don't seem to go anywhere.

I don't get invited there all that often. Producing a book is a complicated enough business, I suppose, without the author getting in the way, but actually I look forward to every visit. It takes me about eight months to finish a book and in that time I'm completely alone. It's one of the paradoxes of being a writer that, physically, there's not a huge difference between the debut novelist and the international best-seller: they're each stuck in a room with a laptop, too many Jaffa Cakes and nobody to talk to. I once worked out that I've probably written more than ten million words in my lifetime. I'm surrounded by silence but at the same time I'm drowning in words and it hardly ever leaves me, that sense of disconnection.

But everything changes the moment I walk through the swing doors with the famous Penguin logo up above. I'm always amazed how many people work there and how young so many of them seem to be. Like writing, publishing is a vocation as much as a career and I get a sense of a shared enthusiasm that would be hard to find in most other businesses. Everyone in the building, no matter what their level, loves books – which has to be a good start. But what do they all do? It embarrasses me how little I know about the actual process of publishing. What's the difference between a proofreader and a copy editor, for example, and why can't one person do both jobs? Where does marketing end and publicity begin?

I suppose it doesn't matter. This is where it all happens, where a thought that may have begun years ago in the bath or on a walk is finally turned into reality. When people talk about the 'dream factory' they usually mean Hollywood, but for me it will always be Vauxhall Bridge Road.

So I was happy to find myself there on a bright June morning, three months before my new novel, *The Word is*

Murder, was due to be published. I'd been asked to come in by my editor, Graham Lucas, who'd surprised me with a telephone call.

'Are you busy?' he had asked. 'We'd like to talk about publicity.' As always, he went straight to the point.

Advance proofs of the book had already gone out and apparently they had been well received – not that I'd have heard otherwise. Publishers are brilliant at keeping bad news from authors.

'What time?' I asked.

'Could you manage Tuesday? Eleven o'clock?' There was a pause and then: 'We also want to meet Hawthorne.'

'Oh.' I should have expected it, but even so I was surprised. 'Why?'

'We think he could make a serious difference to the sales. After all, he is the co-author.'

'No, he's not. He didn't write any of it!'

'It's his story. We see you as a team.'

'Actually, we're not that close.'

'I think the public will be very interested in him. I mean … in the two of you together. Will you talk to him?'

'Well, I can ask him.'

'Eleven o'clock.' Graham hung up.

I was more than a little deflated as I put the phone down. It was true that the book had been Hawthorne's idea. He was an ex-detective who worked as a consultant to the police, helping them with their more complicated investigations.

He'd first approached me to write about him while he was looking into the murder of a wealthy widow in west London, but I'd been reluctant from the start, mainly because I preferred to make up my own stories. Certainly, I had never thought of the book as a collaboration and I wasn't sure I liked the idea of sharing the stage – any stage – with him.

But the more I thought about it, the more I realised that this could play to my advantage. I had now followed Hawthorne on two investigations – and 'follow' is the right word. Although I was meant to be his biographer, he never actually explained anything of what he was doing and seemed to enjoy keeping me several steps behind him, always in the dark. I had missed every clue that had led him to Diana Cowper's killer and because of my own stupidity I had almost got killed myself. I had made even more catastrophic errors on our next case, the murder of a divorce lawyer in Hampstead, and I wasn't entirely sure I could write the second book without making myself look ridiculous.

Well, here was a chance to redress the balance. If Graham Lucas was going to have his way, Hawthorne would have to enter my world: talks, signing sessions, interviews, festivals. It would all be new to him, but I'd been doing it for thirty years. Just for once, I'd have the upper hand.

I had met him that same afternoon. As always, we sat outside a coffee shop so that he could smoke.

'It's eleven o'clock next Tuesday,' I said. 'It'll only be half an hour. They just want to meet you and talk about marketing. When the book comes out, you're going to have to gear yourself up for joint appearances at some of the major festivals.'

He'd looked doubtful. 'What festivals?'

'Edinburgh. Cheltenham. Hay-on-Wye. All of them!' I knew what mattered most to Hawthorne so I spelled it out for him. 'Look, it's very simple. The more books we sell, the more money you'll make. But that means getting out there. Do you realise that there are about a hundred and seventy thousand books published in the UK every year? And crime fiction is the most popular genre of all.'

'Fiction?' He scowled at me.

'It doesn't matter how they describe the book. We just have to make sure it's noticed.'

'You're the author. You go to the meeting!'

'Why do you have to be so bloody uncooperative all the time? Do you have any idea how difficult it is writing these books?'

'Why? I do all the work.'

'Yes. But it's a full-time job making you look sympathetic.'

He looked at me with eyes that were suddenly offended. I'd seen it before, that occasional flicker of vulnerability, reminding me that he was human after all. Separated from his wife and son, living alone in an empty flat, making Airfix models in some echo of a doubtless traumatic childhood, Hawthorne wasn't as tough as he pretended to be, and perhaps the most annoying thing about him was that, no matter how difficult he was, I still found him intriguing. I wanted to know more about him. When I sat down to write, I was as interested in him as in the mysteries he set out to solve.

'I didn't mean that,' I said. 'I just need you to come to the publishers. It's really not that much to ask. Promise me that you will.'

'Half an hour?'

'Eleven o'clock.'

'All right. I'll be there.'

But he wasn't.

I waited for him for ten minutes in the reception area until finally an intern arrived to take me up to a conference room on the fifth floor. I hoped I might find him there but when the door was opened and I was shown into a square, windowless room, there was no sign of him. Instead, four people sat waiting behind a long table with coffee, tea and 'family favourite' biscuits on a plate. They looked at me, then past me. They were unable to hide their disappointment.

My editor had been sitting at the head of the table but he got up when he saw me. 'Where's Hawthorne?' His first words.

'I thought he'd already be here,' I said. 'He's probably on his way.'

'I assumed you'd come together.'

Of course, he was right. We should have. 'No,' I said. 'We agreed to meet here.'

Graham looked at his watch. It was quarter past eleven. 'Well, let's give him a few minutes. Take a seat ...'

I still wasn't sure what to make of Graham Lucas, who had only recently joined Penguin Random House as a senior editor. He was about fifty, slim, with a narrow beard that made him look like an academic. He was wearing a blazer and a roll-neck sweater that might have been cashmere and certainly looked expensive. He had a gold band on his fourth finger and as I sat next to him I detected the flowery scent of an aftershave that didn't really suit him. I think it's fair to say that we had a close relationship, but only professionally. I had no idea where he lived, what he did in his spare time, if he had children and – more importantly – if those children read my books. When we were together, all he ever talked about was work.

'Have you started the second book?' he asked now.

'Oh yes. It's going very well,' I lied. I'd already told my agent, Hilda Starke, that I would probably be late delivering.

She had arrived ahead of me but she hadn't got up when I came in. She was sitting at the table, puffing on one of those vape devices, which was odd because I could never remember her actually smoking cigarettes. I knew she didn't want to be here. She was sitting, bare-armed, with her jacket on the back of her seat, sipping coffee. She had left a bright red crescent moon on the side of the cup.

In a moment of weakness and without telling her, I had agreed to split the royalties fifty-fifty with Hawthorne. That was what he had demanded from the start and I'd found myself acquiescing without consulting her first. Hilda was also annoyed because she had failed to persuade Hawthorne to let her represent him. They had spoken once on the telephone but she hadn't met him yet. So she was stuck with ten per cent of fifty per cent ... which was a much smaller percentage than she would have liked.

Tamara Moore, sitting opposite her, was Random House's publicity director: a very intense and formidable woman in her early thirties. There was a laptop open in front of her and her eyes hadn't left the screen. At the same time, she was holding a fountain pen, twisting it in her slender fingers as if it were a weapon. Briefly, she looked up. 'How are you, Anthony?' she asked. Before I had a chance to answer, she introduced me to her assistant. 'This is Trish. She's just started.'

'Hello.' Trish was about twenty years old and looked tired. She had a wide face with frizzy hair and an easy smile. 'It's a pleasure to meet you. I loved *High Fidelity*.'

'That's the next meeting,' Tamara muttered, quietly.

'Oh.' Trish fell silent.

We spent the next ten minutes chatting but it was hard enough to make even the smallest of small talk when all of us were waiting for the door to open and for Hawthorne to appear. Inwardly, I was seething that he had let me down. Finally, Graham turned to me, tight-lipped. 'Well, there's not a great deal to talk about without Daniel here, but we might as well get started.'

'Nobody ever calls him Daniel,' I said. 'He's just Hawthorne.' This was met with silence. 'I could try his mobile, if you like,' I added.

'I don't see that there's any point.'

'I have a lunch at twelve thirty,' Hilda said, giving me no support at all.

'We'll get you a cab,' Graham said. 'Where to?'

Hilda hesitated. 'Weymouth Street.'

'I'll see to it.' Trish tapped the instructions into her iPad.

Tamara pressed a button on her keypad and an image of the front cover of *The Word is Murder* flashed onto a screen. It was a signal for the business to begin.

'We can at least talk about our strategy for the end of the year,' Graham said. 'When can we expect proofs, Tamara?'

'They'll be in at the end of the month,' Tamara replied. 'We'll be sending fifty copies to bloggers, reviewers and key customers.'

'Radio? TV?'

'We're just making approaches ...'

'What about festivals?' I asked. 'There's Edinburgh, Harrogate next month, Norwich ...' Everyone looked at me blankly so I went on: 'I enjoy doing festivals. And if you really want people to meet Hawthorne, surely that's the best way?'

Hilda sniffed and blew out a cloud of steam that instantly disappeared. 'There's no point doing festivals until you've got the book to sell,' she said, stating the obvious.

'And we can't make any decisions about that until we've actually met Hawthorne,' Graham added, pointedly.

Right then, to my enormous relief, the door opened and the intern came back in, followed by Hawthorne himself. From his blank look and slightly quizzical smile, he seemed to have no idea that he was thirty minutes late. He was wearing his usual combination of black suit, white shirt and narrow tie. I suddenly felt shabby in my sweatshirt and jeans.

'This is Mr Hawthorne,' the intern announced. She turned to Graham. 'Your wife has called twice. She says it's important.'

'I can tell her you're in a meeting,' Trish said, glancing from Tamara to Graham as if she needed a consensus.

'No, it's all right,' Graham said. 'Tell her I'll speak to her later.' He got to his feet as the intern left. 'How do you do, Mr Hawthorne. It's very good to meet you.'

'The pleasure's mine.' Perhaps Hawthorne was sincere. Perhaps he was being sarcastic. It was impossible to tell. The two men shook hands. 'It's been a while since I was in this part of town,' he went on. 'I once busted a brothel in Causton Street – half a dozen sex workers from Eastern Europe. Just round the corner from the Lithuanian embassy. Maybe that's where they got their visas ... not that we ever made a connection.'

'How fascinating.' Graham was immediately hooked. 'It's extraordinary what can happen right on your doorstep without you even knowing.'

'Maybe Tony will write about it one day.'

'Tony?'

'That's me,' I said. 'You're half an hour late.'

Hawthorne looked astonished. 'You told me half past eleven.'

'No. I said eleven o'clock.'

'I'm sorry, Tony, mate. You definitely said half past. I never forget a time or a place.' He tapped the side of his head for the benefit of everyone in the room. 'It's my training.'

'Well, there's no need to worry about it,' Graham said, giving me a sour look. 'Let me introduce Tamara, who's the head of publicity, and her assistant, Trish.'

Hawthorne shook hands with both of them, although I noticed that there was something about Tamara that puzzled him. 'And you must be the amazing Hilda Starke,' he said, sitting down next to her. 'It's great to meet you at last. Tony never stops talking about you.'

Hilda was not easily charmed but right then she was beaming. Hawthorne had this effect on people. I have described him often enough: his slight build, short hair cut to the scalp around the ears, the oddly searching eyes. But perhaps I have never done justice to the way he could dominate a room from the moment he entered it. He had an extraordinary presence that could be saturnine, threatening or magnetic, depending on his mood.

'Congratulations on the book,' Hilda said. Just like my editor, she seemed to have forgotten that I was the one who had written it.

11

'I haven't read it yet,' Hawthorne said.

'Oh?'

'There's not much point reading a whodunnit when you know the end.'

It was a line that he must have prepared in advance. At any event, they all nodded in agreement.

'Aren't you worried about how Tony has portrayed you?' Graham asked.

'It doesn't bother me at all. So long as the book sells.'

Graham turned to me. 'I hope you're not going to write about us,' he said. He made it sound like a joke.

I smiled. 'Of course not.'

Trish offered Hawthorne coffee, which he accepted, and a biscuit, which he refused. He never ate in front of other people if he could avoid it. For the next five minutes Graham talked about the publishing business, current trends, his hopes for the book. 'It's never easy launching a new series,' he said. 'But we have a reasonable shot at the best-seller lists. There's not much else coming out this September. There's a new Stephen King, and of course Dan Brown will grab the top spot, but we deliberately chose a quiet week. How would you feel about doing some radio?'

The question was directed at Hawthorne, not me.

'I'm OK with radio,' Hawthorne said.

'Have you had any experience of the media?'

'Only *Crimewatch*.'

Tamara, who didn't smile often, smiled at that. 'We've approached *Front Row* and *Saturday Live*,' she said, speaking to the room. 'They're waiting to read the book, but the fact that Mr Hawthorne actually worked for the police is definitely of interest.'

'And the fact that he got thrown out?' I was tempted to ask.

Tamara went back to her laptop. 'We were just talking about literary festivals,' she went on. 'And as a matter of fact, we have had an invitation.'

My ears pricked up at that. The truth is that literary festivals are the best thing in a writer's life. To start with, they get you out of the house, out of your room. You meet people: readers and writers. You get to visit beautiful cities like Oxford, Cambridge, Cheltenham, Bath. Better still, you might find yourself being whisked abroad – to Sydney, Sri Lanka, Dubai or Berlin. There's even a literary festival on board *Queen Mary 2*.

'So where is it?' I asked.

'It's in Alderney. They're launching a new festival in August and they'd love to have you both.'

'Alderney?' I muttered.

'It's a Channel Island,' Hawthorne told me, unhelpfully.

'I know where it is. I didn't know they had a literary festival.'

'Actually, they have two.' Tamara tapped a few buttons, projecting the home page onto the main screen. It read: THE

13

ALDERNEY LITERARY TRUST — SUMMER FESTIVAL.
SPONSORED BY SPIN-THE-WHEEL.COM.

'Who are Spin-the-wheel?' I asked.

'They're an online casino.' She obviously shared none of my misgivings. 'Alderney is a world centre for online gambling. Spin-the-wheel sponsor a lot of things on the island.' She brought up another page. 'They have a historical fiction festival in March and it was so successful that they've decided to start another. So far they've invited Elizabeth Lovell, Marc Bellamy, George Elkin, Anne Cleary and ...' she leaned closer to the screen ' ... Maïssa Lamar.'

'I haven't heard of any of them,' I said.

'Marc Bellamy is on television,' Graham said.

'He's a cook,' Hilda added. 'He has a morning show on ITV2.'

'I'm not sure,' I began, although I was aware that I was the only person in the room who was being negative. 'Alderney's a tiny place, isn't it? It seems a very long way to go ...'

'It's forty minutes direct from Southampton,' Hawthorne said.

'Yes, but—' I stopped myself. *Hawthorne* had said that? I looked at him a second time.

'I'm up for it,' Hawthorne continued cheerfully as I stared at him in disbelief. 'I've always had it in mind to visit Alderney,' he went on. 'It's an interesting place. Occupied in the war.'

'But as Hilda just said, we won't have any books to sell,' I reminded everyone. 'So what's the point?'

'It could be helpful with pre-orders,' Graham said. 'Hilda?'

Hilda looked up from her mobile, which was lying on the table beside her. 'I can't see any harm in it. We can look at it as a dry run, a chance for Anthony and Mr Hawthorne to get their act together. And if the whole thing is a complete disaster, there's nothing lost.'

'Well, that's a vote of confidence,' I said.

'Then it's agreed.' Graham was in a hurry to move on. 'What else?'

We spent the rest of the meeting talking about Hawthorne. Or rather, Hawthorne talked about himself, focusing mainly on his work. It was interesting how he could say so much and give away so little, something that had infuriated me when I was writing my first book about him. Shortly after twelve, Trish reminded Graham that he had another meeting and told Hilda that her car had arrived to take her to Weymouth Street. Tamara closed her laptop and Hilda drew on her jacket, heading off for her lunch. It was clear to me that all four of them were delighted with Hawthorne. It was smiles all round as they shook hands.

Even the security guard was beaming at him as we exited onto Vauxhall Bridge Road together. I was in a bad mood and didn't bother to disguise it.

'What's the matter, mate?' Hawthorne took out a cigarette and lit it.

I jerked a thumb back at the office. 'They were all over you! What was that all about?'

'They seem like a nice bunch of people.' Hawthorne contemplated the end of his cigarette. 'And maybe you should be a bit more charitable. Your agent's obviously worried about the results of her test.'

'What test? What are you talking about?'

'And Graham's getting a divorce from his wife.'

'He never said anything about that!'

'He didn't need to. He's having an affair with the publicity director, and that girl, Trish, knows all about it. It can't be too easy for her. Being a new mother and worried about her job.'

He did this every time we went anywhere new together and I knew he was baiting me. But I refused to play his game.

'I don't want to go to Alderney,' I said. I began to walk back to Pimlico tube station. I didn't care if he followed me or not.

'Why not?'

'Because the book won't be out. There's no point!'

'I'll see you there, then.'

The crime rate on Alderney is so low that it doesn't even have a police force of its own. There is a police station with one sergeant, two constables and two special constables – but all of them have been seconded from the neighbouring island of Guernsey and there isn't very much for them to do. Recent offences included 'taking a conveyance without authority' and speeding. It's unclear if they were connected.

If you ignore the atrocities committed when the island was occupied during the Second World War, throughout the entire history of the place there hasn't been a single murder.

That was about to change.

2

Departures

Six weeks later, Hawthorne and I met at Waterloo Station on our way down to Southampton Parkway. It was the second time we had travelled together – the year before, we'd taken the train up to Yorkshire – and he was carrying the same suitcase with no wheels on the bottom that he had probably taken with him to school. He reminded me a little of those children evacuated during the war. He had the same lost quality.

It seemed to me that he was unusually cheerful. By now I knew him a little better, which is to say that although I had learned very little about his past history, I could at least gauge his moods, and I was certain he was keeping something from me. He'd made it clear that he had no interest in literary festivals, but he'd leapt at the chance to go to Alderney. He'd even known how long it would take to fly. He was clearly up to something – but what?

The train left on time and he took out a paperback copy of *The Little Stranger* by Sarah Waters. It's a fantastic ghost story and I guessed he was reading it for his book club. We weren't even out of the station before I'd tackled him. I couldn't wait any longer.

'All right,' I said. 'You're going to have to explain it to me.'

He looked up. 'What?'

'You know perfectly well. All that stuff you said at Random House. You told me that Graham was having an affair with Tamara, that Trish knew about it, that she'd just had a baby and that she was worried she was going to lose her job. You also said Hilda was waiting for test results.'

'That was weeks ago, mate!' He looked at me a little sadly. 'Have you been obsessing about it?'

'Not obsessing, but I would like to know.'

'You were in the room, Tony. You should have seen it all too.'

'Do me a favour, will you, and just tell me ...'

Hawthorne considered for a moment, then turned his book face down and laid it on the table. 'Well, let's start with Hilda. Did you see her arm?'

'She was wearing a jacket.'

'No. She'd taken it off and put it on the back of her chair. There was a little patch where the skin was a bit paler, right over the median cubital vein.'

'I don't even know what that is.'

'It's where the needle goes in for a blood test. She was nervous about something. She was puffing on that vape and she kept on looking at her phone like she was waiting for a text … maybe from the doctor. And that lunch of hers in Weymouth Street. I bet she made it up. It's just round the corner from Harley Street, which is where all the doctors hang out.'

'What about Graham and Tamara?'

'The intern – Trish – told him his wife had called twice and that it was important, but he didn't even ask what it was about. It was obviously something that had been going on for a while. Trish didn't even wait for him to make a decision, which is a bit strange when you think about it. *I can tell her you're in a meeting*, she said. But she was looking at Tamara when she said it.'

'That doesn't necessarily mean they are having an affair.'

'Didn't you smell Tamara's perfume?'

'No. I didn't.'

'Well, I did. And it was all over Graham.'

I nodded slowly. I had thought it was aftershave. 'What about Trish?' I asked. 'I didn't notice any prams or baby photos.'

'Well, something's been keeping her awake at night. She looked worn out. And there was a stain on her left shoulder. The only way it could have got there was from burping a baby. You only have to do that until they're seven or eight months old, so why hasn't she taken the full twelve months' maternity leave? She probably hasn't been at the company that long … she's only about twenty. I imagine she got pregnant quite soon after she arrived and although they can't fire her, she's come back as soon as she can because she's worried about her future.'

He made it all sound so easy but of course that was the whole point. He liked to remind me who was in charge. We didn't talk again after that. Hawthorne went back to his book and I took out my iPad and went through my emails.

From the moment my publishers had accepted the invitation to Alderney, I'd been bombarded with messages from the festival organiser, Judith Matheson, and already I was nervous about meeting her. She seemed quite formidable, chasing me for information and following up if she hadn't had a reply within a few hours. Would I be happy staying at the Braye Beach Hotel? Did I have any special dietary requirements? Did I want to rent a car? Would I be signing books? She had arranged the train and air tickets, booked my hotel room and made sure I had access to an up-to-date festival programme. Only the evening before, she had emailed me to say that a few of the invited writers would be congregating at the airport and that I should join them at the Globe Bar and Kitchen just before security and passport control. *You'll have time for a pub platter and a pint before you take off*, she wrote, even suggesting what I might eat.

I swiped across to the festival website and checked out the writers with whom I was going to be spending a long weekend.

*

Marc Bellamy

Marc needs no introduction, as anyone who has watched his Sunday-morning cookery show – *Lovely Grub* – on ITV2 will know. Marc isn't afraid of ruffling feathers with his no-nonsense approach to cuisine that he promises will be anything but 'haute'. Old-school favourites including steak pie, fried chicken and sticky toffee pudding are on the menu, and in the words of his catchphrase, 'It's cobblers to calories'. He'll be celebrating the launch of the *Lovely Grub Cookbook* on Alderney and has agreed to prepare a Saturday-night supper for the festival organisers and guests.

Elizabeth Lovell

Born with diabetes, Elizabeth Lovell lost her eyesight just before her thirtieth birthday. At the same time, though, she realised that she had developed a unique gift to 'see' into the spirit world and to hear voices from the other side. Her story was told in her auto-biography, *Blind Sight*, which sold two hundred thousand copies online. This was followed by *Second Sight* and her new book, *Dark Sight*, which continues her story. Elizabeth lives in Jersey with her husband, Sid. She gives talks all over the world and we are delighted to welcome her back to Alderney.

George Elkin

George Elkin is Alderney's most famous historical writer. He was born and brought up in Crabby, where he still lives with his wife, and brilliantly described the German occupation of the Channel Islands 1940–45 in his first book, *The German Occupation of the Channel Islands 1940–45*. This was followed by *Operation Green Arrow* and *The Atlantic Wall*, both of which were shortlisted for the Wolfson History Prize. He will be talking about his next book, which examines the construction and running of the four labour camps built by the Germans on Alderney during the war. He is also a keen birdwatcher and amateur artist.

Anne Cleary

Is there anyone under the age of ten who hasn't followed the adventures of Bill and Kitty Flashbang, the super-powered twins? Bill can fly, Kitty turns invisible and together they have saved the world from ghosts, dragons, mad robots and alien invaders! A former nurse, prison visitor and founder of the charity Books Behind Bars, Anne Cleary will be talking about the inspiration behind her work and there will be a special children's session at (appropriately!) St Anne's School, where young people will be encouraged to develop their writing and drawing skills.

Daniel Hawthorne and Anthony Horowitz

You may have read detective stories, but here's your chance to meet a real detective. Daniel Hawthorne spent many years working at Scotland Yard in London before he became a private investigator. He works now as a special consultant on many high-level investigations, the most recent of which has been turned into a book (published later this year) by best-selling author Anthony Horowitz, who also wrote the Alex Rider series. The two of them will be interviewed by States member Colin Matheson and there will be plenty of opportunity for questions from audience members with a taste for true crime.

Maïssa Lamar

We are very pleased to welcome Maïssa Lamar from France, where she has won great acclaim as a performance poet. Born and educated in Rouen, she writes and performs in Cauchois, a dialect spoken in the east of Normandy, which has led Le Monde newspaper to describe her as 'a leading light in the revival of Cauchois culture'. Maïssa is also an associate professor at the University of Caen and has published three collections of poetry. Her performance at the Alderney Summer Festival will be conducted partly in English and partly in French with English subtitles.

So that was it: an unhealthy chef, a blind psychic, a war historian, a children's author, a French performance poet, Hawthorne and me. Not quite the magnificent seven, I couldn't help thinking.

There were just three of them waiting for us at the Globe Bar and Kitchen when we finally arrived. George Elkin was presumably at his home in Crabby. Elizabeth Lovell and her husband, Sid, would be crossing by ferry from Jersey. But Marc Bellamy, Anne Cleary and Maïssa Lamar were already sitting round a table, chatting away as if they were old friends. It turned out that they had all come down on the train ahead of us, along with another young woman, Kathryn Harris, who introduced herself as Marc's assistant.

It's an incredible thought that there are more than three hundred and fifty literary festivals in the UK. I've been to many of them. Appledore, Birmingham, Canterbury, Durham ... It wouldn't be difficult to travel the entire country from north to south, working my way through the alphabet at the same time. I think there's something wonderful and reassuring about the idea that in the rush of modern life people will still come together and sit for an hour in a theatre, a gymnasium or a giant tent simply out of a love of books and reading. There's a sort of innocence about it. Everyone is so friendly and I've hardly ever met a writer – no matter how big a best-seller – who's been difficult or stand-offish; on the contrary, many of them have become good friends.

Somehow, when I think of literary festivals (even Hay-on-Wye, where this is very rarely the case), the sun is always shining.

But I was uneasy as I sat down with the other guests in Southampton. Our surroundings didn't help. The Globe was an airport restaurant serving airport food. That was the best and the worst I could say of it. The bright lighting and open-plan configuration, spilling into the terminal, didn't help. We might just as well have been eating on the runway. Also, I still wasn't convinced that Alderney was a good idea. With just six weeks' notice, I hadn't had time to prepare and I still had no idea how Hawthorne would perform when he was put on a stage. Talking about Alex Rider or Sherlock Holmes was one thing, but having the subject of the book sitting next to me would put me well outside my comfort zone. And it wasn't just that. As I joined Marc, Anne and Maïssa at the table, I immediately felt that I was an outsider, that I didn't belong.

I recognised Marc Bellamy from the photograph I had seen of him on the festival website. He was even wearing the same clothes: a bottle-green jacket, an open-neck shirt with a double-sized collar and a pair of half-rim reading glasses on a gold chain around his neck. Like many of the television celebrities I had met, he was actually much smaller than he seemed on the screen and although his teeth were very white and his tan very deep, he didn't look well. Perhaps that went with his persona. After all, he specialised in

27

unhealthy food, railing against vegans, vegetarians and pescatarians ('the worst of the lot ... there's something fishy about them') on his show. Of course, he was only having fun, delivering his jokey insults with an exaggerated Yorkshire accent accompanied by a nudge and a wink. He was overweight – chubby rather than fat. His hair was swept back in waves with a little silver around the ears. His nose was a road map of broken blood vessels. I guessed he was about forty.

'How do!' he exclaimed when he saw us. This was actually one of his catchphrases. 'You must be Anthony and Mr Hawthorne – or is it the other way round! Hawthorne and Mr Anthony.' He laughed at that. 'Don't be shy. Come and sit down. I'm Marc. This is my assistant, Kathryn. That's Maïssa, with two dots over the *i*, and I'm talking about her name, not her forehead. And Anne Cleary – rhymes with dreary, but she's anything but! Scribblers United ... that's what we should call ourselves. You've got time for a bite. Plane's on the runway, but they haven't finished winding the elastic.' He laughed again. 'Anyway, we've already ordered. What are you going to have?'

We took our places. Hawthorne asked for a glass of water. I went for a Diet Coke.

'Horrible stuff! Be a good girl and put in the order, will you?' These last words were addressed to his assistant. She was in her early twenties, slim and a little awkward, hiding behind a pair of glasses that covered most of her face. She had been staring at her knees, trying not to be noticed, but now she stood up and hurried away. 'She's a good girl,' Marc continued, speaking in a stage whisper, shielding his mouth with the back of his hand. 'Only just joined me. Loves my show, which is just as well. It means I don't have to pay her so much!'

There was something quite desperate about the way he talked, as if he was always searching for the next joke just around the corner but was afraid he would never quite reach it. I didn't quite have Hawthorne's deductive skills, but I'd have bet good money that he was a lonely man, probably on his own, possibly divorced.

'Hello, Anthony.' Anne Cleary greeted me as if she knew me and I felt my heart sink as although I knew who she was, I couldn't remember having met her.

'How nice to see you again, Anne,' I said.

She scowled but without malice. 'You've forgotten me,' she said, reproachfully. 'You and I had a long chat at the Walker Books summer party a couple of years ago. That was when they were still having summer parties.'

'You're with Walker Books?' I asked. They published Alex Rider.

'Not really. I just did a one-off for them. It was a picture book. *Hedgehogs Don't Grow on Trees*.'

'I ate a hedgehog once,' Marc chipped in. 'Roasted in clay. It was actually quite nice. Served up by a couple of Gypsies.'

'I think you mean travellers,' Anne said.

'They can travel all they like, love. They're still gyppos to me!'

Anne turned back to me. 'We talked about politics … Tony Blair.'

'Of course. Yes. I remember.'

'I bet you don't, but never mind. Names and faces! I'm exactly the same. That's the trouble with being a writer. You spend so much time on your own and then suddenly you get fifty people at once. But it *is* nice to see you again. I thought that when I saw your name on the programme.'

I remembered her now. We'd talked for about half an hour and we'd even swapped email addresses, although that had come to nothing. She had told me that she lived in Oxford, that her husband was an artist – a portrait painter – and that she had two grown-up children, one of them at university in Bristol. She was one of those Labour voters who had become disillusioned after the Iraq War and had gone on to join the Green Party. I was annoyed with myself and examined her more carefully, determined that I wouldn't make the same mistake the next time we met. My first thought was that she reminded me of my mother, or somebody's mother. There was something warm, even protective, about her. The round face, the black hair cut in a sensible way, not hiding the flecks of grey, the comfortable clothes.

'What are you doing in Alderney?' I asked. What I meant was, why had she accepted the invitation?

'I don't get invited to many festivals these days. Not like you, I'm sure. Are you talking about Alex Rider?'

'No. I've written a detective story ...' I gestured at Hawthorne on the other side of the table ' ... about him.'

'I'm Daniel Hawthorne.' I had never heard him offer up his first name and, looking at him, I saw that he was actually in awe. 'I'm pleased to meet you, Anne,' he went on. 'My son used to love your books. He's a bit old for them now, but when he was seven and eight I used to read them to him.'

'Thank you!' She smiled.

'*Flashbang Trouble*. That was the one with the pirates. It used to make us laugh out loud.'

'Oh! That's one of my favourites.'

'Mine too.'

This was a completely different Hawthorne to the one I knew and it only reminded me how distant I still was from him. I had met his ex-wife once, very briefly. I had never seen his son. But he and Anne had bonded immediately and as the two of them continued to chat, I turned to the performance poet, Maïssa Lamar, and asked: 'How come you're here at the airport?'

'I am here to take the plane to Alderney!' She picked each word carefully with a French accent that was several coats thick. Or maybe it was Cauchois. She was looking at me as if I had said something ridiculous.

'I just meant ... I thought you'd be coming from France.'

'Last night I give a performance in London. At the Red Lion theatre in Camden.'

I made a mental note to check her out on YouTube. Maïssa was, at a guess, French Algerian. She was wearing a heavily embroidered jacket and loose-fitting trousers. There was a silver stud in the side of her nose and large silver rings on most of her fingers. Her hair had been cut so short that the scalp showed through, although there was enough left to leave a zigzag pattern on one side. Her large, bright eyes lingered on me briefly before dismissing me. There are contemporary poets whose work I love: Jackie Kay, Sia Figiel, Harry Baker. But I already had a feeling that Maïssa and I weren't going to get on.

A waiter arrived with the food and drink: coffee, tea, a salad and a plate of meze, a green tea for Maïssa and a pint of bitter for Marc. We had an hour until the plane left. A few moments later, Marc's assistant, Kathryn, came back with the extra drinks that Hawthorne and I had ordered. She added the bill to the one left behind by the waiter and sat down next to me.

'So you are a writer also?' Maïssa asked Hawthorne.

'Not me, love.' Hawthorne smiled. 'I'm a detective.'

'Really?' Her eyes widened. 'What is it then that you do in Alderney?'

'He's written a book about me.' Hawthorne pointed in my direction. 'He's going to talk about it. I'm just here for the ride.'

'What do you investigate?' Anne asked.

'I'm more of a consultant now. Financial crime. Domestic crime. Murder.' He let that last word hang in the air. 'Whatever comes my way.'

There was a long silence. It struck me that all four of our new acquaintances were a little nervous.

Marc changed the subject. 'I've never got the point of smashed avocado,' he announced, scooping some onto his pitta bread. 'And I hate that word – *smashed*. That's typical bloody Jamie Oliver. Just slice it up with a sharp knife and that's good enough for me. Preferably with some crispy bacon on the side.'

'Would you like me to get you some, Marc?' Kathryn asked. She had ordered a cheese salad for herself.

'No, no. What I'm saying is, it's just another of these modern food fads. When I was growing up, nobody had heard of the bloody things. They used to call them avocado pears and no-one knew what to do with them. There was one geezer even tried to serve them with custard!'

We continued to chat, weighing each other up. Marc ate most of the meze, including all the avocado, and finished his beer. Finally, Kathryn looked at her watch. 'It's forty minutes until the plane leaves,' she said. 'Perhaps we ought to go through.'

I picked up the two bills. 'I'll get this.' I wasn't sure why I said that and immediately regretted it. Was I really so desperate to ingratiate myself with the group? The bill came to £29. I left three £10 notes and, as I had no change, £5 for the tip.

We all got up. Maïssa disappeared in the direction of the toilets while the rest of us queued up at passport control. That was at least one benefit of Southampton. The airport was small and the queues were short.

As I reached the security area, I felt in my pocket, instinctively knowing that something was missing. I was right. I had taken out my telephone to check for messages and must have left it on the table. I'm afraid it's something I do more and more. 'I'll be back in a minute,' I told Hawthorne.

He was still chatting to Anne, his new best friend, and barely nodded.

I hurried back to the restaurant.

As I approached the table, I heard someone speaking rapidly in French and, looking around, I spotted Maïssa outside the toilet, talking to a younger man in a black leather jacket. She had her back to me so she didn't know I was there. The man was in his twenties with long, greasy blond hair, a thin face and a wispy moustache. I suppose he could have been someone she had met by chance but there was something about their body language and the tone of her voice that told me otherwise. Maïssa was speaking very quickly, annoyed about something. I might have been wrong, but I thought I heard her mention the name Hawthorne.

She looked at her watch, then hurried across to passport control. The younger man waited a few moments, then followed. That was odd too. It was as if they didn't want to be seen together.

It didn't take me long to find my phone, which had lodged itself under a serviette. I picked it up and was about to leave when I noticed something else. It was very strange. The waiter hadn't yet cleared the table. The dirty dishes and glasses were still in place, as was the £30 I'd paid.

But the tip that I'd left, the £5 note, had gone.

3

BAN NAB

Marc Bellamy did have a point with his joke about elastic bands. The plane that took us to Alderney was one of the smallest I'd ever flown in – with two propellers and a single wing that could have been strapped across the top. It actually reminded me of one of the models Hawthorne liked to make. He and I were sitting shoulder to shoulder, which made me uncomfortable in all sorts of different ways. He was the sort of person who liked to keep his distance. When I was working with him, we were either confronting each other face to face or I was two steps behind him. A sideways view was strangely unnerving.

The plane rolled along the runway at Southampton Airport, then stopped for a minute as if the pilot was questioning one last time whether it could actually fly. Then the engines rose in pitch and we belted along, finally lurching upwards, our stomachs doing the same but in the opposite direction. We were in the air! We broke through the clouds and buzzed along for about thirty minutes, the clatter of the propellers making any conversation almost impossible. We dipped down again and Alderney came into view. With my face pressed against the window, I looked down on what – from this height – seemed to be a largely uninhabited strip of rock, one that might have been cast loose, floating on the sea. We banked and curved round for landing and I saw a black and white striped lighthouse perched at one end, white froth crashing far below. Hawthorne had been reading his book throughout the journey but as he folded it away, I couldn't resist it any longer. I leaned over and shouted: 'Why did you want to come here?' It was hard to make myself heard against the sound of the engines.

'What?'

'In London. You said you'd always wanted to visit Alderney.'

He shrugged. 'It looks nice.'

In all the time I had known him, I don't think I'd ever heard Hawthorne shout. It wasn't just that he was even-tempered. If I had recorded his delivery and transferred it to a screen like a heart monitor, he would have been a flatliner. This was the first time he had raised his voice.

He was also lying to me. I was sure of it. He was here for a reason and it had nothing to do with the scenery.

We landed and then bumped and jolted our way across another stretch of grey concrete. The pilot turned off the engines and I watched the propellers as they slowed down, becoming visible moments before they stopped. The door opened and we uncurled ourselves and made our way out. The airport's one terminal was right in front of us, managing to look both temporary and thirty years out of date at the same time. We went in through a swing door that led into a small, irregular space: the arrivals hall. *Serving the island since 1968* read the sign behind an empty check-in desk. Nothing much seemed to have changed.

There was a solid, rather aristocratic woman in her forties waiting for us beside a weighing machine. She was wearing a tweed jacket, scarf and pearl necklace and was carrying a sign with ALDERNEY LIT FEST typed in large letters. It had to be Judith Matheson. She had seemed nervous, standing alone in the empty arrivals hall, but her expression quickly turned into surprise and pleasure that we had actually arrived. She had spent a lot of time working on her make-up and even more on her hair, a wispy chestnut, which had been beaten into submission. She was someone for whom appearances mattered. That was the appearance she gave.

'Hello! Hello!' she announced as we gathered around her. 'I'm Judith. Welcome to Alderney! I hope you all had a good flight. Plane nicely on time, I see. The luggage will come through in a minute and if anyone needs to use the loo, it's just over there.'

'How far is it to the hotel?' Anne asked. She seemed a little breathless and I wondered if the flight had made her nervous.

'Ten minutes.' Judith managed to sound enthusiastic about everything. 'Nothing's very far on Alderney. There's a mini-bus outside. Can I get you anything? A glass of water? The luggage really should be here very soon.'

'No. I'm all right, thank you.'

I heard the revving of a motor, a vehicle approaching, and a minute later the first cases appeared, pushed through a rubber curtain onto a silver table. I noticed Kathryn Harris, who had taken her own case but was also struggling with two more belonging to her employer and I went over to her.

'Can I help you with one of those?' I asked.

'Oh – thank you.'

I grabbed one and almost dislocated my shoulder with the weight of it. I was surprised it had even been allowed on the plane.

'It's full of Marc's new book,' Kathryn explained. 'I'm sure it'll be a lot lighter going home!'

Marc Bellamy had overheard us. 'It had bloody well better be!' he chimed in.

My own case came through, then Hawthorne's. Somehow we all managed to disentangle ourselves and made our way out into a car park with taxis and car rentals on one side and a white minibus with *Alderney Tours* painted above the slid-ing door waiting just ahead.

Judith continued to fuss over us as we stowed our luggage and climbed into the bus, then finally we were away. Alderney is just three miles long and a mile and a half wide and my first impression as we drove down the very straight lane from the airport was how little of it seemed to be developed. There were no buildings nearby. Fields stretched out in every direction, the grass strangely etiolated, as if the colour had been swept away by the strong breezes coming in from the sea. We came to a main road – not that there was anything very main about it – and at the junction I noticed a makeshift wooden sign hammered into the soft earth with a message in red paint. BAN NAB. I wondered what it meant. I wasn't even sure what language it was in.

We turned left and passed a farm but no other houses or any buildings, continuing downhill until we came to what looked like a Napoleonic fortress, very square and solid, with tall, evenly spaced windows and a great many chimneys. It was sitting on its own in a swathe of grass with the sea behind. In front of me, Kathryn Harris held her iPhone against the window and took several shots. My eyes were drawn to an old oil drum standing abandoned in the grass with, once again, the same words – BAN NAB – painted in red letters on the side. I wanted to ask Judith Matheson about them but she was deep in conversation with Anne Cleary.

'Did you see that?' I asked Hawthorne.

'What?'

'Ban Nab. It's a palindrome.' He said nothing, so I added: 'It reads the same forwards and backwards.'

'Do geese see God?' Hawthorne asked.

'I'm sorry?'

Hawthorne shook his head and looked away.

The road curved round and we came to an ill-defined harbour area that should have been prettier than it was: too much of it had been given over to retail and industry. Even the chip shop could have been more welcoming, standing on its own, surrounded by concrete. But things changed when we reached the Braye Beach Hotel on the other side. This was a traditional seaside hotel, the sort of place I associated with childhood, long summers and ice-cream cones. It was made up of several houses joined together with a conservatory at one end and a long veranda looking out over the sand. The bus pulled up in front of the main entrance and Judith led us inside, talking all the while.

'If you want to collect your keys and pop up to your rooms, you've got free time until the first session at half past four this afternoon. That's George Elkin talking about the occupation of Alderney at the town hall on the rue de l'Église, which opens the festival. You'll find welcome packs with maps and telephone numbers on your beds. We thought we'd all meet for a drink straight afterwards at The Divers Inn, which is right next door. Dinner tonight is at the hotel. If anyone has any questions they can call me any time.'

The inside of the hotel was bright and airy, with comfortable, mismatched furniture, dried flowers, ships made out of driftwood and books on shelves.

'I'll see you later, Tony.' Hawthorne started to move towards the reception desk.

'What are you going to do?' I asked.

'Drop my stuff ... then I thought I'd go out and explore.'

'Do you want me to come with you?'

'No. It's all right, mate. I'll catch you later.'

The other writers had piled in behind Hawthorne, eager to get to their rooms, and I wandered into the lounge, where I found myself alone with Judith. For a few moments we looked at each other uncertainly. I decided to break the ice. 'So this is your first festival,' I said.

'Yes. We have the history festival earlier in the year, but this is our first crack at general fiction and poetry.'

'Have you always lived in Alderney?'

'Absolutely. It's a wonderful place. I hope you're going to find time to explore. You can't miss Gannet Rock, and there are some lovely walks. We have a house at Les Rochers.'

'We?'

'My husband, Colin. Plus three children, although two of them are away at boarding school. Actually, you'll meet Colin tomorrow. He's agreed to interview you and Mr Hawthorne.' I already knew this from the programme. 'I had to twist his arm,' she went on. 'He would have preferred to do George Elkin.'

I wasn't sure how to take this so I smiled and said: 'Can I ask you something?'

'Of course.'

43

'What does "Ban Nab" mean?' Her face fell and she seemed unwilling to answer. 'It's just that I saw it on a couple of signs ...' I tried to make light of it.

She fumbled with her pearl necklace, at the same time giving me a nervous smile. 'I rather hoped you wouldn't notice. It's actually quite upsetting. Alderney is normally such a close community, but I'm afraid this has completely divided us.'

I waited for her to go on. She did so reluctantly.

'NAB stands for Normandy-Alderney-Britain. A company called Électricité du Nord is planning to build an electric power line to connect France and the UK and they want to route it through Alderney. It will actually benefit the island in lots of different ways. Cheaper electricity, cheaper internet and a payment of £60,000 a year, but naturally there are some people who've decided it's a bad idea and they've been demonstrating against it.'

'Why?'

She sighed. 'This is rather difficult for me, Anthony,' she explained. 'Colin happens to be the head of the NAB committee that's been deciding on the issue and so he's very much at the centre of things. He's a barrister and he's also a member of the States, which is what we call the island's parliament, so he was a natural choice. But it has rather put our heads above the parapet.'

'And he's for it?'

'There was a vote and although it wasn't unanimous, the committee recommended that we go ahead.'

'So what is it that people don't like?'

'Well, there are some issues.' Judith Matheson glanced around her as if afraid of being overheard. 'There will be some local disruption and there are questions over which route the line will take. Generally speaking, people in Alderney are hostile to change.' As she spoke, she had been looking past my shoulder in the direction of the balcony and suddenly she beamed. 'Oh, look! Mrs Lovell and her husband are sitting in the sunshine. Why don't you let me introduce you? She's a remarkable woman.'

It was obvious that Judith had grabbed the moment to change the conversation, but before I knew it, I found myself being ushered outside.

The terrace ran the full length of the hotel with really lovely views. There was a stretch of wild grass, then a sandy beach curving round in a bay and, on the other side, a rocky hillside with another ancient fort holding its own against an enemy that had never actually bothered to arrive. The only invaders were the clouds, a puffy armada floating across an otherwise blue sky.

Elizabeth Lovell and her husband were finishing their lunch at a table about halfway along. Elizabeth had her back to the sea, but then she had no interest in the view: her round black glasses spoke for themselves and in the loudest possible way, making it difficult to focus on any other part of her face, which was perhaps just as well. She did not look healthy, with pale skin, sunken cheeks, grey lips. Her black hair was tightly permed. Despite the warm weather, she was wearing a long-sleeved dress and a shawl. Her husband – in polo shirt and baggy cotton trousers – was small, plump and bald and was drinking a glass of wine. She had ordered soup. He had been eating lobster. The broken shell and claws were all around him.

'Hello, Elizabeth. Have you had a good lunch?' Judith had regained her good cheer.

'Lovely, thank you.' Elizabeth turned towards us, craning her neck awkwardly. Her words sounded strangled, as if they were trapped in her throat.

'I'm with Anthony. He's just arrived with the other writers.'

'Dark hair, untidy, going grey. Jewish. Late fifties. Didn't shave this morning. Short-sleeved shirt, linen trousers … crumpled. Doesn't look too pleased to be here.' This not entirely flattering portrait of me was rattled out at speed and without emotion by her husband. 'Hope you don't mind,' he went on. 'Liz likes to know who she's talking to.'

How could I be offended? 'It's nice to meet you,' I said.

But it wasn't. I don't believe in ghosts. I don't believe in an afterlife. And it's always been my feeling that anyone who calls themselves a professional medium can only be exploiting the all-too-real sadness of people who have suffered a loss. I once had dinner in an expensive restaurant with an actor whose wife was supposedly psychic. She insisted that my mother, who had been dead for thirty years, was standing next to me and continued to pass across messages from her. My mother was happy. She hoped I was happy too. It quite put me off my fish pie.

I didn't say any of this to her, of course. Instead, I asked her, 'When did you arrive?'

'Yesterday,' Elizabeth said.

'Flew from St Helier,' her husband added. 'Via Southampton and Guernsey. Took half the day. The ferry's no better.'

'Well, we're delighted you're here,' Judith said. 'Have you got everything you need?'

'Top-notch.' Sid picked up a lobster leg, gripped it between his teeth and sucked out the meat. 'Will you join us, Anthony?'

'That's very kind of you,' I said, 'but I've just got off the plane. I'm sure we'll see each other later.'

Why did I say that? Why is it that whenever I meet someone who has lost their sight, I'm unfailingly clumsy? Elizabeth didn't seem to notice. Her husband poked around for another piece of flesh. She ate her soup. I nodded at Judith and left.

Judith came back with me to the reception area. By now all the other writers had taken their keys and mine was the only one remaining.

'I'll see you at four thirty,' she said. 'And then afterwards at The Divers Inn. Call me if there's anything you need.'

I took my key and my suitcase and went up to the second floor. The rooms at the hotel had been given various designations – Platinum, Silver, Premium and so on. I noticed from the card that had been given to me with the key that mine was simply a Guest Room. It was small, with two single beds, two chairs, two pictures of Braye and, disappointingly, a view over the car park. But it was comfortable enough and I would only be here for two nights.

I unpacked and took out my laptop but I was too tired to work. It had been a long day and I'd had to get up early to meet Hawthorne at Waterloo. I had a book to read but in the end I dozed off, stretched out on the bed.

I was woken by a loud banging on the door. As I opened my eyes and stumbled to my feet, slightly ashamed to be found asleep in the middle of the afternoon, I realised that it was not actually my door but the one belonging to the neighbouring room. It opened and closed again.

Almost at once, an argument began on the other side of the wall. Some of the words were indistinct, but as the two people raised their voices I was able to hear whole sentences.

'Why didn't you tell me he'd be here?'

'I'm sorry, Marc. I didn't know.'

'You accepted the invitation.'

'I asked you! You said it was all right!'

It was Marc Bellamy and his assistant, Kathryn Harris. He was the one who had knocked on the door so the room must be hers. His voice grew louder and more violent.

'I can't bloody stay here!'

'I'm sorry ...' She sounded on the edge of tears.

'You've really screwed up.'

I heard the sound of an impact. He had either kicked something or thrown something at her and it was enough to get me to open my door, half afraid for her safety.

I was just in time to see Marc Bellamy go storming past. He didn't notice me. His fists were clenched. He was staring straight ahead.

He had murder in his eyes.

4

The Ace of Spades

I'm afraid I missed George Elkin and the occupation of Alderney. I should have gone to his talk, but I'd managed to sleep for two hours and I spent the rest of the afternoon catching up with my emails, texts, Twitter feed and WhatsApps – my tenuous links with the outside world. The welcome drinks began at half past six and that was when I came down. I asked for Hawthorne at reception but he hadn't got back from his walk.

The sun was dipping down towards the horizon as I left the hotel and in the evening light the island seemed to have retreated even further into the past. Two rows of terraced houses painted the colours of Neapolitan ice cream mirrored each other across a narrow street joined by a line of bunting that zigzagged from one side to the other. The road didn't seem to go anywhere. In the distance, a hillside rose steeply, blocking anything that might tell me which century I was actually in. There was nobody around. The shops had already shut and I couldn't help wondering what everyone actually did with themselves in the evenings in such a small place. I suppose a literary festival was a welcome diversion.

I didn't have far to go. The Divers Inn was right next to the hotel, actually part of the same building. There was a brand-new Mercedes coupé parked outside, pristine white, with the registration CLM 16. It looked a little incongruous, sitting on its own, with seagulls wheeling overhead. It was as though it had been driven into the wrong advertisement.

The Divers Inn was a traditional bar with wooden tables and a dartboard, bells and bottles, and arched ceilings lined with ships' badges. A Victorian diving suit, complete with helmet and faceplate, sat propped up in a corner. There were drinks laid out on the bar – red and white wine, orange juice and water – as well as a few plates of snacks. About thirty people had gathered inside but the space was small enough to make them feel like a crowd.

I immediately saw Marc Bellamy and his assistant, Kathryn, standing next to each other. He was nibbling a cocktail sausage. She had a stick of celery. They were avoiding each other's eye and although several hours had passed since their argument, some of its rancour had followed them here. Anne Cleary, the children's author, was talking to the festival organiser, Judith Matheson, and another man standing at her side. He had the look of an academic, bald and bearded with fanatical eyes, wearing a jacket with patches on the elbows. Colin

Matheson? Somehow, I couldn't imagine them together as a pair. I looked for Maïssa Lamar, but she wasn't in the room and nor was there any sign of the man in the black leather jacket whom I'd seen at the airport. I hadn't yet told Hawthorne about that. I was sure he would only make fun of me.

In fact, Hawthorne had seen me come in and made his way over to me.

'Where have you been?' I asked him.

'Out and about.' His eyes were innocent. Nothing else was. 'What about you?'

'Working.'

'You work too much. You should have come out and had some fun.'

He was saying that now. Earlier he had been less keen on my joining him. Even so, I was glad to have caught up with him. Like it or not, we were a double act – at least while we were on the island – and without him I felt very alone. We went over to Anne Cleary and Judith Matheson, who introduced me to the other man. 'This is George Elkin,' she said, adding, 'I was sorry not to see you at his talk. It was a brilliant start to the festival.'

'I'm very sorry,' I said. 'We had to work …'

I had included Hawthorne in my excuse and I thought he'd be grateful but he looked at me in surprise. 'No. I was there, Tony. I found it very interesting.' He turned to Elkin. 'You mentioned that your grandfather was in the Sylt concentration camp.'

53

'Yes.'

'How did that happen?'

'He was one of the very few Channel Islanders who refused to leave in 1940, although my grandmother did make it to England. It was only when she arrived that she discovered she was pregnant.' It was a story he had told many times and there was little emotion in his voice. 'My grandfather was considered a troublemaker and was sent to Sylt. We don't know when he died.'

'Was Sylt a labour camp or a concentration camp?' Anne asked. 'I can never remember the difference.'

'It was run by the SS. It followed a policy of *Vernichtung durch Arbeit*, which means "extermination through work". There was almost no chance of survival.'

'So it was a concentration camp.'

Elkin frowned. 'You could say that the entire island was a concentration camp. More than forty thousand people died. They're buried all over Alderney, but mainly in the area of Longis Common.'

It was a cheerful conversation for a literary drinks party and I was searching for a way out of it when there was a bray of laughter and a voice called out: 'My God! I don't believe it! It's Tea Leaf!'

We all looked round.

The speaker was a very handsome man with thick, prematurely grey hair falling in waves from a high forehead. He had already announced himself with a loud public-school accent and it fitted his aristocratic looks: clean-shaven with an aquiline nose and bright blue eyes. He was expensively dressed. It was impossible not to notice the cashmere polo neck, the Armani jacket, the brand-new jeans and loafers, the chunky Rolex watch weighing down his wrist. He had the perfect tan of the yachtsman or the millionaire. He was quite probably both. He was about forty years old, slim, athletic, pleased with himself.

He had rounded on Marc Bellamy, who was gaping at him with a mixture of shock and resignation. The crowd had parted as if to give them space for the encounter.

'How do, Charles,' Marc said. He still used the Yorkshire epithet but all the confidence that he had shown at Southampton Airport had, for the moment, drained away. *Why didn't you tell me he'd be here?* I had no doubt that this was the 'he' Marc had been referring to.

'I couldn't believe it when I saw your name on the programme. You've done very well for yourself! I love your show, by the way. You always did like to get your hands on a steak pie. Even when you were thirteen.' The new arrival spread his hands, explaining himself to the crowd. 'Tea Leaf and I were at school together at Westland College.'

'Why do you call him that?' Anne asked.

'We all had stupid nicknames for each other,' Marc replied, before Charles had time to embarrass him further.

'We haven't seen each other for ...' Charles tried to work it out.

'Twenty-five years.'

'You left so suddenly!'

'Well, life moves on ...'

They had been to the same school, but they were very far from old friends. I could feel the tension between them.

'Did you ever marry?' Charles asked.

'Married and divorced.'

So I had been right about that.

'I never thought you'd end up as a TV celebrity. I always remember you as being the quiet type, stealing up into the dorm! What's your show called?'

'*Lovely Grub*.'

'That's the one!' Charles laughed. 'Never watch it myself but Helen says it's a lot of fun. It's great to see you, Tea Leaf. We've got to catch up and have a proper chat.' He turned to the assembly. 'The stories I could tell you about this chap!'

It was all said in jest with plenty of smiles, but as Charles walked over to us I could see Marc Bellamy gazing at him with complete loathing. Kathryn Harris was watching the two of them with dread. She was the one who had brought Bellamy here. This was her fault.

Charles reached us and once again Judith did the introductions. 'This is Charles le Mesurier. He lives on the island and it's thanks to him that this festival is happening.' The words sounded well practised but they were unenthusiastic. She kept her distance from him. 'It's his company that's sponsored us and we're very grateful.'

'Always happy to give something back to this island.' Charles had developed a certain bonhomie that was entirely surface. I had seen it in his dealings with Marc Bellamy. He'd been complimentary enough, but every word he had spoken had carried its own little knife. 'It was my parents who first brought me to this island. Or rather, they sent me with the bloody nanny! Never thought I'd end up living here, but I'm hoping you're all going to come up to my place tomorrow night. We only completed The Lookout last year and it's quite spectacular. The weather forecast couldn't be better. It's the big party, with Marc knocking off the snacks! Seven o'clock to ten thirty. You're all invited.'

'Will Helen be there?' Judith asked in a tone of voice that made me wonder if she would actually be happier if she wasn't.

A shadow of annoyance crossed Charles's face. 'She's stuck in Paris. A shopping trip that won't end until there's nothing left in the bloody shops. She said she'd be back in time for tonight, but I guess we won't see her until tomorrow.'

The drinks lasted about another forty minutes, although Hawthorne slipped away long before the end. He didn't tell me he was going but I guessed he wanted to eat alone in his room and then hang around in the car park, smoking. Maybe I'd see him later. Meanwhile, Anne Cleary had invited me to join her for dinner and I'd accepted gratefully, hoping to make up for my clumsiness at the airport when I'd failed to remember her.

I found myself leaving at the same time as Charles le Mesurier, who had worked the entire room and seemed to be in a particularly good mood. From the way he behaved, it wasn't as if he just sponsored the festival. He owned it. I had already decided that he wasn't the most attractive of characters, but what happened in the last few moments as we made our way to the door really shocked me. You have to remember that this was a year before Harvey Weinstein was arrested and the Me Too movement really took off, but even so there were standards of behaviour, lines that no man would dare to cross. Or so I'd thought.

I was standing only a few feet away so I saw it quite clearly. Kathryn Harris had positioned herself near the door, keeping her distance from her boss. I have described her as being young, in her twenties, with glasses that covered too much of her face, but I should have added that she was very attractive, slim, with grey eyes and sand-coloured hair curling down to her shoulders. As he made his way towards the exit, Charles le Mesurier noticed her for the first time and I saw him smile in an unpleasant way. He could have moved around her but instead he brushed against her and at the same time his hand suddenly snaked round and took hold of her bottom. She started but before she could break free, he leaned towards her and muttered something in her ear. Kathryn blushed, an angry red.

I was only a few feet away and what I was witnessing could easily have been described as a fully fledged sexual assault. I was actually quite disgusted and I wondered if I should do something. But I was nervous. If I went charging in, the white knight to the rescue, there was every chance that I would only make the matter worse. It might even seem patronising to suggest that Kathryn needed my help, that she couldn't look after herself. I stood there, momentarily frozen, but mercifully, before I could make a decision, it was over. Le Mesurier released her. She looked at him with eyes that were full of anger and humiliation. He smiled and moved away.

I didn't see what happened next. A couple of people I'd met earlier came over and talked to me and the next time I looked, Kathryn had gone and le Mesurier was just disappearing through the door. I waited a few moments before following him out. I didn't really want to talk to him again, not after what I had just seen.

Unfortunately, he was waiting for me in the street. 'So you write kiddie books, do you?' he asked, lazily.

Kiddie books. There it was again. The art of the insult.

'Actually, I write adult fiction too,' I told him.

'Oh, yes. You're here with the detective.'

'Hawthorne. Yes.'

'I've often been tempted to murder my wife. Maybe he can give me some advice.' He smiled. 'What time are the two of you on?' he asked.

I told him that my session with Hawthorne would be happening the next day at four o'clock.

'I thought I might come,' he said. 'I don't read much crime fiction myself, although I'm quite fond of Dan Brown. He's sold millions. Do you know him?' He didn't wait for an answer. 'But there's a chap who works with me who's very keen and I said I'd join him. He wants to hear all about Detective Inspector Hawthorne.'

He was playing with me in exactly the same way that he had with Marc Bellamy. Of course I sold fewer copies than Dan Brown. And why should he have bothered to read anything I had written? At that moment I saw him as a schoolboy at Westland College with Marc Bellamy and knew without any doubt that he would have been absolutely horrible.

'I'm sure you can still get a ticket to my event,' I said.

'Oh yes. I've asked and there are still plenty available.'

We had been walking down the high street while we talked and we stopped as we reached his car. It was, of course, the Mercedes with the personalised number plate that I had seen earlier. But as le Mesurier pressed the key fob to open the doors, I noticed something had been lodged under the windscreen wipers. It was a playing card. He saw it too and pulled it free. He showed it to me.

'Look at that!' he exclaimed. 'Must be my lucky day.'

The card was the ace of spades.

He got into the car, taking the playing card with him. The door closed with a soft clunk and about a dozen lights came on in unexpected places, filling the interior with a soft glow.

I watched as he started the engine and drove away, and all the time I was thinking that the ace of spades wasn't necessarily something I would have associated with good luck. Quite the contrary: the card had been printed with a skull and crossbones inside the spade. I had seen it clearly.

I like decks of playing cards. I have a lot of them. And I remembered that the double-sized black pip at the centre of the ace is often thought to resemble, even to have been inspired by, the spade used by an undertaker. The Americans deployed it as a weapon in the Vietnam War, dropping it on the bodies of the soldiers they killed in order to frighten the survivors. In Iraq, the ace of spades was the card that identified and targeted Saddam Hussein.

Charles le Mesurier thought it was lucky. I knew better.

It was the death card.

5

Blind Sight

❧

When I say that I had breakfast with Hawthorne the next morning, I mean that I tucked into scrambled eggs and bacon, tea and toast, while he sat, slightly aloof, watching me over black coffee and a cigarette. It's hard to be close to anyone who refuses to eat with you, but then Hawthorne had an equally difficult relationship with food as he did with people. I had once visited his London flat just next to Blackfriars Bridge and had remarked on his pristine kitchen, his empty fridge. He survived mainly on processed food, the sort that came in plastic trays and never looked anywhere near as appetising as the pictures on the packet. The only alcoholic drink he'd been able to offer me was a rum and Coke and he himself had stuck to water.

The only time we'd actually sat down to dinner had been at the Station Inn in Ribblehead, Yorkshire. The two of us had been investigating the murder of Richard Pryce, a wealthy divorce lawyer, and we had gone to find out about a potholing accident that had taken place a few years before. Had he been particularly communicative that night? Not really. If I remembered the meal, it was only because of a chance encounter. A complete stranger had wandered into the pub and recognised Hawthorne, but had referred to him as 'Billy', insisting that the two of them had met in a nearby village called Reeth. Hawthorne had denied it. Far from bringing us closer together, the meal had left me more mystified than ever.

As for breakfast, I might as well have been eating it alone, a complete contrast to my dinner with Anne Cleary the night before. That had been warm and increasingly easy-going. I had ordered a bottle of wine but she had told me she wasn't drinking – she was on antibiotics – and so I'd ended up drinking most of it myself. We had plenty to talk about: Walker Books, other writers, Alderney and the festival so far. Since I had last seen her, Anne had separated from her husband. She told me that she'd been having a bad time – how bad, I was to find out soon enough.

I looked for her now but guessed that she had left early for her session at St Anne's School. A few of the other guests were out on the terrace, however. Kathryn Harris was sitting on her own at the table next to us, stabbing with a teaspoon at a bowl of muesli and yoghurt. Marc Bellamy was at the far end, still keeping his distance, his head buried in a copy of the *Daily Mail*. Elizabeth Lovell and her husband had just finished their breakfast and he nodded at us as they left. Her session was taking place that afternoon and according to Judith Matheson it was sold out.

I waited until they had gone, then I turned to Hawthorne. 'Maybe it would be a good idea if we found somewhere quiet and rehearsed how we're going to run our session,' I suggested.

He looked surprised. 'You think there's any need?'

'Of course there is!' This was what I'd been waiting for all along. For once, I knew what I was talking about. 'People are bound to ask you questions as well as me. You're the subject of the book, so everyone's going to be interested in you. It's much more sensible to prepare the answers and make sure we don't contradict each other.'

'It's not a performance.'

'Actually, it is. We're going to be on a stage, with an audience. They'll have paid money for their tickets.' He looked doubtful, so I went on. 'Maybe we should track down Colin Matheson. He's interviewing us. He can give us an idea of how he wants it to go.'

Hawthorne shrugged. 'It's only questions and answers, mate. And there'll probably only be half a dozen people there. You're worrying too much.'

Out of the corner of my eye I saw Maïssa Lamar approaching the hotel, wrapped in tight-fitting black spandex with a headband, wires trailing from her ears. She had been out jogging. As she disappeared from sight I was reminded of what I had seen at the airport. I told Hawthorne.

'It was very strange,' I said. 'She seemed to be on her own, but the moment we all got up and left she went and met someone.' I described the man I had seen. 'Their conversation seemed very intense.'

'It's not so unusual to meet someone you know at an airport,' Hawthorne said.

'At Southampton Airport? And she was talking about you. I'm sure I heard her mention your name.'

'They're all interested in me. You just said so yourself.'

It was exactly what I'd expected. He wasn't taking me seriously. But still I went on. 'There's something else,' I said. 'Someone stole £5 off the table at that restaurant in the airport.'

'You think it was Maïssa?'

'I don't know.'

'Maybe it was the waiter.'

'It could have been any of them.' He still didn't seem interested so I finished up with the playing card, the ace of spades that had been planted on Charles le Mesurier's car.

Hawthorne shook his head. 'Tony, mate. You're putting this stuff together like it's a book. But nothing's happened. Nobody's been killed. So none of it's of any interest.'

'Is that what you think?'

'I just think maybe you should relax.' How could he be so reasonable and so irritating at the same time?

I got up as soon as I could and walked away, leaving him to his own devices. As I went past the next table, I caught

Kathryn Harris's eye and smiled at her. 'Is everything OK?' I asked.

'Oh yes. It's lovely here and I'm so excited to be helping. We've got the big party tonight. Have you seen Charles le Mesurier's house?'

'Not yet.'

'It's amazing.' She looked up at the sky. 'It's going to be a hot one. I'd love to get out and explore the island. But I'm going to be busy most of the day getting things ready.' She glanced over at the far table. 'Marc's putting together quite a feast.'

She seemed completely unaffected by what had happened the evening before, both her argument with Marc Bellamy and her encounter with Charles le Mesurier at The Divers Inn. It made me think that I might have read too much into them. She was much younger than me. Perhaps she saw things differently.

Alderney is a lovely place. I had managed to rent a bicycle and spent the rest of the morning exploring the island, captivated by the sense of anachronism, the cobbled streets, the Jane Austen architecture, all the defences – the forts, the barracks, the German pillboxes, the batteries and the bunkers – that had been constructed with almost insane extravagance but never actually used. I cycled all the way from Fort Clonque, a nineteenth-century fortress sitting on its own rocky outcrop at the western end of the island, to The Odeon, a brutalist naval range-finding tower perched on a hillside at the far east. I stopped at Gannet Rock and stood at the edge of the cliff, looking vertiginously down to the churning, crashing sea. In front of me, two rocks of biblical proportions rose out of the water, covered with thousands of brilliant white birds. It was a breeding ground for gannets and one of the wildest and most isolated places I'd ever seen.

I wasn't going to make the same mistake as the day before when it seemed I'd been the only writer to miss George Elkin's presentation, so just before one o'clock I was back at the Alderney cinema in time to catch the last twenty minutes of Maïssa's performance. The cinema was not a huge place. From the outside it looked more like a shop or perhaps a solicitor's office and once you were in there, there were only about a dozen rows of bucket seats, upholstered in the red plush of another age. Even so, Maïssa had signally failed to fill it. Only thirty people had come to hear her and they weren't having a good time.

Maïssa's delivery was dreadful. She hadn't even learned her own work by heart and she stood behind a dais, reading it out with a sort of carelessness as if she just wanted to get it over with. She introduced her poems in broken English and didn't seem to understand fully what she was saying. The poems themselves, in Cauchois, were indecipherable and the translations – which were being projected onto the screen behind her – weren't actually much help. As I came in and took my place at the very back, she was in the middle of a poem about Joan of Arc, but I'm afraid, to my ears, it came over as little more than a collection of random words.

She finished and there was a smattering of the sort of applause that always sounds embarrassing in a half-empty room. Maïssa smiled briefly. 'Thank you very much,' she said and she too did not sound enthusiastic. 'I will end, please, with a haiku. I write it for my boyfriend after we split up. It is my thought for him and it is short, so I can translate.'

She paused, turned the page and began to speak.

> 'I look to the light
> But a dark shape pursues me.
> Your shadow or mine?'

She bowed her head for a moment. I joined in the applause but at the same time there was something that puzzled me. I'd read that poem before. I was sure of it. But how could that be possible when I'd never heard of Maïssa Lamar before I'd been invited to Alderney?

I was still thinking about it as I came out of the cinema and it was while I was standing there on the pavement that I saw him: the fair-haired man from the airport. He had taken off the leather jacket and wore a polo shirt that clung to him, showing off the muscles in his chest and arms. There was a gold chain around his neck.

On an impulse, I went up to him. 'Hello,' I said. 'Are you here for the festival?'

He looked at me blankly.

'I think I saw you at the airport. You were talking to Maïssa.'

'I'm sorry. You're making a mistake.' He turned round and walked away from me but I'd learned two things from the exchange. He was definitely French. And he hadn't wanted to be recognised.

I watched him disappear, then crossed the road.

The festival had organised a sandwich lunch at The Georgian House, a gastropub and B & B just opposite the cinema, and it was here that I caught up with Hawthorne, who was talking to a man I didn't know. About forty, lank black hair framing a crumpled face with troubled eyes, he looked like a junior doctor about to break bad news.

'This is Colin Matheson,' Hawthorne told me.

I was completely thrown. At breakfast I'd suggested meeting Colin Matheson, but Hawthorne had shown no interest at all. 'Oh – you've met!' I said.

'Yes. We've just had a bit of a run-through ... how we're going to do the session.' He looked at me accusingly. 'Where were you, mate?'

'I was listening to Maïssa Lamar.'

'I'm afraid I decided to give that one a miss,' Matheson said, managing to sound both regretful and relieved. Judith had told me he was a barrister and I have to say I was surprised. He was softly spoken. He didn't seem assertive enough. 'I've just been going through some of the questions with Mr Hawthorne,' he went on. 'We've almost sold out, by the way.'

I wasn't sure if that 'almost' was good or bad news. After all, the cinema only had about ninety seats.

'Maybe you and I could have a quick chat about it?' I suggested, weakly.

'I'm not sure we've got the time.' Colin smiled. 'Anyway, I'm sure you don't need any rehearsal, a pro like you.' He glanced at his watch as if that settled the issue. 'We thought we might go to Elizabeth Lovell's session after lunch,' he added. 'Judith managed to snag some seats. You've probably heard, they're a bit of a hot ticket! Would you care to join us?'

I'd had no intention of going, but if Hawthorne planned to be there …

'I'd love to,' I said.

'Good. Good. I've heard her talk before and she is quite remarkable. If you believe in that sort of thing …'

'And do you?'

'I try to keep an open mind.'

I became aware of a figure moving towards us, making his way through the lunchtime crowd with obvious determination. It was the historian, George Elkin, and he didn't look happy. Colin Matheson turned round, saw him and visibly flinched. He knew what was coming.

'I've just heard the news …' Elkin said.

'George! Have you met—'

71

'The power line. You've decided on the route.'

Matheson had no fight in him at all. His eyes seemed to sink deeper into his head. 'Actually, George, we haven't announced it yet.'

'I know you haven't announced it. I can understand that you wouldn't want to announce it. But you've done it all the same.' He turned to Hawthorne and me. 'There are five mass graves on Longis Common. A thousand poor souls murdered by the Nazis, finally at peace. My grandfather is one of them. Think of it! He was in his twenties when they starved him and worked him to death. But these people ...' There were actually tears in his eyes as he fought for control. 'They'll desecrate the whole area, tear it up for a handful of euros and to hell with what everyone else thinks.'

'Actually, there are quite a lot of people on the island who support NAB,' Matheson said.

'And there are a great deal more that don't.' Elkin stood there, seething. 'This is all about Charles le Mesurier, isn't it? He's the guiding light behind NAB and you're all dancing to his tune.'

'That's completely untrue.' Matheson looked more uncomfortable than angry. 'And to be honest with you, this really isn't the best place—'

Elkin cut in. 'You know what the prisoners used to call this island? *Le rocher maudit.* "The accursed rock". It seems to me that very little has changed.' He spun on his heel and walked away.

Matheson folded his hands and shrugged in apology. 'I'm afraid tempers are running a little high when it comes to the power line,' he explained. 'I'm very sorry you had to witness that. George is a good man and he means well, but that was really inappropriate.'

'Is it true what he said?' Hawthorne asked. The encounter had pricked his interest. 'Le Mesurier is in charge?'

'Not at all.' Now Matheson was blushing. 'I made the decision. Or rather, the States-appointed committee did. Mr le Mesurier has been a strong advocate for NAB because he believes it will bring wealth to the island. I can assure you he has the best intentions, as does everyone who's involved!' He looked into the crowd, trying to find Elkin. 'It really was too much of him to attack me in that way. Of course, George lost his grandfather in the most terrible way, killed by the Nazis. But even so ... !'

We finished our sandwiches with a certain amount of awkwardness and then made our way back to the cinema. By now a queue had formed, but Matheson led us in round the side and down to the front where three seats had been reserved. Very quickly, the room filled up. Soon every seat was taken and there were more people standing along the sides and at the back. There were two armchairs on the stage in front of the screen and as the lights dimmed, Judith Matheson marched across the stage, followed by Elizabeth Lovell, who was being guided by her husband. She waited while they took their places.

'Good afternoon, everybody,' Judith began. She deliberately paused while the room settled down, very much in the manner of a primary-school head teacher, severe but kind. 'How lovely to see such a packed house at this very special event. Elizabeth Lovell needs no introduction, but to those of you who missed her the last time she was here, I should explain that the gentleman sitting next to her is her husband, Sid, and although he won't be taking questions himself, he will be assisting her during the next hour. Elizabeth is unsighted, so his first job is to connect her with you. As I'm sure you'll understand, Elizabeth can become very emotional when she speaks at these events, so she likes him to be with her on stage.' She turned to him. 'Sid, I'd like to welcome you back to Alderney.' He smiled and nodded. 'Just two more things. You all know where the exit is in the event of a fire, and Elizabeth has asked me to remind you that there will be a signing afterwards at The Georgian House across the road. I'm very happy to tell you that books are being sold at a ten per cent discount. So without further ado, please welcome Elizabeth Lovell.'

Judith left the stage and the audience burst into sustained applause. At the same time, I looked around. George Elkin had not come, which was hardly surprising, and nor was there any sign of Maïssa Lamar. (Where had I read that poem? I was still wondering about it.) Marc Bellamy and Kathryn were probably in the kitchen of The Lookout, preparing for the evening, and Charles le Mesurier hadn't shown up either. But Anne Cleary was there, sitting just a few places away from me. She lifted a hand and smiled.

'Good afternoon.' Elizabeth Lovell seemed to be focusing on a point in the middle of the audience, a few metres above our heads. Her head was tilted back so that the black discs of her glasses caught the lights being trained on her and flashed them back at us. She was sitting so rigidly, her shoulders could have been nailed to the back of the chair. Her hands were resting on her knees. She was dressed in the same colour palette as the day before and it occurred to me that if I could have looked at her from the side, she might have had an uncanny resemblance to the famous painting of Whistler's mother.

'Packed house,' Sid muttered. He was wearing a blazer, white shirt and slacks. 'Nice crowd ... maybe a hundred people. No children. Raked seating. Standing at the back. More women than men.'

'Thank you, Sid.' She lifted her voice. 'It's been a very long time since I lost my physical sight but I still like to know where I am and who I'm talking to. I have an ability to sense the atmosphere and I know that I'm surrounded by friends. At the same time, though, I sometimes find it hard to be sure on which side of the mirror those friends can be found. For that, ladies and gentlemen, is the difference between life and what most people call death. They are reflections of each other. Two different sides of the mirror.'

This was her introduction and for the next thirty minutes she talked about her life and philosophy, expanding on what I had already read in the festival programme. Born in Exeter, she'd had a happy childhood, an ordinary education, loving parents, a job as a librarian. She'd always had an interest in books and had dreamed of becoming a writer. She had met Sid on holiday in Jersey. He was the taxi driver who had picked her up from the airport.

So far so ordinary. Her story, which she had clearly told many times, became more interesting, and more occult, after she lost her eyesight due to diabetes. This had happened twelve years ago, when she was about to turn thirty.

'Of course, I was angry,' she told the audience. 'I was shocked. I was in denial. But at the same time, I realised that although this side of the mirror – your side – was closed to me, the other was opening up. I began to call it Blind Sight. I cannot see what you can see. But you cannot see what I see, and I can tell you, ladies and gentlemen, that what I see is wonderful. There is no such thing as death. We are surrounded by friends and family who wish us no harm, who – quite the opposite – want to guide us. I never call them ghosts. That's a word used to frighten children. Nor are they even spirits. That makes them sound angelic and I can assure you, not all of them are. To me, they are reflections. With Blind Sight I can see them. I am looking at them now.'

And so the fairground ride – the ghost train – began. I glanced at Hawthorne, wondering what he was making of all this, but he was giving little away, listening with polite interest. Elizabeth continued to describe 'the other side of the mirror', then suddenly pointed. I followed her quivering finger to a poster on the wall advertising *Mission: Impossible – Rogue Nation* but I don't think that's what she had in mind.

'There!' she said. 'I'm seeing a lady. Her name was Mary or Margaret. She was here for seventy years before she crossed to the other side ...'

I'd seen it all before, starting with the choice of 'Mary or Margaret', which immediately doubled her chances of making a score. Put a hundred people in a room and the odds were huge that one of them would know a Mary or a Margaret who had died, and if those names didn't work, she could move on to Mabel, Miranda and Miriam.

'She has wet hair,' Elizabeth added.

I had to admit, I wasn't expecting that.

There was a short silence. Elizabeth was still gazing in the direction of Tom Cruise. Then someone shouted: 'That's Mary Carrington!'

'Lady in the fourth row. Fifties. Glasses,' Sid muttered. He hadn't spoken for a while.

Elizabeth's head swung round. 'Who was Mary Carrington?' she asked.

The same person replied. 'She lived in town. Everyone knew Mary. She used to have a sweet shop. She slipped getting into the bath. She hit her head and drowned.'

'She is with her husband ... Eric.'

'It wasn't Eric! It was Ernest!' a man called out from the back.

'She wanted to be with him and now they're happy together, even though they miss you. They miss the island.'

'She always said she hated it here,' the man remarked.

'She said it but she didn't mean it. Now ...' Elizabeth took a deep breath as if she had heard someone creeping up on her from behind. 'There is another presence here. A young man. He left us far too soon. His name is ...' She hesitated, unsure. 'William?'

I knew it was all trickery. I have an interest in magic and have read biographies of Harry Houdini, who spent half his life exposing fake mediums. I used to watch the Canadian magician James Randi on television and he explained exactly how it worked. If nobody in the audience knew a William who had drowned or been run over or whatever, Elizabeth would make something up and move on. The audience wanted to believe her and that was the weapon she was using against them. How had she known about Mary Carrington? It would have been easy for her to find out. Maybe she had come across the story in a back edition of the Alderney *Journal*. I was sure it would have been reported.

She was waiting for someone to respond to the arrival of William and I was expecting her to move on to Walter or Wayne when she added, in a surprised voice, 'Is Anne here?'

I hadn't noticed it until now but it had become very warm in the cinema. There was no air conditioning and although they'd left the door open at the back, the flow of air was sluggish. I felt the one hundred people pressing in on me and heard their collective breathing. In the half-darkness, the blind woman on the stage seemed almost threatening. I remembered going to pantomimes when I was a boy and living in terror that I would be chosen by one of the actors for a sing-song or a bit of fun on stage. I felt the same way now. My father had died young. I hoped with every fibre of my being that he wasn't going to show up next – although he'd never taken that much interest in me when he was alive.

'Anne?' Elizabeth scanned the audience sightlessly.

Sid reached out to her. 'Do you mean Anne Cleary?'

'Yes.'

'Second row. Just to your left.'

Elizabeth tilted her head in that direction. 'There's someone called William. He was very close to you. Was he your son?'

I looked at Anne, three seats away, and my heart went out to her. All the blood had drained out of her face. She was in a state of shock. 'Please ...' She didn't want Elizabeth to continue.

'William was very troubled and he made a terrible decision. He was very young when he left you. And he knows how sad you are. He caused you pain. He wants you to forgive him. He died—'

'He died of an overdose while he was at university.' Anne's voice cut in, supplying the information, perhaps trying to short-circuit this before it went any further. All around her, the audience had become very still, uncomfortable to be witnessing this personal tragedy.

'Yes ...' Elizabeth nodded slowly, her gaunt face full of compassion.

'He was an addict. He didn't know what he was doing.' Anne's voice cracked. She hadn't mentioned her son when we'd had dinner the night before, although she had said she had a daughter living in London. Even as we had laughed together it had struck me that there was an air of sadness about her, a sense of something unsaid. I hated what was happening to her now. It was horrible and unfair.

'Don't be sad, Anne,' Elizabeth said from the stage. 'There is no sadness on the other side of the mirror. He's left all that behind him.'

'That may be true.' Anne stood up. 'But he's left me and his family behind him too and the pain has never gone ... not for us.' She had said enough. I saw her make the decision. Breathing heavily, she pushed her way to the end of the row, passing close to Hawthorne and myself, and without looking back left the cinema.

'It can be hard, I know, to accept the truth of what I see.' After what had just happened, Elizabeth Lovell was having to fight to win back the audience, who might easily have turned against her. She touched the fingers of one hand against her heart. 'Believe me, I feel her pain, but I also know that there will be comfort for her too. We talk about losing people, but the truth is that they are never lost.'

She continued in this vein for another ten minutes but there were no further visitations. Judith climbed back onto the stage and, after thanking Elizabeth and Sid, directed the audience over to the book signing. They were eager to cross to the other side – of the road, that is – and there was quite a scrum at the door. Meanwhile, Sid helped his wife down from the stage. Judith was waiting to escort them to The Georgian House, but for a moment the two of them were in front of me. Colin Matheson was on one side, Hawthorne on the other.

'That was extraordinary,' I said.

Elizabeth was leaning on Sid. 'I hope I didn't upset Anne,' she said. 'It's not my choice, you know, who comes to me.'

'She'll be fine.' Sid patted her hand.

'Have you met my friend, Daniel Hawthorne?' I asked. I wanted to introduce them because I was interested to hear what Hawthorne would say.

She held out a hand vaguely in his direction. He took it and smiled.

'Very nice to meet you, Mr Hawthorne.'

'And you, Mrs Lovell.'

'Did you enjoy my talk?'

'It was memorable,' Hawthorne said. 'You must find it very tiring.'

'Oh yes. I'm quite exhausted.' She drew herself up, still resting against Sid. 'But I'm afraid I have to go. There are books to sign.'

'Mustn't keep your fans waiting.' Was Hawthorne mocking her? I couldn't tell.

We watched Sid and Elizabeth leave the cinema. He was guiding her with his hand around her waist.

'Her last book sold half a million copies,' Colin Matheson muttered, as if he couldn't believe what had just happened.

'Online,' I reminded him.

Hawthorne glanced at me. 'Yes. But she gets seventy per cent of the royalties.'

And we got much less. It was something we'd discussed more than once before, but I was disappointed that he had chosen this moment to bring it up again.

Suddenly, we were alone in the cinema with just a couple of volunteers clearing up the litter. I looked back at the stage. 'I don't know how she did all that,' I said. 'But you do realise that she's a complete fraud?'

'Oh yes.' Hawthorne nodded. 'I saw that from the very start.' He paused. 'But those ghosts were definitely real.'

6

The Man in the Third Row

It turned out that the question-and-answer session with
Hawthorne and myself had attracted about eighty people;
not quite up there with ghosts and mirrors, but still a reason-
able crowd. As I took my place on the stage with Colin
Matheson in the middle and Hawthorne on the far side, I
quickly cast an eye over the audience. First, the absences.
Over dinner, Anne Cleary had said she would definitely
come, but I could hardly blame her for changing her mind.
Marc Bellamy and Kathryn Harris were at The Lookout,
preparing their thousand-calorie treats for the evening party.
More surprisingly, there was no sign of Judith Matheson and
I leaned over to ask Colin what had happened.

'She sends her apologies,' he said. 'We had a problem at the
house this afternoon and she had to stay behind to sort it.'

'Nothing serious, I hope.'

'No. Just annoying ...'

On the plus side, Elizabeth Lovell and her husband were sitting in the back row with George Elkin. Maïssa Lamar had also decided to show up, although without her mysterious friend from the airport. And Charles le Mesurier had been true to his word. He had arrived at the last moment and was making his way down to two reserved seats near the front.

He was not alone. He had said he was going to come with someone who worked for him and sure enough he was being followed by a second man who was supporting himself with a walking stick. He had clearly done serious damage to his left leg, which moved almost with a life of its own, out of sync with the rest of him. He was at least ten years older than le Mesurier. Dressed, unnecessarily, in a suit and tie, he was already sweating in the crowded cinema. There was something bullish about him: his steel-rimmed glasses, ruddy cheeks and black hair like a streak of oil across his head. He was scowling, perhaps with the effort of keeping up. It didn't help that he had a reserved seat right in the middle of the third row. Sitting next to an aisle would have been easier. Part of me even wondered if le Mesurier had chosen it deliberately? He was smiling as his friend manoeuvred himself across with difficulty and tumbled rather than sat down.

The house lights dimmed.

Colin Matheson began. 'Ladies and gentlemen, it's my pleasure to introduce ex-Detective Inspector Daniel Hawthorne, who was for many years a highly respected investigating officer based at Scotland Yard in London. When his career with them ended, he became a consultant – ' he allowed himself a smile ' – helping the police, as it were, with their enquiries. He is now what you would call a private detective. Of course, we've all heard that expression bandied about in books and on TV, but I can assure you that what we have here today is neither a *Poirot* nor a *Midsomer Murders* but the real thing, and – this is a special treat for Alderney – today will be the first time that he has spoken publicly about his work. I had the opportunity to chat with Mr Hawthorne for a short while before we came in and I can safely say that the next hour is going to be a treat. He is called in to solve only the most difficult cases and, from what I understand, he succeeds every time. He has made many notable arrests, including the killings in Riverside Close that took place in Richmond a few years ago and which you may have read about in the newspapers.'

The killings in Riverside Close. That struck me as a rather good title for a book. I made a mental note to ask Hawthorne what had happened.

Hawthorne, in his suit and tie, had sat perfectly still through all this. He showed almost no emotion apart from a hint of embarrassment, a sense that he was surprised that anyone could be saying such nice things about him.

Then Matheson turned to me. 'Anthony has written a great many scripts for television, including the two shows I just mentioned. He was personally chosen by Mr Hawthorne to be his biographer, although the first book, *Hawthorne Investigates*, has yet to appear in print. I'm sure he'll have lots to tell us about the challenge of moving from fiction to true crime, and hopefully I'll be able to persuade him to read an extract from the new book.'

There was polite applause.

Colin Matheson turned to Hawthorne. 'I'd like to begin, if I may, Mr Hawthorne, with some facts about you. How long were you a detective?'

I was expecting Hawthorne to be monosyllabic at best but to my surprise he sounded completely relaxed. Perhaps he had rehearsed this with Matheson before I'd met them at lunch. 'I started off in uniform,' he began. 'These days, you can become a trainee DC with two years' work experience and a decent university degree but it wasn't the same back then. So I had to climb the ladder: trainee DC, then a full detective constable and after a while I got accelerated promotion to DI. In total I was with the Met for eleven years.'

'How old are you now, if you don't mind my asking?'

'I'm thirty-nine.'

'Have you always investigated crime?'

'I spent a couple of years in child protection but I felt more comfortable with the CID.'

'Why did you want to go into policing in the first place?'

Hawthorne sat perfectly still. 'I read books when I was a kid. Maigret and Father Brown. It interested me.'

'Did you have any brothers or sisters?'

'No. I was the only one.'

I was beginning to feel a sense of dismay as I listened to all this. I had known Hawthorne for months. I had worked with him on two murder investigations and I was in the middle of my second book about him. But in the space of one minute he had told Colin Matheson more than he had ever told me. I had never known his age, for example. And I had written that he had spent ten years as a detective, not eleven. Why was Hawthorne answering these questions so readily in front of an audience in an Alderney cinema when with me he'd always been so guarded about his private life? Was he being deliberately provocative or could it be that he had some perverse sense of duty, that having accepted the invitation to come here this was the price he had to pay? As always, his face gave nothing away.

I expected Matheson to turn to me but he still hadn't finished with Hawthorne.

'What, for you, is the best thing about being a detective?'

It took Hawthorne a few moments to process that one. 'That's a good question, Colin,' he said, eventually. 'I suppose the answer's got to be making the arrest. That's the bit I always enjoy the most. The thing about murderers is that most of them are as thick as shit, if you'll excuse my language. Even the clever ones are never quite as clever as they think they are. I've met so many of them who think they can get one over on me, but they still make mistakes, and if you ask me what the best thing about being a detective is, it's that moment when I know that I've got them, when the mask comes off, when the whole thing is solved.'

'So it's not a question of protecting people, upholding the law?'

'Well, of course that's part of it, and you being a barrister, I can imagine that's important to you. But that's not my job. I mean, I'm not protecting anyone because when I'm called in, the one person I might have protected is already dead. As for the law, I leave all that to the judges and the lawyers. I don't like going to court, if I'm going to be honest with you. All these people arguing all day. And ten years in jail, twenty years ... what difference does it make? My job's done.'

I was still waiting to join in but at the same time I was fascinated. I had never heard Hawthorne talk so much – certainly not about himself. And it was true what he had just said. When you think about it, just about every murder mystery you read ends with the arrest. You never see the detective giving evidence. And once the killers have been drawn into the legal process, they become quite uninteresting. They disappear.

'But you are making the world a safer place,' Matheson insisted.

'Is that true?' Hawthorne blinked. 'As I've already said, by the time I arrive, the murder's been committed. Nobody's been saved. And more often than not, the killer's got what he wanted. He's inherited the money. He's got rid of his wife. It's very unlikely he's going to kill anyone else.'

'So the work you do ... it's just part of a process.'

'You could say that. You can't have law without law enforcement. That's what I do.'

'But you're good at it.'

Hawthorne nodded. 'I think so ...'

'Have you met many murderers?'

'Yes.'

'And ... ?' Matheson waited with a half-smile, wanting more. But there was no more so he moved on. 'Are all murderers caught?'

'All the ones I've met have been.'

This got a ripple of laughter from the audience.

'What gives them away?'

'It could be anything.' Matheson still wanted more and this time Hawthorne obliged. 'There's so much pressure and the stakes are so high that it's hard to stay in control. There'll always be a little detail – it could just be a tic – that gives you away. It's like you're playing poker and you've been dealt a royal flush. Ace, king, queen, jack, ten. It could be worth a million quid. But you've got to be a real pro to know how to keep it to yourself and most killers aren't.'

Out of the corner of my eye I saw Charles le Mesurier nod at that. He was the CEO of Spin-the-wheel, the online gaming company that had sponsored the festival, so it was an analogy he appreciated. His friend or business partner was leaning forward, listening intently. He didn't seem to be enjoying the talk.

I hadn't spoken a word for what seemed like a very long time now but Matheson hadn't finished with Hawthorne. 'Does it worry you, appearing in a series of books?' he asked.

'Not really.'

'It was your idea.'

'That's right.'

'Why did you want to do it?'

Hawthorne shrugged. 'I needed the money.'

There was more laughter. If this was a dry run for Edinburgh and Hay, it was clear that Hawthorne was going to be fine. He didn't need me at all.

'And was Anthony your first choice of writer?'

'Let's just say he was the first one who was available.'

I smiled gamely. The audience applauded.

Finally, Matheson turned to me. 'So what was it that persuaded you to write *Hawthorne Investigates*?' he asked.

I had sat in silence for so long that for a moment I didn't even know what he was talking about. Then I remembered. 'Actually, that's not the title. The book's going to be called *The Word is Murder*.'

'Oh.' With that single syllable Matheson let me know that he preferred Hawthorne's title.

'I wrote it because I thought it would be interesting,' I said.

My answer clearly wasn't interesting enough. Matheson turned back to Hawthorne. 'I presume you've read the book,' he asked.

'No. Not yet. Tony hasn't shown it to me.'

'Are you nervous about how you may appear? Especially as you've put yourself into the hands of a writer known for fiction.'

Hawthorne shook his head. 'It doesn't really bother me. It's only a book.'

'Two books,' I said.

'People can think what they want. I know the truth.'

'Finally, Anthony, a question for you. What's it been like, writing about Mr Hawthorne?'

I had to think for a moment before I answered that. 'Well, it was different—' I began.

That was only the start of what I was going to say but Matheson assumed that I had finished and cut straight in. 'You've kindly agreed to read a few pages for us,' he said.

'Yes . . .' I had brought the typescript on my iPad and flicked it open.

It had taken me a while to choose a section from the book. Obviously, the audience would want to hear a scene in which Hawthorne actually appeared, but I didn't want to read out anything that might sound critical of him, certainly not when he was sitting right next to me. Nor did I want to give too much away. I'd finally settled on an extract from Chapter Four: Hawthorne looking over the crime scene. I had to cut a couple of personal observations but otherwise he appeared in a good light and there was a scattering of applause when I finished.

'Thank you, Anthony.' Matheson signalled for the house lights to be raised. 'And now I'm sure there are plenty of things the audience would like to ask ...'

For the next twenty minutes, we took questions, although almost all of them were directed at Hawthorne and had very little to do with the books. He went through several of the cases he had investigated, including the brothel in Causton Street that he had mentioned at Random House and, more annoyingly, the murder of Diana Cowper, which I had just described. Unlike me, though, he didn't stop at the scene of the crime. I would have to remind him, before we ever did another talk, not to mention, quite so casually, who had done it.

I got three questions. An elderly lady in the front row asked me about *Foyle's War*. A kid at the back wanted to know if there was going to be another *Alex Rider* and if so, would it have better gadgets? And a strikingly attractive fair-haired woman with ice-blue eyes made a lengthy speech about the importance of school libraries and asked me what I would do to save St Anne's, by which I think she meant the school rather than the entire town. This is actually something I know quite a lot about and I remarked that under UK law, libraries are statutory in prisons but not in schools. This happens to be true and, with this audience, it went down well.

But after that it was all Hawthorne. Did he believe in the jury system? Did he support capital punishment? Did he like reading detective fiction? Had he ever watched *Midsomer Murders*? (No.) Was his picture going to be on the front cover of the book? Who would play him in the TV series? On and on it went until Matheson raised a hand and said that we were out of time.

There was one person in the audience who hadn't been allowed a question, even though he had tried several times to attract Matheson's attention. It was the man in the third row who had come in with le Mesurier, and before anyone could stop him, he pulled himself laboriously to his feet and called out: 'I have a question.'

'Actually—' Matheson tried to cut him off.

'Detective Inspector Hawthorne hasn't told us why he left the Metropolitan Police. If he was so successful at his job and they liked him so much, why did they kick him out?'

I looked at Hawthorne. To the audience, it would seem that nothing had changed. He seemed relaxed. His face gave nothing away. But sitting with him, I got the sense of a coiled spring. Right then, I was quite certain that the two men knew each other.

'You're mistaken,' Hawthorne said. 'I wasn't kicked out. I decided to leave.'

'So there's no truth in the story that you were dismissed following an assault on an innocent man while he was in your custody?'

'Not me,' Hawthorne replied, mildly. He cocked his head. 'And not innocent, as I recall.'

The audience was looking from one man to another, puzzled and a little concerned.

'So there was no IOPC investigation? No dismissal for gross misconduct?'

'Definitely not.'

'Well, my mistake.' The words were laced with sarcasm. The man had made his point. He sat down.

The session came to an end. There was to be no signing session because we hadn't yet produced any books. As the audience filed out, Colin Matheson leaned across. 'I'm so sorry about that,' he said. 'Derek Abbott is an absolutely vile human being. He works for Charles le Mesurier, advising him on his investments and various financial matters. You saw the two of them come in together? I don't know why he was here. He hardly ever appears in public and quite frankly, if I'd known he was going to be in the cinema, I might have declined to take part. He lives on the island and he's pure poison.'

'What did you say his name was?' I asked.

'Derek Abbott.'

Suddenly, everything was clear. This was the reason Hawthorne had been so keen to come to Alderney. Derek Abbott! He was the child pornographer who had 'fallen' down a flight of stairs while Hawthorne was escorting him to the interview room. And he lived here! What was in Hawthorne's mind? Was he pursuing some sort of vendetta? Did he mean to have a second go at finishing him off? And why hadn't he told me? The bastard! Didn't he think I'd find out?

I had been told the story of Abbott's life-changing accident by another police officer and although Hawthorne had denied it, I had always assumed that he must have known exactly what he was doing. I had tried not to allow it to affect what I thought of him. How could I make a hero out of a man accused of police brutality – even if his victim had been about as repulsive as it is possible to be? Wouldn't that make me complicit?

In the end, I had done everything I could to put the whole thing out of my mind and maybe that was why I was so angry when we got out into the street. 'Why didn't you tell me that Derek Abbott lived here?' I almost shouted at him as soon as Colin Matheson had left the two of us alone. 'Why didn't you tell me he was on the island?'

'I didn't think it was any of your business, mate.' Hawthorne was unruffled, which only made me angrier.

'Of course it's my business. I'm writing about you.'

'You don't have to write about him, though.'

'What? You think I can lie? Or just pretend it never happened?' I tried to collect my thoughts. 'Why did you even want to see him again?'

'I was interested to find out what had happened to him.'

'You know perfectly well what happened to him. You turned him into a cripple!'

'He tripped. He fell. I did nothing.'

95

'So why are you here, then? What are you going to do to him this time? Push him off a cliff?'

Hawthorne had had enough. He was already walking away.

'I just can't believe you've done this!' I shouted.

'I'll see you at the party,' he called back.

He turned a corner and he was gone.

7

The Lookout

I spent about an hour in my room before I came down to the reception area that evening. I tried to read a book I'd been given, a history of modern Greece, but I was too out of sorts to focus on the words and I couldn't make sense of Venizelos and the so-called National Schism. The party was supposed to begin at seven o'clock, but I didn't want to be there until half past. In fact, I wasn't sure I wanted to be there at all. I lay on the bed, staring at the ceiling. Finally, I got up, showered, changed and took the lift downstairs.

My information pack had told me that The Lookout, Charles le Mesurier's house, was a ten-minute drive away, but I intended to walk – with or without Hawthorne. I really didn't care. I'd be following the coast the whole way and I liked the idea of watching the evening light glisten on the surface of the water and listening to the rhythm of the waves.

I left my room and went downstairs. As I came out of the lift I heard Anne Cleary's voice. She sounded upset. 'Are you sure nobody's handed it in?' She was standing at the reception desk with her back to me. 'It's not that it's particularly valuable. But it does mean a lot to me.'

'I'm sorry, Mrs Cleary. I've looked in the lost-property drawer but it's not there. I can ask the cleaners for you tomorrow.'

'It was in my room, by my bed.'

'I'm sure they wouldn't have taken it, but I'll ask them.'

I took a few steps forward and she turned and saw me. 'What's happened?' I asked.

'Oh – it's nothing. It's just that I've lost my fountain pen. It's a particularly nice one, a Sakura, made in Japan. It was given to me by my agent.'

'When did you last see it?' I asked.

'I was just saying. I thought it was in my room.'

'Did you lock the door?'

'It locks itself.' She took a deep breath. 'Maybe I left it at the school. I signed a whole lot of books, although I'm sure I put it in my handbag.'

I couldn't help feeling sorry for her, particularly after what had happened that afternoon. I'd been meaning to ask her what she thought about her encounter with Elizabeth Lovell. Surely she was far too sensible to believe that her dead son, William, had somehow communicated with a so-called psychic. She must have known that she had been the victim of a cruel confidence trick. But I didn't say anything. I didn't know her well enough and I didn't want to intrude. 'Are you coming to the party?' I asked.

She had dressed for it in a black jersey with silver sequins and a long skirt, and sure enough she nodded. 'To be honest with you, I don't really feel like going to any party tonight, but I suppose it would be rude not to and there's no real point sitting on my own in my hotel room. So, yes, I'll look in for a short while.'

'I was going to walk round if you'd like to join me.'

'No, thank you. I'm waiting for George Elkin. He's offered me a lift.'

That was when Hawthorne arrived. He'd taken the stairs, not the lift, and came straight over to us. From the look on his face, you'd have thought the argument between us had never happened. 'You all right, Tony?' he asked.

'Yes,' I said. 'I'm about to walk to the party.'

'I'll join you.'

'I was just talking to Anne,' I said. 'She's lost her pen. She thinks someone may have taken it.'

'A black Sakura with a silver nib?'

'You've seen it?' Anne's face lit up.

'No. I noticed you using it yesterday when you signed into reception.'

He wasn't showing off, but that was absolutely typical of Hawthorne. I had no idea how he did it but there wasn't a single detail that he ever missed and somehow he filed it all away in that remarkable mind of his, to be dredged up whenever it was needed. That was why I would never solve a case before him. I couldn't even remember what I'd had for lunch.

The two of us set off together.

I had already decided not to say anything more about Derek Abbott and his presence on the island. I didn't want to spoil the evening. Instead, I walked in silence until we had reached the edge of Braye Beach and then I asked: 'How do you think she knew?'

'What?'

'Elizabeth Lovell knew that William Cleary was a drug addict and that he killed himself with an overdose.'

'Are you sure that's what she said?'

'She was vague. But she seemed to know what she was talking about.'

Hawthorne shrugged. 'It would have been easy enough to find out.'

I nodded. 'I did a search on the internet. There's almost nothing about William except that he took an overdose and died when he was twenty-one. The real story was the university. A lot of the newspapers claimed they weren't giving their students enough support. They had a very bad record on youth suicide. You might be interested to know that Bill and Kitty Flashbang – those two characters you liked – were named after her own children and that's why she stopped writing about them. Her marriage also broke up. Her husband is an artist. He had a nervous breakdown and now he lives in Cornwall.'

'You've been busy,' Hawthorne said.

'I just think it's very sad. And it makes it inexcusable, what Elizabeth Lovell did.'

We both fell silent after that. Lost in our quite different thoughts, we continued our journey across the island.

It was a beautiful evening. We were walking along the rue de Beaumont, which followed the curve of the beach with a vista of grassland, then rocks, then white sand and finally a dark sea, turning crimson as the sun began to set. To one side, the stone breakwater at Braye Harbour stretched out an improbable distance, as if the architects had set themselves the task of walking all the way to the horizon. On the other, a series of quite ordinary houses stood side by side, almost ignoring the view. We passed a classic Gilbert Scott telephone box, painted blue not red, and the thought occurred to me that if I ever wrote a book about Alderney, I'd recommend featuring it on the cover.

Eventually, we left the houses behind us. A few seabirds circled overhead, silhouetted against the sky, and as we continued, the grass became wilder, the rocks more rugged and I could hear waves crashing against the cliffs. We were overtaken by a few cars and then by the minibus that had met us at the airport. It was full of people dressed up for the party and I caught a glimpse of Maïssa Lamar leaning against one of the windows, clutching a beaded handbag and wearing a colourful headdress. She might have seen us but she made no acknowledgement as the bus swept past, kicking up a cloud of dust behind it.

Now the road took us past Fort Albert, which I had seen from the hotel. Isolated on a headland at the end of the bay, the construction looked ancient, almost Arthurian. The land around it was hostile, full of dark magic. Hawthorne knew where he was going. He pointed to a track that led to the beach, with more German defences scattered on both sides. I saw lights. There were cars parked ahead of us, along with the airport minibus. We had arrived.

The Lookout was a celebrity house, built to impress. It was shaped roughly like an arrow – or perhaps more like an American stealth bomber, about to blast off across the sea. Its two wings reached out to enclose us as we walked towards it. Spotlights set at ankle level washed over the asphalt approach. Charles le Mesurier had told me that it had only been completed a year ago and the narrow horizontal windows in their steel frames and the double front doors were aggressively modern. But the architect had also been inspired by art deco: the walls were covered in white stucco and there were three flat roofs forming terraces, rising up one above the other, which added to the building's sense of dynamism and thrust.

The front doors were open and I could hear live music, a local jazz band launching into an enthusiastic rendering of 'Fly Me to the Moon' arranged for snare drum, banjo and synthesiser. The minibus was empty. Maïssa and the other passengers had already gone inside. Looking into the house, I could see the silhouettes of people passing back and forth like puppets in one of those Indonesian puppet plays. There had to be a chandelier somewhere because it was casting tiny sparkles of light. I got the sense that I was entering another world.

From the moment I went in, I saw that Charles le Mesurier had spared no expense in the creation of his island Xanadu: it was every bit as spectacular as he had promised. Sure enough, a splendid chandelier – modern rather than antique – dominated the hallway above a floor that was a gleaming expanse of white marble. The art on the wall included prints by Damien Hirst and Banksy. An archway in front of us led into a living room with a sun lounge on one side and a dining room with an archway into the kitchen on the other, but sliding walls had been drawn back to turn these rooms into one huge space. I don't think I'd ever been in a house where the people furthest away were actually diminished in size simply by perspective.

Looking ahead, I saw the floor-to-ceiling windows had also been slid aside. Light from the interior spilled out onto emerald-green lawns and perfectly cut flower beds, while a gravel path lit by tiny lights set in the ground continued all the way to the bottom of the garden. A square stone building with two windows – some sort of pavilion – had been built at the very end. I could hear the soft murmur of the sea beyond.

This wasn't a house. It was a movie set. The art, the hard-wood floors, the rugs, the grand piano, the Italian lighting and furniture, they had all been chosen to make an impression. It suited the character of Charles le Mesurier – or what I knew of him. The big fish in the small pond. When you visited him at home, he wanted you to know what he was. This wasn't just a home. It was a monument to himself.

I glanced at Hawthorne. He didn't seem particularly impressed by his surroundings, but he would never have shown it if he was.

About a hundred people, some of them in black tie, had already arrived and Marc Bellamy was working the room, having appointed himself master of ceremonies. He was dressed in the full regalia of a traditional chef: white jacket with two rows of buttons, baggy grey trousers and a red bandana. All that was missing was the hat.

He saw us and came over.

'How do!' He began with the inevitable greeting. 'How are you, Tony? And you, Mr Hawthorne? Busy day?' He didn't wait for an answer. 'I hope you've brought your appetites with you. What are you going to have to drink?' He waved a hand at Kathryn, who was carrying glasses on a tray. She was wearing a black dress and a white apron, like a French waitress. It was as if the two of them had decided to come in fancy dress. 'What do you think of this place, then? Not quite my cup of Tetley's, but it must have cost a bob or two. Versailles on the island of Alderney.' His pronunciation of the French chateau moved it directly to Yorkshire. 'Let's hope the locals don't rise up and chop off the owner's head!' he added with a twinkle.

He sauntered over towards some other new arrivals and I looked past him into the room. Charles le Mesurier was standing beside the piano, dressed tonight in a loose-fitting silk jacket, T-shirt and white trousers, talking to a group of people who were hanging on his every word. Elizabeth Lovell was sitting on a sofa with Sid next to her. He was whispering descriptions of the other guests, cradling what looked like a large whisky on his lap. There was one particular person I was looking for and I spotted him at once, standing next to the entrance to the kitchen. Derek Abbott was leaning on his walking stick, talking to a woman I didn't know: short, strawberry blonde hair, lots of make-up, expensively dressed. Hawthorne had seen him too.

'Did you know he'd be here?' I asked.

'No.'

'Are you going to stay?'

Hawthorne shrugged. 'Why should I leave?'

It was true that there was plenty of space for them to avoid each other. In fact, we still hadn't made it out of the hallway and Abbott might not even have seen us. Just then, I heard a car door slam on the drive and looked round in time to see Anne Cleary and George Elkin getting out of the dusty green Volkswagen that had brought them here. I waited for them to come in. Elkin hadn't made any effort to dress up for the party. He was wearing the same jacket with the elbow patches and a check shirt. He didn't look happy to be here.

I smiled at Anne. 'Did you manage to find your ... ?' I began.

But Anne wasn't looking at me. She seemed stunned. I followed her eyes and realised that she was staring at Derek Abbott and the woman. She was shocked.

'Anne?' I asked. 'Are you all right?'

She noticed me for the first time. 'That man ... !' she faltered. 'Who is he?'

'His name is Derek Abbott,' I said. 'Do you know him?'

'I've seen him ... somewhere.'

'Maybe you met him in prison,' I suggested.

It was a stupid thing to say. But Anne and I had spent quite a bit of time talking about her prison charity, Books Behind Bars, and there was a part of me that wanted to stir things up. I was still annoyed with Hawthorne and my comment was actually a gentle stab in his direction. He didn't respond.

But Anne had gone quite pale. 'Oh my goodness!' she exclaimed. 'I think you're right. That's exactly where I met him. He was in one of my reading groups ... I'm sure of it!' She turned to Elkin. 'I wonder if I should even stay here. What do I say to him if he remembers me?'

'Best not say anything,' Elkin muttered. 'Nobody really talks to him anyway. I'm surprised he's here.'

'I don't know ...'

She was saved by the arrival of Kathryn Harris, who had come hurrying out of the living room and now imposed herself between us with the drinks tray. 'Red, white or rosé,' she announced cheerfully. 'Or there's beer on the far table, as well as lemonade and sparkling water.'

Anne and I each picked a glass of wine. Hawthorne chose lemonade.

'We'll be bringing out the chicken satay in a moment,' Kathryn continued. 'But save some room for the steak and kidney puddings. They're Marc's speciality!'

By the time she had finished her recommendations, Abbott had turned his back on us and limped over to the sun lounge. I had to smile. There were now three of us who would have to keep our distance from him to avoid any further embarrassment.

Even so, the evening passed pleasantly enough and, despite my earlier reservations, I was glad I'd come. The music was being provided by three men in striped jackets, white trousers and straw hats; they called themselves The Channelers and according to the advertisement propped up in front of the synthesiser, they could be heard every other Thursday at The Divers Inn. The sun had fully set by now and the garden was shrouded in darkness, but there were pinpricks of electric light on either side of the path and a soft yellow glow behind the windows of the pavilion at the end. To be fair to Marc Bellamy (and to Charles le Mesurier, who had paid for it), there was plenty of food. The chicken satay was followed by Welsh rarebits, chicken vol-au-vent, stuffed Yorkshire puddings, sausage rolls and shrimp skewers – all very retro and 'cobblers to calories'. The shrimp even came with a Marie Rose dip.

I chatted to several of the guests, including Judith and Colin Matheson, the first time I had actually seen them together. It was strange how unsuited they were. She was a couple of inches taller than him and quite a bit broader and as he stood next to her he shrank into himself even more than usual, glancing nervously around the room whilst clutching a glass of clear liquid.

'Gin and tonic?' I asked.

'Perrier.' Colin grimaced. 'I'm the designated driver.'

'I've had very good feedback from your session this afternoon,' Judith said.

'I was sorry not to see you there.'

'I was sorry I had to miss it. I hope Colin told you. I had some issues at home.'

Issues at home. She'd chosen the words carefully, not wanting to give too much away, and she quickly steered her husband into the next room before he could add anything more.

Once again I caught sight of Derek Abbott. It was impossible to avoid him completely. He had retreated to the far corner, lowering himself into an armchair with his walking stick resting against the arm. He was sitting there managing to be both defensive and aggressive. Most people seemed to be ignoring him, but he had been invited and so he had come, to hell with what they thought. That was what he seemed to be saying. If he hadn't seen me on stage, I might have been tempted to go over and talk to him myself. But he knew who I was and what was I going to say to him? 'Is it true that Hawthorne pushed you down a flight of concrete steps because you were dealing in child pornography?' Hardly the perfect ice-breaker at a social gathering like this.

Hawthorne, for his part, never came close. I noticed him in the kitchen, in conversation with Colin Matheson. Although we had arrived together, we had hardly spoken a word all evening. Perhaps we had nothing to talk about. All the time we had spent together – in London, Kent and Yorkshire, in taxis and trains, his home and mine – we had been pursuing an investigation. He was the detective. I was the writer. That was what defined us as far as he was concerned.

Even so, we had come to Alderney as a team. I had thought we might enjoy our time on the island but even that small hope had been dashed by the appearance of Derek Abbott. Was I wrong to have been so angry? The trouble with Hawthorne was that he had his own way of doing things, his own code of conduct. He wouldn't care if you disagreed with him. But if you tried to argue with him, you'd almost certainly come off worse and maybe that was what I was discovering now.

I was just going over to join him when Charles le Mesurier stepped in front of me, blocking my way. He was closer than

I would have liked and I could smell the alcohol on his breath. 'I enjoyed that little chat of yours this afternoon,' he said.

'Thank you. I like your house.'

'Yes. I had a whole load of designers in, but in the end I came up with most of it myself.' He was quite drunk, not exactly slurring his words but a little too emphatic in the way he spoke. I noticed that while we had all been given wine or beer, he had a crystal flute of champagne, which he was holding with his thumb and first finger on either side of the rim.

'What's the building at the bottom of the garden?' I asked.

'That was put there by the Germans in the war. It's actually a gunnery, but after I bought the place I turned it into a sort of summer house ... somewhere private to hang out.' He leered at me. 'I call it the Snuggery. I rather like that. Gunnery to Snuggery.'

'Do you spend a lot of time here?'

'God, no! As little as possible! You know what they say about this place? Two thousand alcoholics clinging to a rock. I'd go mad if I stayed here more than a couple of months at one go. I have my business interests. Spin-the-wheel and all the rest of it. But I like to move around. London, the South of France, New York ...'

'And you're involved with the power line.' I was remembering what Elkin had told me.

He looked at me queerly. 'Who's been talking to you about that?'

'I've noticed the signs.'

'Ban NAB.' He laughed mirthlessly. 'That's exactly what I mean about Alderney. The people here are stuck in the nineteenth century. Give them anything that will actually make a difference – cheap electricity to the UK and a nice little earner in their pocket – and half of them think the sky's going to fall in.'

He was going to continue but then Marc Bellamy walked past with a plate of devilled eggs and he spun round. 'Hey, Tea Leaf!' he exclaimed. 'I'm going to lift one of those, if you don't mind.' He snatched half an egg and slid it into his mouth. 'Not bad at all,' he said – with his mouth full. 'I have to say, you've done really well for yourself,' he went on. 'Your own show on Channel 5!'

'ITV2,' Marc said.

'Maybe you should be a guest on *I'm a Celebrity … !* I'm sure you'd be completely at home with those mealworms and kangaroo testicles.'

Marc stared at him with bleak hostility and I thought he was going to snap back, but then he swallowed his words and moved on.

There really was something uniquely offensive about Charles le Mesurier, particularly after he'd had too much to drink. The alcohol accentuated his public-school accent, so that everything he said came out with a sneer. His good looks – the swathe of grey hair, the aristocratic nose – only made him seem all the more superior and self-assured. He wasn't an easy man to like.

'You haven't met the wife,' he said.

I didn't know who he meant but then I turned round and saw her. 'The wife' was the woman who had been talking to Derek Abbott when I arrived. She had crept up behind me and now stood facing her husband, hands on hips and a scowl on her face.

'I'm going to bed,' she announced.

'You're not serious.'

'I'm exhausted, Charles.'

'How much money did you manage to spend?'

'I don't know. You'll find out at the end of the month.'

He still didn't want her to go. He pointed at me. 'Helen, this is Anthony. He's a famous writer.'

'Hello,' I said. 'I heard you were in Paris.'

'I got back this afternoon.'

'Are there direct flights?'

She gave me a look. 'We have a PJ,' she explained.

Of course, she was rich. She looked it. The dress she was wearing screamed haute couture – a combination of pink toile, beading and feathers that actually covered very little of her body but at enormous cost – and there was a cascade of diamonds around her neck. She was tired and she was irritated but she still exuded sexuality from her strawberry blonde hair to her Marilyn Monroe lips to the generous curves of her body.

It was hard to gauge her relationship with Charles le Mesurier. There was a careless quality to the way they spoke to each other, even in front of me. They would probably have no qualms about having a full-blooded row in public. And yet there was definitely some sort of affection there. It was as if they had known each other so long that they no longer cared about pretences. You had to accept them for who they were and if you didn't like it, that was your problem.

Charles le Mesurier tried one last time. 'We're having a party, baby. You can't go to bed.'

'*You're* having the party, Charles. Nobody knows who I am and nobody gives a damn. You can manage without me. Just try not to wake me when you come upstairs.'

'All right. All right.' He leaned towards me, cupping his hand over his mouth as if he didn't want her to hear. 'We've been together fifteen years and I don't know what I'd do without her. Look at her! The face that launched a thousand chips.' He smiled at his own witticism and weaved away.

Helen and I were left together and suddenly she relaxed a little. 'I'm sorry about that,' she said. 'Charles is a darling really. But he can be so boring when he's had a few drinks. There are times when I literally want to kill him.'

'What did he mean?' I asked. 'A thousand chips?'

She laughed. 'That's what he always says. It goes back to the time when I used to work for him at Spin-the-wheel.' I still didn't get it so she added: 'Roulette chips.'

'Oh.'

'God knows why he decided to sponsor a literary festival. He never reads. Maybe he thought it would make him look respectable. I'm sorry. What did you say your name was?'

I told her.

'And you're a writer? I'm afraid I haven't read anything by you, but then I don't read much either. Well, you're going to have to forgive me. I really have had a long day. It was nice to meet you. Good night.'

She disappeared in the direction of the hallway. I saw her turn left, presumably heading for the stairs. I looked at my watch and saw that it was ten past nine. I thought of leaving too.

Charles le Mesurier must have been waiting for her to go because the moment she was out of sight, he meandered across to the archway leading into the kitchen. He had noticed Kathryn Harris – in her French-maid costume – standing on the other side, helping herself to the last cheese puff on one of the plates. The crowd was beginning to thin out a little – perhaps people didn't keep late nights in Alderney – so I saw what happened next quite clearly.

Before Kathryn had managed to eat, le Mesurier sidled up to her, placed his lips very close to her ear and whispered something, then leaned back with a twisted smile. I didn't need to hear the words to know what he was suggesting. It was virtually a repeat performance of what had happened at The Divers Inn. The girl took a step away from him and now the kitchen wall separated her from me so I couldn't see her response. But whatever it was, le Mesurier seemed amused. He took another swig of champagne, then lurched into the dining room and another group of guests.

This time I couldn't just let it go. Despite my misgivings, I went into the kitchen – ultra-modern, of course, with gleaming surfaces and brand-new equipment – to find Kathryn at the sink, plunging glasses into foamy water. There were twenty or thirty lined up on one side. 'Excuse me,' I said. 'Are you all right?'

She spoke with her back to me. 'I'm fine, thank you.'

'It's just that I saw what happened ...'

'Nothing happened.' She turned round and I saw at once the tears of indignation pricking at her eyes. 'Honestly. Thank you for being concerned, but it really doesn't matter.'

'He shouldn't be allowed to get away with it ... behaving that way. I know it's his house and his party. But even so—'

'Please! Don't say anything.' She sounded almost afraid. 'I don't want to lose my job. He didn't actually do anything. He's just a dirty old man. Like they all are.' She turned back to the sink. 'I need to get these glasses done. We stop serving at ten.'

'Are you sure?'

'Absolutely.'

'Well, I'm sorry ...'

Feeling very uncomfortable, I walked out of the kitchen and went in search of Hawthorne. I got the sense that the party had developed a stale, sated quality, the sort that comes after two hours of overindulgence. It was time to move on. The Channelers had launched into a jazzed-up version of *The Blue Danube*, but they were sweating and out of sync. There were plates of half-eaten food everywhere. I looked for Hawthorne in the sun lounge and the living room. Then I went out onto the patio. It was always possible that he had gone out for a smoke.

The evening was cool and very dark. I could see the lights on either side of the path and, almost lost in the shadows, the solid bulk of the building at the end. What had le Mesurier called it? The Snuggery. There was no sign of Hawthorne, but glancing to one side I noticed a solitary figure sitting on a wooden bench and realised it was Elizabeth Lovell. She was on her own, some distance away, lighting a cigarette, which somehow surprised me. There was no reason why a woman who was blind and psychic shouldn't be allowed a cigarette, but somehow it felt at odds with her public persona. Her husband wasn't with her and I was glad to be able to slip back inside without being seen.

Hawthorne had left without me. Suddenly, I was glad that this time tomorrow I would be home again. I was missing my wife. There was absolutely no reason for me to be here. An open door led back into the kitchen and from there I continued into the hall, where a pile of books had been set up on a table: *Lovely Grub* by Marc Bellamy. His photograph, in which he was cradling a mixing bowl with a ladle, was on the cover. It was on sale for £20.

I picked up a copy and opened it at random. I found myself looking at a recipe for Chicken Cordon Bleu, a dish that had revolted me even when I ate it back in the seventies. The ingredients – oil, butter, cheese, cream, breadcrumbs – felt like signposts on the way to a heart attack. I snapped it shut just as Maïssa Lamar appeared, coming downstairs. I don't know which of the two of us was more surprised. I got the sense that she had hoped not to be seen.

She came over to the table. I handed her the book. 'Cookery,' I said.

'I'm sorry?'

'*C'est un livre de cuisine.*'

'You speak French?'

'*Un petit peu.*'

If I'd been trying to impress her, it hadn't worked. She tried to push the book back into my hands, but I wanted to keep her talking. 'I enjoyed your performance this morning,' I said.

'Thank you.'

'And I met your friend.'

'I'm sorry?'

'Fair hair. Moustache. He was at the airport.'

She looked at me blankly. 'I'm sorry. I have no friend.' Abruptly, she dropped the book onto the table and went into the living room.

It was definitely time to go. I walked out of the house and climbed into the first taxi I saw. I had to wait a few minutes until two more guests arrived to fill the other seats, but then we set off. Without realising it, I'd had too much to drink. I wasn't drunk, but I could feel the self-disgust that alcohol always inspires when it doesn't make you happy. Ten minutes later, we arrived at the hotel. I grabbed my key and went up to my room. I got undressed, throwing all my clothes onto one of the armchairs. I cleaned my teeth. I went to bed.

The next thing I knew, it was morning and I was aware that I was no longer alone in the room. Someone had woken me up. I opened my eyes and then closed them again. Hawthorne was standing at the end of my bed. I couldn't believe he was there. How had he even got into the room?

'Hawthorne ...' I muttered. It was outrageous. I was asleep, unshaven, in my undershorts, in bed.

'Tony, mate, get up and get dressed,' Hawthorne said. 'There's been a murder.'

8

The Snuggery

'Who's been killed?' I asked. It was the one thing Hawthorne hadn't told me. Actually, so far he hadn't told me anything.

'Charles le Mesurier. Who do you think?'

It was true. Le Mesurier was rich. He was also obnoxious. He had sneered at almost everybody he met. And since we were sitting in the back of a taxi on the way to The Lookout, the victim could only have been him or his wife.

'Who told you?' I asked.

'Colin Matheson. Helen le Mesurier found the body and called him over to the house. He's waiting for us there.'

The driver had been listening to all this. He twisted round. 'There's never been a murder in Alderney!' he told us, his voice full of excitement. It was as if he had been waiting for it all his life.

'What's your name?' Hawthorne asked.

'It's Terry.'

'All right, Terry. Do me a favour and keep your eyes on the road.'

'Yes, sir. Whatever you say.' He stayed silent for about thirty seconds but then he couldn't stop himself. 'Did it happen last night? There was a party and I was there! Maybe I gave the killer a lift!'

There were more cars parked outside The Lookout, but none of them had any police markings. The front door was open and we walked straight into the three rooms, which still hadn't been reassembled. Someone had cleared away all the plates and glasses but the furniture hadn't been moved back into place and there was a sense of emptiness, heightened by the fact that the man who had designed and created all this had been permanently taken from it. Colin and Judith Matheson were already there waiting for us, along with a third man who had not been at the party and who was introduced to us as Dr Queripel.

'Thank you for coming, Mr Hawthorne,' Matheson began. I had never seen a man more out of his depth. It was as if he had no idea why he had been summoned here and, worse than that, no idea what to do. His wife was sitting in an armchair, as white as the pearls around her neck, clutching a ball of tissue in her fist. She didn't look as if she had been crying, though. If anything, she looked angry.

'I didn't know if it was right to call you or not, and you may consider it an impertinence – but this couldn't have happened at a worse time,' Colin began. 'There's no good time for it to have happened, but what I mean is that, unfortunately, two of our constables are on holiday and the third, Sergeant Wilkins, is in bed with a bad back. To be honest, I think this would be beyond his pay grade anyway. We've sent for backup from Guernsey and there are two officers on their way, but in the meantime I thought it sensible to get at least some sort of investigation started. Strike while the iron is hot, so to speak.'

'You did exactly the right thing,' Hawthorne assured him. He turned to the doctor. 'You examined the body?'

'It's the most horrible thing I've ever seen,' Dr Queripel replied. He was in his thirties with fair hair that was already thinning and a lean face. He looked thoroughly decent in his old-fashioned suit. I could imagine him walking a dog, smoking a pipe. Perhaps not at the same time.

'Cause of death?'

'Mr le Mesurier has been stabbed with a paperknife. I think the knife belonged to him, by the way.'

'You'd seen him use it?' Hawthorne asked.

'Yes. I wasn't actually his GP but I'd come over to the house once or twice. He has an office upstairs and it was on his desk.' He lowered his voice and took a step closer so that Judith Matheson wouldn't hear. 'As far as I can see, there's a single deep incision at the front of the neck. I imagine the knife will be lodged in the vertebral body and may have penetrated the spinal cord. There's quite a lot of blood, so it could have nicked the carotid artery too.'

121

'No chance of suicide?'

'Absolutely not. You can see for yourself.'

Hawthorne nodded. 'I should take a look ...'

'Of course. We have to go out through the garden.' Dr Queripel glanced at me, acknowledging my presence for the first time. 'You'll go alone?'

'Actually, if you don't mind, I'll take Tony with me. I always find him very helpful.'

'I suppose I'd better come too,' Matheson said with reluctance.

'Well, all right.'

The four of us went out of the sun lounge and into the garden. I was completely thrown by what Hawthorne had just said. How was I ever helpful? All I ever did was write about him, but of course that was exactly what he was hoping for now. Without realising it, I had stumbled onto – or into – the third book in our three-book contract. For anyone reading this, I suppose it will have been obvious from the start. I wouldn't have been writing about Alderney if we'd just gone to the island, answered a few questions about books and flown home again.

But for me, everything had changed. To give one example, most of what I have described up to now has been done from memory because I had no idea I was going to need any of the finer details, but from this point onwards I began to take careful notes. It was strange, really. I had come to Alderney in the hope that I would be introducing Hawthorne to my world: books, lectures and all the rest of it. But instead, I had once again been dragged into his.

We followed the path that had been illuminated during the party and for the first time I got a proper view of the gun emplacement at the far end of the garden and its relationship to the house. The Lookout, as its name implied, had views of the sea, presumably visible from the upper floors. The garden actually ran from the back of the house to the edge of a cliff, with a beach some distance below. As we drew nearer, I could see the water through the trees.

In the daylight, the Snuggery presented itself as a grey cement box about the size of a single-car garage with metal doors that swung open like shutters and a modern glass door behind. There was a flat roof that doubled as a viewing platform, with three narrow windows just below. A flight of concrete steps climbed steeply up the side. The whole thing was enclosed by shrubs and wild flowers, as if it was trying to hide away from the modern world. It was actually quite a distance from the main house: with the party in full swing and the jazz band playing, it would have been quite possible for Charles le Mesurier to cry out without being heard.

The metal doors had been pulled back and the glass door was half open too. Colin Matheson stayed where he was, not wanting to go back in, so Hawthorne continued without him, accompanied by Dr Queripel. I hesitated for a moment too. Then I went in.

From gunnery to snuggery: there was something distasteful about the change of use. Originally built for killing Allied seamen, the concrete box had been turned into something like a Turkish harem, the walls concealed behind heavy velvet curtains, with a thick Persian rug and an ornate coffee table surrounded by cushions on the floor. The curtains on the back wall had been pulled to one side, revealing a second set of metal doors, identical to the ones through which we had entered. It might have been possible to come in this way, climbing up from the beach, but they were bolted from the inside.

Two low leather banquettes with an arrangement of dark-coloured cushions had been set against the long walls, facing each other, and an elaborate light hung from the ceiling, the wooden shade perforated with tiny triangles, circles and crescent moons. An equally exotic drinks cabinet stood to one side, one door open to reveal a selection of glasses and bottles on mirrored shelves. All that was missing was the hookah and the belly dancers.

Charles le Mesurier was sitting in a high-backed wooden chair – actually it was more like a throne – facing the garden, with his back to the second door. I've described many deaths in the course of my work, in books and on TV, but I'm not sure I've ever managed to capture the absolute horror of the real thing. It's the smell that hits you first, sickening and unmistakable. Dead actors look nothing like dead people. Once the blood has settled and life has drained away, the human body doesn't look remotely human. Knife wounds are particularly disgusting. And I write about these things for entertainment! Sometimes I wonder what I'm doing.

The first thing I saw was the knife handle protruding from Charles le Mesurier's throat. It was slim, silver, ornate; a letter opener, Dr Queripel had said. The silk jacket and trousers he had worn at the party clung to him, glued there by the blood that had fountained down from the wound. There was a dark pool of it around his tasselled suede loafers.

'It's merciless,' Dr Queripel muttered.

It seemed an odd choice of word, but then, with a jolt, I realised what he meant. Before he had been killed, le Mesurier's wrists and ankles had been tied to the chair with brown parcel tape. At least, three of them had. His right hand had been left free and now lay palm upwards, limp, the fingers curled as if he was asking for money. It was a bizarre detail. What could possibly have been done to him before he was murdered, and what had his one hand been needed for?

'You've seen?' Dr Queripel asked. He was talking to Hawthorne.

Hawthorne had approached the body, avoiding the blood. He looked carefully at the entrance wound made by the knife, then examined the back of le Mesurier's head. Finally, his eyes travelled down to the dead man's hands. 'Was he left-handed or right-handed?' he asked.

'I don't really know. Why do you ask?'

'His watch,' Hawthorne said. 'He wore a Rolex, but it's gone.' It was true. The shirtsleeve, saturated in blood, hung open, revealing a wrist that was bare.

'I don't know.' Dr Queripel was aghast. 'I have a feeling he was right-handed. But are you really suggesting that somebody did all this to steal his watch?'

'There's no sign of any break-in and he's wearing the same clothes he had on at the party, so it looks as if he came straight here, either alone or with someone. Maybe he'd arranged a meeting. There's a contusion on the back of his head – I'd say he's been hit with a blunt object. He was forced into the chair and tied down. One wrist was left free. There has to be a reason.'

'Maybe the killer ran out of tape,' I said.

This suggestion was greeted with silence.

Dr Queripel took a step closer and Hawthorne held up a hand. 'Please be careful!'

The doctor stopped and Hawthorne pointed to an area of carpet about halfway between the chair and the door into the garden. The dark red and mauve pattern made it difficult to make out what he had seen, but looking closer, I noticed the shape of a partial footprint. There was a curve where the toecap had come into contact with the blood. It could have been left behind by a man or a woman, but from the size I got the impression that it was someone with small feet.

'Dear God!' Queripel exclaimed. The footprint pointed towards the door. 'This is how he made his getaway!'

'Yes. The trail continues back into the garden.'

'So he was knocked out, tied down and then killed,' Queripel said. 'And whoever did it went back to the house ... presumably while the party was still going on.' He thought for a moment. 'I suppose that narrows the field.'

I was really hoping we had finished in the Snuggery, but before we left Hawthorne gently pulled back the curtains on both sides to reveal bare concrete walls with no windows. He examined the second set of doors and, using a handkerchief, slid back the bolt. He opened the door and the sunlight blazed in, as if determined to purify the grim scene. All three of us breathed in the fresh air with gratitude. Finally, Hawthorne closed the door and locked it again, leaving everything as it had been when we arrived.

He made his way back towards us, then stopped and knelt down. As I stood there watching, he reached into his jacket pocket and took out a business card from the Braye Beach Hotel and used it to scoop up a coin that had been lying on the rug near one of the curtains. He held it up and showed it to me. It was a two-euro piece.

'Do you think that was his?' I asked.

'Your guess is as good as mine, mate.'

'We use English currency on Alderney,' Dr Queripel said. 'But France is only eight miles away.'

'His wife, Helen, had just come back from Paris,' I added. 'And the performance poet Maïssa Lamar is French.'

I thought I was being helpful but it was as if Hawthorne hadn't heard.

'I think, maybe, you should leave it for the police,' Queripel said with a touch of admonition in his voice.

'Whatever you say,' Hawthorne replied cheerfully, and he slid the coin gently back onto the floor.

We went back outside where Colin Matheson was waiting for us, still looking queasy. 'Have you seen enough?' he asked.

'More than enough,' I said.

Hawthorne was unfazed. 'Well, Charles le Mesurier certainly didn't have a very nice end to the evening,' he said. 'How's Mrs le Mesurier getting on?'

'She's gone back to bed. She's in shock.'

'When did she find him?'

'This morning.' Colin Matheson looked exhausted. 'She woke up at half past seven and realised he wasn't in the bed. She looked for him in the spare rooms and downstairs. Then she saw the door of the gunnery was open and so she came over here.' He shook his head. 'It must have been absolutely ghastly for her.'

'I've given her a mild sedative,' the doctor said.

Matheson turned to Hawthorne. 'I don't know if you have any thoughts, Mr Hawthorne ...'

'Well, first of all, nobody must leave the island.'

'Absolutely. Mr Torode said the same thing.'

'Who is Mr Torode?'

'He's the deputy chief officer of the Guernsey Crime Services. He's one of the officers who's coming over.'

'Right.' If Hawthorne was put out, he didn't show it. 'Let's not waste any time while he's on his way. I'd like to talk to Helen le Mesurier. And it would be helpful if you could pick up Marc Bellamy and that girl he was working with and bring them across.'

'Why?' Matheson was surprised.

'They organised the party and they were looking after the guests. If le Mesurier decided to slip off into the garden – and, for that matter, if anyone followed him – they might have noticed.'

That made sense. With a wall completely enclosing the garden and the back door locked, the killer would surely have had to approach the Snuggery from the house. So it had to be someone who had been at the party. Someone I had seen.

We began to walk back towards the sun lounge.

'What was your relationship with le Mesurier?' Hawthorne asked. He directed the question at Dr Queripel.

'I'm sorry?'

'I'm interested to know what you were doing in his study. You said you'd been in there a couple of times and that was how you knew about the paperknife. But you weren't his GP and there was obviously no love lost between you ...'

'How can you possibly say that?'

'Well, you haven't exactly been shedding tears over his demise. You referred to him as Mr le Mesurier, so you weren't on first-name terms, and I didn't see you at the party last night. Given that Alderney isn't exactly a whirl of social activity, I'm assuming you weren't invited.'

Dr Queripel was the sort of man who blushed easily and he did so now. 'As a matter of fact, there's plenty to do on Alderney,' he replied. 'And last night, my wife and I had a very pleasant evening playing bridge. But you're right. I was not on friendly terms with Mr le Mesurier and the reason I saw him on two occasions was strictly business.'

'What business?'

'The power line.'

'Dr Queripel is one of the most vocal opponents to the Normandy-Alderney-Britain power line,' Matheson cut in. He looked embarrassed. Or maybe he was angry. He was certainly uncomfortable. 'He's actually organised quite a few demonstrations against it.'

'So you're the one painting "BAN NAB" all over the place?' Hawthorne asked.

'Not at all. I would never take part in that sort of activity. But those of us who are opposed to this awful scheme are entitled to have their voices heard and I had two meetings with le Mesurier, in his study, to get our point across.'

We had stopped walking about halfway between the Snuggery and the house. Colin Matheson and Dr Queripel were facing each other like two boxers squaring up before a fight and at that moment all thought of the murder seemed to have vanished.

'What did you say to him?' Hawthorne asked.

'The obvious. The power line and the construction around it will rip the heart out of Alderney. The cable landing chambers, the transition posts, the converter stations. There are almost no foreseeable benefits and the damage to the environment, to wildlife and to tourism will be irreversible.'

'Why did you feel you had to talk to le Mesurier?' Hawthorne asked. 'I thought Colin here was in charge of the committee making the decisions.'

Dr Queripel nodded. 'Colin is the head of the committee set up by the States, but everyone knows that it's le Mesurier who's pulling the strings.' He stared across at the other man. 'I still don't know how he got to you, Colin, or how he made you dance to his tune. Or maybe it's just a question of how much he offered you—'

'That's outrageous!'

'—but it was le Mesurier who wanted this bloody thing and he was the one who was going to benefit the most.'

'In what way?'

'Well, for a start, he'd sold his own land for the converter station. He wouldn't disclose how much he'd made out of that, but I bet it was a damn sight more than anyone else on this island was going to see—'

'You should be careful what you say, Henry,' Matheson cut in, glaring at Dr Queripel. 'And it might help if you were a little less hypocritical. Everyone knows that the only reason you're against this project is because you're worried about your view.'

'What is Alderney without its views?'

'It's a beautiful island and it's a shame that the converter station has to go between your house and the sea, but it had to go somewhere.'

'And it's just a coincidence that it goes on le Mesurier's land?' Queripel was fighting to keep his self-control. 'Who knows what deals he was making with Électricité du Nord? Without him, this whole thing would never have got as far as it did and – with a bit of luck – now that he's dead, perhaps it'll all go away.'

'You don't sound too sorry he's been killed,' Hawthorne remarked.

'I'm not. Tying him to a chair and putting a knife through him? I can think of fifty people on this island who would have been happy to do it. And before you interrupt me, Colin, you're probably one of them. He had you twisted round his little finger. I've known you half my life. You'd never have voted for NAB if you weren't being forced into it, and if it turns out that you decided you'd had enough and had to put an end to it, I'd be the first to shake your hand.'

Henry Queripel spun on his heel and continued towards the house. Colin looked at us, trying to find something to say. 'It's all nonsense,' he muttered. 'I hardly knew Charles. I mean, obviously I saw him from time to time. I gave him legal advice and more recently, of course, there was the festival, which he sponsored and my wife organised. But to suggest he had any influence over me … that's plain wrong. I supported the power line because I thought it was the right thing for the island.'

'And will you still support it now?' Hawthorne asked.

'Of course. Well … I suppose we'll have to see.'

The three of us went after the doctor. Hawthorne was smiling and I could see he had enjoyed the whole encounter. After all, we'd only been at the murder scene a few minutes and already two possible suspects had revealed themselves to him. And all he'd had to do was watch.

9

Roses and Butterflies

'I don't understand. Who are you? What are you doing here? Why do I have to talk to you?'

It looked as if Helen le Mesurier had been crying ever since she had made her grisly discovery. There were balls of damp tissues all over the bedroom floor and her eyes were red and swollen. Was she exaggerating? She had been tired and tetchy the night before, but even allowing for that, she hadn't seemed entirely devoted to her husband. *There are times when I literally want to kill him.* I remembered her saying those very words and frankly, when Hawthorne had told me who'd been murdered, she had immediately come to mind as the most likely suspect.

The bedroom was large, in the very centre of the house, with two long windows slanting towards one another, providing two different views of the garden, the Snuggery and the sea. It was filled with expensive reproduction furniture that was pretending to be eighteenth-century French. The bed was a great pile of silk and wooden cur-licues. The dressing table, curving under the weight of so many perfumes and cosmetics, could have come straight out of a French farce. Helen was sitting on a gilded sofa that boasted embroidered cushions and bow legs. She was wearing a Ricky Martin T-shirt that came down to her thighs and black leggings. Someone had brought her a cup of tea in a porcelain cup and saucer. It was on an orna-mental table beside her.

Hawthorne was sitting opposite, perching on the stool that he had taken from the dressing table. Matheson had intro-duced him as a detective helping the police with their enquiries but Helen wasn't having any of it. 'Where are the *real* police?' she asked Colin, angrily. 'Who asked this man to come into my house? And what's *he* doing here?'

That was me. Her finger stabbed out in my direction even though I'd done my best to blend into the background – not easy when the wallpaper had a pattern of roses and butterflies. I tried to avoid her eye.

'They're trying to help,' Colin said, uneasily.

Hawthorne leaned forward. 'We just want to know who killed your husband,' he said reasonably. 'The police are on their way from Guernsey, but the first twenty-four hours after a crime has been committed are the most important of all and we don't want to waste any of them. It was a very unpleasant act of violence. He was killed in an extremely nasty way – as you saw.' He paused. 'You wouldn't want anyone to think you were unwilling to help.'

'I don't care what people think.' Helen le Mesurier turned to Colin. 'Do I have to talk to them?'

'I think it might be a good idea,' Colin replied.

'I don't know.' She pulled out another tissue. 'He was sitting in a chair. He was tied up. And that knife! I bought him that knife. I got it in Barcelona.' She began to cry again.

'I can understand how upset you are,' Hawthorne said, speaking softly. 'But I need to ask you about your movements last night.'

'I can't help you. I don't know anything. I came in and went to bed. I didn't see anything.'

It was a start, anyway. 'You'd just come back from Paris?' Hawthorne asked.

'I got back in the afternoon.'

'What were you doing there?'

Helen dabbed at her eyes as she considered the question. 'I went shopping.'

'Where?'

'I don't remember. The Marais. Palais-Royal. Boulevard Haussmann ...'

Hawthorne cast an eye around the room. 'I don't see any shopping bags.'

That stopped her short. I actually saw the change come over her as she realised she wasn't just being asked questions: she was under attack. 'I didn't see anything I wanted to buy.'

'But you were in Paris for . . . two days?' She didn't answer, so he went on. 'Where did you stay?'

'The Bristol.'

'Were you alone?' Again she didn't speak. Hawthorne looked at her almost sadly. 'The thing is, Mrs le Mesurier, the police are going to ask you the same questions and you can't lie to them. They'll talk to the receptionist. And these days, there's CCTV, phone records . . .' He spread his hands. 'I know it's not very nice having to talk about personal matters, but it's all going to come out anyway, so you might as well get it over with.'

'I want a cigarette.'

'Have one of mine.' He took out a packet and they both lit up. It was strange to see two people smoking indoors, but I suppose it was her house. Their lungs. 'So who were you with?' Hawthorne asked.

The two of them had bonded in some strange way over the cigarettes. Suddenly, she was less antagonistic. 'You have to understand,' she said. 'I did love Charles. I'd been married to him for fifteen years.'

'No children?'

'It didn't happen for us, but we didn't want children anyway. I've got nephews and nieces. That's good enough for me.'

'How did the two of you meet?'

'I was an actress. He saw me in a production of *The Sound of Music*. I was one of the nuns. He offered me a job and things developed from there.'

'What job?'

'Modelling. PR. I helped him with his internet business and then we started going out together and in the end we got married. You didn't know him so you may not understand, but actually I always knew what I was getting myself into. Charles was never going to stay at home and sit in an armchair, watching TV. He wasn't that sort of man.'

'What sort of man was he, Mrs le Mesurier?'

'He liked life. He liked women. Lots of women. There was no stopping him.' She looked to me for confirmation. 'You must have seen him last night. Even that girl who was serving the drinks . . . he couldn't keep his eyes off her. That's how he was . . . in New York, in Saint-Tropez, in London. He was always on the move, always after the next conquest. I just had to live with it.'

'Are you saying you didn't mind?'

'Why should I have minded, Mr Hawthorne? I had a lot of fun with Charles. He was witty. He was generous. And if he could be a complete prick some of the time, there were plenty of compensations.' She counted them on her fingers. 'I had an allowance. I had this house. I had expensive presents. I could travel. Charles might be out there being photographed with different floozies for the gossip columns, but I was the one he always came home to. And for what it's worth, he wasn't the only one who played the field. We both did. We had an open marriage. No secrets from each other.'

'He knew who you were with in Paris?'

Helen shook her head. 'No. I hadn't told him yet. I would have eventually. I didn't get the chance.'

'So who was he?'

For the first time, she looked vulnerable. 'If I tell you his name, will you contact him?'

'I might.'

She didn't know whether to go on or not, but she knew she had no choice. She put the cigarette to her lips and the tip glowed red. 'Jean-François Berthold,' she said. The answer came out in a swirl of smoke. 'I met him when he came to Alderney.'

'And what was Jean-François Berthold doing in Alderney?'

'He's a land surveyor. He was working for a French company.'

'Would that be Électricité du Nord?'

'Yes.' She was surprised he knew. Or perhaps she'd hoped he didn't. 'He's part of the NAB project ...'

'Which your husband supported.'

'I really don't think that's an appropriate question,' Colin Matheson cut in. He had been so quiet up to now that I'd almost forgotten he was in the room.

'Why not?' Hawthorne demanded.

'Charles has just been killed. Helen is in shock. And you're suggesting some sort of ... conspiracy?'

Hawthorne turned back to Helen. 'Are you in shock, Mrs le Mesurier?' he asked.

Helen sniffed. 'I'm upset. Of course I am.'

Hawthorne got up and went over to the window. 'You arrived yesterday from Paris. You didn't stay long at the party. You went upstairs. Do you know what time that was?'

She didn't know, so I helped her out. 'It was ten past nine,' I said. I remembered looking at my watch.

'Did you go straight to bed?'

'I unpacked and had a bath first.'

'Were the curtains drawn?'

Helen thought back. 'No. I drew them myself. After my bath.'

Hawthorne looked out of the window. 'You can see the Snuggery from here.'

'I didn't see anything! I mean, I didn't see anyone go in or come out, if that's what you're getting at, Mr Hawthorne. Even if I had looked out of the window – and I didn't – it would have been too dark to see the bottom of the garden.' She paused. 'I think I did notice that the lights were on inside, but that's all I can tell you.' She was almost daring him to challenge her. 'Is there anything else?'

'Did you hear anyone come upstairs? During the party or immediately afterwards.'

'No. Who would have come upstairs? Only Charles, and he didn't, did he?' She reached forward and stubbed out her cigarette. When she looked up again, there were fresh tears in her eyes. 'And now we know why.'

Hawthorne took pity on her. 'Thank you, Mrs le Mesurier. You've been helpful. There is just one last thing. Was your husband left-handed or right-handed?'

'Why would you want to know that?' She shook her head and sighed. 'He was right-handed.'

'Did he wear his Rolex on his right wrist?'

'Yes.'

'And do you know where he got it?'

'He bought it in Hong Kong. It was gold – and very expensive.'

'How expensive?'

'He told me he'd paid £20,000, but it might have been more. Why do you want to know?'

'The watch has gone. Do you know if he was wearing it last night?'

'Of course he was. He never took it off.' She corrected herself. 'Only sometimes ... before he went to bed.' She looked uncomfortable. 'He'd do that as a signal.'

'What sort of signal?'

'When he wanted to be intimate, he took off his watch.'

Hawthorne considered this. 'But he didn't come to bed.'

'Not with me.' She reached out and picked up her cup of tea as if to say that she'd had enough of these questions and wanted to be left alone. Hawthorne examined her for a moment. Then, with a nod, he left. Colin Matheson and I followed.

'The office ...' Hawthorne said, as we stepped outside.

Matheson looked at him blankly.

'I want to see where the paperknife came from.'

'Oh, yes ... This way.'

He led us down a corridor painted white with a single dazzle of colour at the end: a photomontage of Charles le Mesurier done in the style of Andy Warhol. There was an open door beside it and the three of us went into a modern home office with lots of bookshelves but very few books. An angular black wooden desk dominated the room. Buy two and put them together and you could have made a swastika. A black leather chair with a high back stood behind. A gleaming chrome desk lamp – possibly Italian, certainly expensive – curved towards a giant computer screen. A mobile phone, presumably le Mesurier's, lay to one side. Using a handkerchief, Hawthorne picked it up and examined it. He showed it to me.

'What do you make of that, Tony?'

There was a smear of something rust-coloured on the back. 'Blood?' I asked.

'I think so.'

'But how is that possible? If he was killed in the Snuggery, how did the phone get to be here?' I thought it through. 'Maybe it's somebody else's blood.'

'We'll have to get a test.' He laid the phone down again.

The room was so neat and minimalist that it was impossible to tell if anything had been disturbed. Hawthorne said nothing as he opened three of the desk drawers – the fourth was locked – and tapped the computer to see if it was turned on. It wasn't. There was another vibrant artwork on the wall, matching the one outside in both size and style. This one showed Helen le Mesurier standing beside a roulette wheel, holding a paddle. *The face that launched a thousand chips.*

'I'm not sure we should really be here,' Colin Matheson said.

'Nobody's asking you to be here,' Hawthorne replied, affably.

He searched around, possibly looking for the key to the locked drawer, then gave up. There was nothing here. But at least he had established a sequence of events ... or so I imagined. Whoever had killed Charles le Mesurier had come back into the house from the Snuggery and continued upstairs. They had searched for something in the study while Helen le Mesurier slept a few doors away. Perhaps they had picked up the mobile phone, transferring a blood-stain to the back. Could that even be the reason why he had been murdered? Was there something on the phone or in the computer that the killer needed? Le Mesurier had been tied down. Perhaps he had been threatened with torture unless he gave up the password. Yes. That made sense.

We heard the front door open and I heard Kathryn Harris's voice coming from downstairs. She sounded indignant. That reminded me of what had happened the night before in the kitchen: Charles le Mesurier almost assaulting her. Quickly, I drew Hawthorne aside and told him what I'd seen.

'If anyone had a motive to kill him,' I said, 'it was her.'

'When was this?' Hawthorne asked.

'It was just after his wife had gone to bed.'

Hawthorne smiled. 'At least he had the decency to wait until she was out of the way.'

We made our way back downstairs to the entrance hall. Marc Bellamy and Kathryn Harris had arrived together. He was looking very much the worse for wear, pale and dishevelled, as if he had slept badly. Someone had just woken him up, bundled him into a taxi and brought him here. I probably didn't look much better.

'What's all this about?' Marc asked. No 'How do!' today. He was wearing a hoody from his own television show, with the words 'Lovely Grub' stitched across the chest. He hadn't had time to shave and the stubble did him no favours, emphasising his poor skin, his jowls. 'What's happened?'

'Let's talk in the kitchen,' Hawthorne suggested.

'I've made some tea,' Judith Matheson said. Of course she had. She was the sort of woman who would always make tea no matter what the crisis. Lose your leg in a hideous industrial accident and she'd be there with a nice cup of Earl Grey.

The Mathesons followed us into the kitchen, then left us together: Hawthorne and me and our two witnesses.

'So what's going on?' Marc demanded. 'Has someone died?'

'Charles le Mesurier has been killed,' Hawthorne told him.

I could see all sorts of things going through Marc's head as he digested the news. 'Well, I'll be ... ! You're not serious?'

'Are you saying he's been murdered?' Kathryn cut in. She was sitting next to her employer and out of the two of them she seemed the more relaxed. Perhaps she had got out of bed earlier, but she looked showered and refreshed, her hair neatly combed, dressed in a tracksuit, her eyes quite calm behind the oversized glasses.

'That's exactly what I'm saying.'

'Well, I'll go to the foot of the stairs!' Now that he'd been given a bit of time to consider what had happened, Marc Bellamy couldn't hide a smirk. 'How did they do it?'

'He was stabbed.'

'Serves the bugger right. I shouldn't say it. But he was a nasty piece of work . . . all that sneering and sniping. No-one's going to miss him now that he's gone.'

Kathryn looked at him in surprise – not because of what he had said but because he had said it at all. 'Why are we here?' she asked. 'You can't think I had anything to do with this. I never even met him until I came here.' Another thought occurred to her. 'And if you don't mind my asking, what exactly has it got to do with you anyway? You're just here as part of the festival, the same as us.'

'You don't need to talk to me if you don't want to, Ms Harris,' Hawthorne replied, gently menacing. 'I'm just trying to work out where everyone was and at what time and it seems to me that you and Mr Bellamy here are best placed to tell me that. You were looking after the guests. It was part of your job to keep an eye on them.'

'I don't mind talking to you,' Marc exclaimed. 'I haven't got anything to hide. I was working all evening. I was mainly in the kitchen. Left about ten fifteen.' He stared. 'Don't tell me it was a kitchen knife! He had a nice set of Sabatier. Did someone shove one of those into his neck?'

'Who said anything about his neck?' Hawthorne said.

Marc faltered. 'Just a figure of speech.'

Hawthorne turned his attention to the assistant. 'How long have you worked for Mr Bellamy?' he asked.

'Kathryn only joined me six months ago.' Marc had decided to answer for her. 'My last assistant – Jo – went on to *Saturday Kitchen*.' His little eyes brightened. 'She was poached!' It was a joke he had made many times before but this time it fell flat and he knew it. 'I was about to advertise but Jo recommended Kathryn. I interviewed her and we got on like the proverbial burning bungalow, so I hired her on the spot.'

'I spent two years working for a party planner when I came out of uni,' Kathryn explained. 'Jo and I were roomies and I was always jealous of her. I thought Marc's recipes were the best. When she told me she was leaving, I asked her to put in a word for me and she did.'

Hawthorne glanced across at Bellamy. 'You were at school with Charles le Mesurier.'

'Westland College. Yes. That's right.'

'How did you get on?'

Marc might have been reticent while le Mesurier was alive, but he wasn't afraid now and he let loose. 'We didn't bloody get on. Nobody did. He was a bully and an arsehole and everybody hated him. I spent my whole time there avoiding him.'

'He said that you left the school early.'

'I did and he was part of the reason.' It wasn't particularly warm in the kitchen, but he was sweating. He took out a handkerchief and wiped his face. 'I was born and brought up in Halifax. But my dad was in the navy and he got a posting to the south coast. That's how I ended up in a bloody boarding school. I didn't like it there from day one. I was never happy.'

'Why did he call you Tea Leaf?'

'Because I drank a lot of tea! Why do you think? We all had stupid names for each other. We used to call him Flash after the character in those books. Flashman. He hadn't changed much, growing up, I can tell you that!'

'Did he bully you?'

'Oh, come on!' Marc Bellamy sneered. 'What are you try-ing to say, Mr Hawthorne? That I stuck a knife in him because he bullied me at school? No. I just told you. I avoided him like the bubonic and he never came near me.'

'So why did you agree to come to Alderney? You must have known he'd be here.'

'I had no idea.' Marc folded the handkerchief away. He scowled at his assistant. 'That was her fault.'

'Actually, that's not really fair,' Kathryn said. 'I told Marc about the invitation and it seemed like a good idea because we weren't filming and the festival was happening just after his new book came out. I didn't know anything about Charles le Mesurier and by the time I found out it was too late.'

'I saw his name as the sponsor in the festival programme,' Marc growled.

That had been on the Friday evening. I remembered Marc shouting at Kathryn in the room next to mine.

'Did you talk to him last night?' Hawthorne asked.

'I could hardly avoid him, could I?' Marc replied. 'I was in his bloody house. But I wasn't going to be intimidated by him. I did my job and I left. Sold quite a few books too, for what it's worth, so the whole thing wasn't a complete waste of time.'

'Did you notice him go into the garden?'

'No. I can't say I did. I noticed he wasn't there at ten o'clock, which was when we stopped serving food. I looked round for him to say goodbye and sod off, but there was no sign of him.'

'Did you see any of the guests go outside?'

Marc thought back. 'Only the blind woman. She went out onto the patio quite a few times. Puffing away on a pack of fags. Her husband took her out the first time – that was quite early on – but after that I suppose she was able to find her way on her own.'

'What about Maïssa?' Kathryn said.

'Who? Oh, you mean the black lady.' Marc made a little face, as if correcting himself for his casual racism. He pointed towards the corner of the kitchen where another door that I hadn't noticed before led outside. 'Yes. She went out that way. But that was much earlier ... about half past seven.'

'Did she go down to the Snuggery?'

'I've no idea. Kathryn and I were just taking out the s and k's.'

'Steak and kidney puddings,' Kathryn said.

'The secret is to catch the little bastards at exactly the right moment. If you leave them in too long the suet goes soggy.'

Hawthorne got up and went over to the door. He looked out into the garden, judging the different angles. It was just possible to see the Snuggery from here, but I imagined that Elizabeth Lovell, sitting on the other side of the house, would have been invisible. He tried the handle and was surprised when the door opened.

'You didn't lock this when you left?' he asked.

Marc Bellamy shook his head. 'I'd told Kathryn to mind the fort from ten o'clock, when we stopped serving. It was her job to clean up and check that the place was secure.'

Kathryn scowled, but she didn't argue with her employer. 'I assumed Mr le Mesurier would lock up before he went to bed,' she explained.

Hawthorne closed the door, then opened it again. There was something wrong. He took out a pen and inserted it into the strike plate, the rectangular opening into which the latch bolt should have slid. There was something blocking it – a little ball of newspaper. He let it fall into his hand, examined it, then showed it to me. The writing was in French. He folded it carefully and slipped it into his pocket.

He sat back at the table. 'How did you get home?' he asked.

'The history bloke gave me a lift in his VW. I left Kathryn with the washing-up, sorry to say. But that's the job.'

'Can you remember seeing any of the other guests on their way out?'

'Not really. No.'

'I'm afraid I can't really help you either,' Kathryn said. 'I was in the kitchen until a quarter to eleven, give or take. I heard the band packing up their things and I cadged a lift with them back to the hotel. They had a van.' She suddenly remembered. 'I did see the children's writer leave, if that's any use. Mrs Cleary. That was a few minutes before half past nine.'

'How can you be so sure?'

'I met her as she was going out of the front door. She was in a bit of a hurry and she asked me the time. She said she had to get back to the hotel for a call.'

There was a pause while Hawthorne took all of this in. 'I wonder if I could have a word with you on your own, Ms Harris?' he asked.

'Of course. But please call me Kathryn.'

'Don't you want me any more?' Marc Bellamy was offended. He was too used to being the star of the show.

'Not for the moment, thanks, Mr Bellamy.'

'All right. But you be careful. Anything that girl says about me is not true, unless she's being nice about me, in which case it's an understatement!'

It was his last hurrah. He got up and left.

As soon as he was gone, Hawthorne began again. 'Do you understand why I want to have this conversation with you in private, Kathryn?'

She looked him straight in the eye. 'Not really.'

'Well, it's fairly clear that Charles le Mesurier was taking an interest in you.'

She blushed. 'I don't know what you mean.'

'What I mean is that he fancied you. I saw it for myself when we were at the opening-night drinks. It didn't take him long to start pawing at you. And according to my mate Tony here, the same thing happened again last night – the two of you in the kitchen with his tongue halfway down your ear.'

'That's not quite how I described it,' I muttered.

'What exactly did he say to you?' Hawthorne demanded.

He was being deliberately hard on her. I had seen him do it before when he was interrogating someone. If Hawthorne thought you were standing in his way, he would knock your feet from under you. That was his technique.

Kathryn was angry now. 'Why should I tell you?' she demanded. 'What he said has got nothing to do with you.'

'This is a murder investigation. It's got everything to do with me.'

She stared at him defiantly. 'If you tell Marc Bellamy, I'll lose my job.'

'I'm not telling anyone, Kathryn, but I need to know.'

She paused, then said in a low voice: 'He asked me to go with him to the gunnery at the bottom of the garden. He called it his "snuggery", which just made me feel sick. He wanted me to—' She broke off. 'He suggested something really obscene.'

'And what did you say?'

Before she answered, she removed her glasses and wiped them with a serviette. By the time she had put them on again, she was back in control. 'I don't know what you think of me, Mr Hawthorne, but I already told you I've worked in the hospitality industry and I've met enough middle-aged men who've had too much to drink and think I can be served up like a canapé. I told Charles le Mesurier to get lost and I didn't see him again. I'll tell you this, though. I think Marc may have had a point. If somebody's killed him, they've probably made the world a slightly better place.' She smiled briefly. 'Anything else?'

But before Hawthorne could answer, Colin Matheson appeared in the doorway. He was looking pleased.

'Mr Hawthorne,' he said, 'I thought you should know. The police have arrived.'

10

Bad Blood

Two police officers were in the hallway. They had not come alone. A group of men and women were passing through the house carrying metal cases, cameras and other equipment. A couple of them were dressed in those white overalls you see on TV programmes. There were more of them in the garden. I could see a spool of police tape fluttering in front of the Snuggery.

'Mr Hawthorne, I believe! What a great pleasure to meet you and how fortunate for us that you were here!'

I had shadowed Hawthorne on two investigations and it would be fair to say that the regular police had not taken kindly to him on either occasion, resenting his interference as much as they needed his expertise. However, this time I was pleasantly surprised. The man who had spoken was very tall, with a crumpled appearance, pockmarked cheeks and fair hair hanging down in strands. He was dressed in plain clothes – a jacket and tie. But the most remarkable thing about him was that he was positively beaming. His blue eyes had lit up at his first sighting of Hawthorne.

'Allow me to introduce myself,' he went on. 'Deputy Chief Jonathan Torode. This is Special Constable Jane Whitlock.'

Whitlock was standing behind him, holding a hat that she was twisting out of shape. She was quite a bit shorter than him and older too, dressed in a dark blue uniform with a knee-length skirt and dark stockings that did her no favours. Her hair was dark brown and limp, falling over a square forehead and sullen eyes. The two of them could have been a nephew and aunt, visiting Alderney for a day trip and recovering from a particularly rough crossing.

'It's a nasty business. Very nasty. We've just been over to the building at the bottom of the garden. What is it? An old battery? I have to say, I've never seen anything like it. You know, there's never been a murder on Alderney and we don't have any experience of it in Guernsey either. I've been in the force for twenty-six years and the only dead body I've ever seen was some chap who fell off a ladder and broke his neck. Anyway, this is a completely different kettle of fish. John Le Mesurier. Was that his name?'

'Charles, I think.'

'Yes. That's right. I'm getting him confused with the actor. I understand he was wealthy.'

'So I hear.'

Torode looked at Hawthorne curiously for a moment, then broke into laughter. 'Ha ha! Yes! Keeping your cards close to your chest. I can understand that. Look, why don't we go into the kitchen and have a chat?' He noticed me for the first time. 'Who are you?'

'I'm working with him,' I said.

'Good. Good. Whitlock, would you mind making us some tea? And while you're at it, maybe you can take a peek at what's in the fridge. I got up too early for breakfast this morning and of course there was nothing on the plane.'

I was surprised he could treat his deputy so haughtily, but Whitlock was evidently used to it. She grimaced and went into the kitchen ahead of us. We followed, taking our places at the table.

'Now, look, I'm going to come straight to the point,' Torode began. 'Quite frankly, I could use any help I can get with this one. I've been over to the crime scene and I can tell you, I don't like the look of it. Tied to a chair with parcel tape and one hand left free. What the hell's that all about?'

Hawthorne didn't reply.

'All right. It's clear that we need to come to an arrangement, you and I. You work as a consultant now. Is that the right job description?'

'It'll do,' Hawthorne said.

'Well, I know your reputation. I made a few phone calls before I came over and I can say, hand on heart, that it would be wonderful to have you on board. I'd be the first to admit

157

that you've got much more chance of solving this than me, but I'm sure we'd both agree that's irrelevant anyway. The most important thing is to catch the bastard who did it and make sure he's put away.'

'There are a lot of small-size steak and kidney puddings, sir.' Whitlock was peering into the fridge. 'There are also some sausages on sticks.'

'Chuck some of them into the microwave. And where's the tea?'

'On its way …'

Torode rested his elbows on the table and clasped his hands in front of him. 'So here's what I'm proposing. I'll run the police investigation. I'll do it by the book – interviews, fingerprints, CCTV and all the rest of it. At the same time, you can mount a second investigation, in parallel. You can talk to whoever you like, go wherever you want. I'll give you complete carte blanche. You're going to be stuck on Alderney for the foreseeable future anyway, as obviously we can't let anyone leave. But this way you won't be wasting your time.'

'Are you going to pay me?'

'I have to be honest with you, Hawthorne. We may run into a little difficulty there budget-wise. I'll be happy to put in a word with the Committee for Home Affairs, but I can tell you now they're not going to like it, and they control the purse strings. It's against the rules. Or rather, there aren't any rules regarding the use of freelancers, as far as I know. But I'm reasonably confident that we'll be able to work something out … some sort of special contract. How does that sound?'

Hawthorne shrugged. He didn't really have any choice.

'How's that tea coming, Jane?'

'It'll just be a minute, sir.' Whitlock was rummaging through the cupboards. It was hardly a testament to her investigative skills that so far she had been unable to find a tea bag.

'Well, if you're in agreement, I'll get Jane to liaise with you and any information we manage to muster, we'll pass on to you. Where are you staying?'

'The Braye Beach.'

'Nice place! I looked it up on the internet but unfortunately they're full. We're staying up the road. Actually, that's for the best because I don't think it would be a good idea for us to be seen together. Official and unofficial … let's not get the lines crossed. What do you say?'

'It's all right with me.'

'Good. Good. Good. Is there anything you need straight off?' He took out a pen and a leather notebook.

'Anything you can get me on le Mesurier would be useful,' Hawthorne said. 'A full profile of his life and business activities. Any criminal record, of course. Plus a list of all his appearances on *Dad's Army*.'

Torode had been writing this all down but now he stopped, his pen hovering. He laughed briefly. 'That's funny. Yes. I saw what you did there.'

'It might also be useful to know what happens to his money now that he's dead,' Hawthorne went on.

'We might have to wait until Monday for that, but once I've got the information I'll get Whitlock to bring it over. Anything else?'

'That'll do for the moment.'

There was a ping and Whitlock opened the microwave. Steam from half a dozen miniature steak and kidney puddings came wafting out.

Torode closed his notebook. 'Just a couple of things before I let you get on your way,' he said. 'I hope you won't mind me bringing them up.'

'Go ahead.'

'Thank you.' He slipped the notebook away. 'The first thing is that I've been made aware that Charles le Mesurier has a financial adviser by the name of Derek Abbott.' He paused. 'That wouldn't be the same Derek Abbott that you pushed down the stairs, would it?'

Hawthorne's face was stony. 'I didn't push him. He fell.'

'Well, from what I'm told, there was quite a bit of bad blood between you.' Perhaps there was more to Jonathan Torode than I had thought. It seemed to me that he was suddenly harder and more dangerous. 'I think it might be best if you kept away from him. We wouldn't want there to be any more misunderstandings, would we?'

'I thought you said I had carte blanche.'

'Leave Abbott to me. I'll make sure you get a complete transcript of any interview I conduct.'

'And the other thing?'

'Well, I'm sure it goes without saying. But if you do happen to crack the case, and I have every confidence that you will, you will make sure that I'm the first to know, won't you? I wouldn't dream of taking credit for anything you do, but there is the reputation of the States of Guernsey Police Service to consider. I'm sure you understand.'

'Completely.'

'Excellent. In which case – ah, thank you, Whitlock! Here's my tea, at last. I'll wish you a good day!'

It was a dismissal, delivered with a genial smile, but a dismissal nonetheless.

The two of us walked out of the front door to where Terry, the young taxi driver who had brought us here, was still waiting. Hawthorne exchanged a few words with him and we both got into the car. I thought we would be heading back to the hotel, but after we had joined the main road, we travelled just a short distance before we stopped again.

'You can follow the path down from here,' Terry told us.

'We'll be about twenty minutes,' Hawthorne said.

'Can I come?'

'No. Wait for us here.' We got out of the car and began to make our way down. 'I've hired him,' Hawthorne told me. It took me a moment to realise he was talking about

Terry. 'He's going to drive us the whole time we're on the island.'

'That's a good idea.'

'I said you'd pay.'

'Oh.'

We had arrived at a crescent-shaped beach – more shingle than sand – and I wondered what Hawthorne had in mind. We turned left and walked back the way we had come. Looking up, I saw the top half of the Snuggery looming above the edge of the cliff – except that it wasn't really a cliff at all, more a rocky wall that rose up about ten or fifteen metres with a well-defined walkway zigzagging towards the top. I rather doubted that the path dated back to the war. Why would the Germans have made it easy for Allied forces to climb up to their defences? Charles le Mesurier must have constructed it himself so that when he had finished whatever he did in the Snuggery, he could come down here for a swim.

'Could someone have got in this way and killed him?' I asked. I assumed this was the reason we had come down here.

'It's a possibility. Except that the door was bolted from inside ... or at least it was when I looked this morning.' Hawthorne glanced left and right and I found myself thinking of the trip we had made to Deal in Kent together, the last time we had stood beside the sea. 'If someone went up to the house from here, they'd have to have had someone at the party to let them in.'

'What time was le Mesurier killed?' I asked.

'The police will tell us that. But we can assume that he went to the Snuggery sometime between ten past nine, which is when he talked to his wife, and ten o'clock, when Marc Bellamy noticed he was missing.'

Hawthorne had been examining the ground. Suddenly, he stopped and pointed. He had found a footprint in a patch of sand just at the foot of the path leading up to the Snuggery. I couldn't say for sure, but the perfect curve of the toecap looked remarkably similar to the bloody footprint we had found near the body.

'You're right, Hawthorne!' I exclaimed. 'I don't know how you do it. But it's perfectly clear.' I looked up at the Snuggery. 'Someone unlocked the door. They had an accomplice who climbed up from the beach. The two of them hit le Mesurier on the head and forced him into the chair. And after they'd killed him, they separated and each went their own way.'

'It could have happened like that.' Why did Hawthorne have to sound so unsure when it was perfectly obvious to me? 'But there's a problem.'

'What problem?'

'Well, for the whole thing to work the way you just described – one inside, one outside – they'd have to know that le Mesurier was planning to visit the Snuggery and at what time.'

'They could have texted from the house.'

Hawthorne took out his phone and looked at it. 'No signal.'

I did the same and sighed. 'Mine too.'

'Your set-up only works if the accomplice is already there and waiting *before* le Mesurier arrives – maybe hidden behind one of those curtains. Le Mesurier comes in with someone and that's when the two of them incapacitate him and force him into the chair. They tie him up – we still don't know why – and then they kill him.'

'Suppose they unlocked the door earlier? Someone could have climbed up from the beach and hidden behind the curtains. They could have been inside the Snuggery all evening.'

'They'd still have to be sure that le Mesurier would go in there. And on his own …'

Hawthorne was still holding his mobile phone. He took a photograph of the footprint.

'Are you going to tell Torode about this?' I asked.

'I'm sure he'll find it for himself, but I'll send him a picture if you think it will make him happy.'

He slipped the phone back into his pocket and was about to leave, but I stopped him. 'Hawthorne,' I said. 'There's something you've got to tell me.'

'What's that, mate?'

'Why are you here? Why did you agree to come to Alderney? And don't tell me it was anything to do with our book. This is about Derek Abbott, isn't it? I know you don't want to talk about it, but you've got to tell me. You knew from the start that he was living here. When we were invited that day in London, I guessed you were up to something. I don't want to have an argument with you, but you can't keep me in the dark, especially if I'm going to end up writing about all this. So what's going on?'

Hawthorne took his time before replying. We were standing on the very edge of the beach, with the rocks behind us and nobody else in sight. It was still early and the great stretch of sand looked wild and unwelcoming. With the wind tugging at the seaweed and the steel-coloured waves rolling in relentlessly, this was not a beach for deckchairs and pedalos. A seagull hovered overhead. The sun was behind the clouds.

'I will tell you about Abbott,' he said. 'But only if you never ask me again. All right? It makes me sick even to talk about him.'

'He was a paedophile.'

Hawthorne nodded slowly. There was a terrible bleakness in his eyes. 'He was more than that,' he began. 'Mr Derek bloody Abbott. He wasn't some barrow boy selling dirty DVDs off the back of a lorry. And he wasn't weird and bearded, downloading stuff off the net and sharing it with his friends. He was a businessman. He was respectable.'

Hawthorne made that last word sound the exact opposite.

'He started out as a teacher, but when that didn't work for him he moved into classified advertising and by the end of his twenties he was advertising manager for a big group of leisure magazines. Sailing, horse-riding and – as it happened – naturism. From there it was a small step to founding his own company, Free for All. Their first big success was a listings magazine given away outside tube stations. He was ahead of his time. I'll say that for him.

'Listings didn't pay, so he moved into lifestyle and celebrity and from there it wasn't such a huge step into porn. This was the early nineties, Tony. We hadn't quite arrived at the day when you could get it all at the touch of a computer keyboard, so Abbott's girlies often came folded in the middle with staples running down their chest. And it was all legal. *Bored Housewives*. *Ladies of Leisure*. *My Secret Fantasies*. The sort of stuff you'd find on the top shelf of any corner newsagent.

'But Abbott moved with the times. Come the millennium, he had his own satellite TV station: the Adult Channel. At the same time, all his publications had moved online, of course. And in the middle of it all, inside this great spider's web of filth, there was one website that was only available to a very select group of subscribers. The title didn't give very much away either, even though it described exactly what it was offering. It was called Asia Minor.'

'Child pornography.'

'Kids from Thailand, Vietnam and the Philippines, mainly. And it was in a different league to the rest of his stuff. He'd be looking at a twenty-year sentence for supplying and distributing hard-core pornography with young children. So here's the question you might like to ask yourself. Why would a man who was making millions out of legal porn, as well as all his other business interests, want to risk the whole thing on a single website that hardly even paid for itself? By the time it was closed down, it only had a few hundred subscribers, dirty old men paying twenty quid a month. Why was he doing it? That's what the Paedophile and Child Pornography Unit who were running the investigation wanted to know, and in the end they found out. Derek Abbott, the CEO of Free for All, was getting access to the models. That was his little perk. Some of those kids were eleven and twelve years old, and Asia Minor was giving him a constant, fresh supply.'

He took out a cigarette and lit it with cupped hands.

'When Derek Abbott was arrested in London, he didn't care. I still remember the day he came in, sitting there with this look on his face like he was the lord of the manor who'd accidentally wandered into the servants' quarters. The police weren't going to get anywhere near him, not in a hundred years! He knew from the start that he'd set up his business in a way that made him untouchable and he'd brought in a team of lawyers who didn't care who he was or what he'd done so long as they got their retainers. He'd pay his way out of trouble no matter how much it cost – and that's exactly what happened. No-one could connect him to Asia Minor. His own staff had been paid off or intimidated. None of the

witnesses, the kids he'd abused, came forward. He'd cocked
his nose at us from the very start and he was right.'

'But he went to prison.'

'Yeah. In the end, he made one mistake – a bit like Al
Capone and his tax returns. It would almost be funny except
that it wasn't. You see, he had to keep souvenirs. He couldn't
resist it. He was a subscriber to his own channel and the vice
team managed to crack into a private account on one of his
computers and they found a cache of about five hundred
images. They arrested him a second time and brought him
in for further questioning, and that was when he had his
accident on the stairs. And it *was* an accident, Tony.'
Hawthorne jabbed a finger in my direction. 'Never say
otherwise.'

'How many years did he spend in prison?' I asked.

Hawthorne looked at me bleakly. 'Not even one,' he said.
'That's the law. If he'd been done for the manufacture or
distribution of child pornography – I told you – that could
have meant twenty years, which is what the bastard deserved.
Unfortunately, all they could get him for was possession,
which carries a maximum two-year sentence.' He paused.
'Because of his injuries, which put him in hospital, and the
fact that his lawyers made a formal complaint about his
treatment in custody, the judge did him a favour. He was
given six months, which destroyed him and brought down
every single one of his businesses – but it still wasn't
enough.' Hawthorne rolled the cigarette between his thumb

and finger. The smoke twisted away in the wind. 'Not nearly enough.'

I thought for a moment before I spoke.

'I'm sorry,' I said. 'I can understand your frustration. But I still don't see what you hoped to gain by coming here.'

'I didn't plan to come here until we were invited,' Hawthorne reminded me. 'But ... all right. I was interested to see what had happened to him.'

'Why?' Hawthorne didn't answer, so I tried again. 'You must have met lots of unpleasant men who've committed crimes that are just as bad. What's so special about this one?'

But Hawthorne had said enough. He held up the cigarette and allowed the wind to snatch it out of his fingers. Then he turned on his heel and set off across the sand. I followed him, and without saying another word, we climbed back up to the waiting car.

11

Shades of Grey

✤

Our driver's full name was Terry Burgess. He was twenty-six years old, worked for his father's taxi company and had spent most of his adult life ferrying passengers from the airport to Braye and back again, with occasional excursions to Fort Clonque or Gannet Rock. His clients were either tourists who ignored him or elderly residents who criticised his driving. On Saturday nights he picked up the occasional drunk and fined them £10 if they threw up in the back of his car.

Hawthorne's arrival had given Terry a new sense of purpose. In the ten minutes it took him to drive us from the beach to the hotel, he managed to tell us his entire life story and give us the background he was certain we'd need to crack the case.

'It's this power line. NAB. Ever since they said they were going to dig up the island, everyone's been at each other's throats. I bet that's why someone did in Mr le Mesurier.'

I thought Hawthorne would be irritated, but he seemed amused. 'Why do you say that?'

Terry adjusted his driving mirror so he could look into the back where we were sitting. He had curls of ginger hair, blue eyes and a boxer's nose. 'Nothing ever happened on this island without his say-so,' he explained. 'Talk about a finger in every pie! He's got shops, restaurants, pubs, the post office ... he was even talking about setting up his own taxi service! And as for that house of his, you know he spent five million quid building it? How he got planning permission right on the edge of the sea, and his own private pillbox, is anyone's guess.'

He hooted at another car. Not because it was in the way but because he knew the driver.

'Did I tell you I was actually outside The Lookout last night? I was working all evening. And I must have been parked there when ... it happened. It's incredible, really. Crazy! There's never been a murder in Alderney before.'

'I didn't know that,' Hawthorne said.

I was glad the journey wasn't any longer. It was already mid-morning and, like Deputy Chief Torode, we'd left without breakfast. We pulled up in front of the hotel and Hawthorne instructed Terry to wait outside while the two of us went in, making for the restaurant.

It wasn't to be. Anne Cleary was sitting in the reception area. She had been waiting for us. The moment she saw us, she stood up and came over.

'Is it true?' she demanded. 'Charles le Mesurier has been killed?'

'I'm afraid so.' Hawthorne didn't sound too sorry, but then, of course, the murder had provided him with another case – and perhaps another source of income.

'And none of us can leave the island?'

'They've sent a couple of officers over from Guernsey and that's their instruction ... yes.'

Anne Cleary was on the edge of tears. 'But I have to get back to Oxford. I have a doctor's appointment first thing tomorrow.'

'It'll have to wait.'

'It can't wait. You don't understand.'

Hawthorne just looked at her blankly, so I stepped in. 'We were just going to have breakfast. Would you like to join us?'

'I think they've stopped serving.'

She was right. By the time we went into the restaurant it was after eleven o'clock and the tables had been cleared. Even so, we sat down next to a window with a view of the harbour and I managed to persuade a waitress to provide us with two pots of tea, some toast for me and a black coffee for Hawthorne.

'I shouldn't have come here.' Anne was still distressed. She had the sort of face that folded itself easily into grief. The greying hair, the grey eyes, the grey scarf that surely wasn't needed in this warm weather: she was like one of those figures you get in mythology that stand on the shore as the ship sails away carrying the bodies of the dead. 'My agent advised against it and I'm actually far too busy right now to be away from home.'

'So why did you come?' Hawthorne asked.

She sighed. 'Because I'm a soft touch. They sent me a letter saying the island only had one school – St Anne's – and that it was in danger of closure because of the falling population. They were also raising money to support the library. I don't know why my giving a talk there would be any help, although I suppose having a high-profile author is always a good thing. Actually, I had a very good session there in the end: the children were lovely and the teachers couldn't have been nicer. I really shouldn't complain. Alderney's beautiful and I love this hotel. But after that business yesterday, I just wanted to leave.'

She was referring, of course, to Elizabeth Lovell's session and the revelations that had been made about her son.

'I don't believe any of that nonsense,' she went on. 'Life after death and ghosts and mirrors and all the rest of it. I'm not even sure why I went to her session. I suppose I was being polite. Well, more fool me. She had obviously done her research. It would have been easy to find that story on the internet. There was a lot of press interest in the lack of pastoral care at Bristol University and although we did our best to keep him out of the newspapers, William's name was mentioned. What I don't understand is how anyone could use information like that as part of a performance to promote their own work. It seems so cruel.'

'Maybe she believes what she says,' Hawthorne said.

'She believes in the money she makes.' Anne was indignant. It seemed to me that real anger wasn't in her nature.

'You still went to the party,' Hawthorne said. 'You must have known she'd be there.'

I thought he was being unnecessarily rough on her, particularly as, when they'd first met, he'd made a point of telling her how much he and his son had enjoyed her books. But she didn't seem to notice. 'I didn't want to go,' she said. 'I told Anthony as much. I'd had a really rather difficult day, not just with that woman but also my pen! I'm quite sure somebody's stolen it and it really upsets me because it was given to me by my agent after *Flashbang Wallop* got into the top ten. That was the first in the series. The books are in six languages now and they've done very well, but it's always the first one you remember.'

'What changed your mind?'

'I don't know. I just decided that there was no point sitting in the hotel on my own. That would only make me more depressed. But I didn't want to join Elizabeth Lovell and her husband on the bus so I was very happy to accept a lift from George Elkin. And once I arrived, I made sure I steered clear of both of them – Mr and Mrs Lovell – for the whole evening. George is a very interesting man, by the way. Absolutely steeped in the history of the Channel Islands.'

'Is that what you talked about?'

'No. We talked about birds. He's a keen birdwatcher. He'd seen a black-winged kite.'

'Had he?'

'It's very rare, apparently. It's hardly ever been seen in the UK.'

'So you got to The Lookout at about seven thirty.'

'You know that. You actually saw me come in.' She paused. 'I had quite a shock when I arrived. There was a man there I knew, although at first I couldn't remember where I'd seen him. Anthony reminded me.'

Hawthorne had been standing right next to me at the time. 'He was in one of your reading groups,' he said.

'No.' Anne shook her head. 'I'm not certain that he was now that I think about it. But I had definitely seen him when I was visiting Wormwood Scrubs in London. It was the walking stick that reminded me, although at the time he had a crutch, if I remember rightly. We were taken through the central area of the prison on the way to the library and I saw him there.'

'Did you talk to Derek Abbott yesterday evening?'

'No, I'm afraid I didn't. I didn't want to embarrass him.'

'But you knew his name.'

'I didn't know his name until Anthony told me, and it didn't mean anything to me then.' She paused a second time. 'Funnily enough, Charles le Mesurier talked to me about him a short while later.' The tea and coffee had arrived while we were talking and she took a sip. There were also four slices of toast with some jam and butter, but it didn't feel right to eat in the middle of an interview so I left them sitting on the table in front of me. 'I spoke to Mr le Mesurier for quite some time,' she went on. 'And I know I shouldn't say this, but he didn't strike me as a particularly nice man.'

'Why do you say that?'

'Well, he had everything, hadn't he! Good looks, wealth, that house, a gorgeous wife. But he didn't have anything nice to say about anyone.' She turned to me. 'I'm sorry to say this, but he went on quite a bit about your session and how much he disliked it. He said that the extract you read was too long and he didn't think it was well written.'

'Oh. Did he?' Charles le Mesurier had been brutally murdered but I was still annoyed.

'It wasn't just you. It was everyone. He really disliked George Elkin, although they'd known each other since they were children. He thought the people living on the island were thick, particularly the ones opposed to the power line. And he resented how much money he'd spent on the festival. At least, that's what he told me.'

'What did he say about Derek Abbott?'

'Well, that's exactly what I mean. I actually asked him about Derek Abbott because I thought I knew him and he immediately told me that he'd been in prison and that he should never have trusted him. He said that Mr Abbott worked for him, helping him with his finances and advising him on some of his online publications, but that the two of them had fallen out. They'd had an argument ... something to do with money. He didn't have anything very nice to say about him. In fact, he told me he was about to fire him. Heaven knows why he thought I'd be interested.' She thought for a moment, as if trying to come up with some way to excuse him. 'I have a feeling he'd been drinking,' she concluded. 'He must have started some time before we arrived. Champagne.'

'Did he tell you why Abbott had been in jail?'

Anne Cleary pursed her lips. 'Oh yes. He said quite clearly that he was on the register of sexual offenders. He almost seemed amused. But it does beg the question as to why he would ever employ such a man in the first place!'

'And did Abbott hear any of this?'

'No. I don't think so. He was in the room, but he was keeping his distance. He was in the corner and there were quite a few people between us.'

'Did you see either of them go to the Snuggery?'

'That was that building at the bottom of the garden – Mr le Mesurier told me about it. He said it was his "private space", whatever that means, and he was obviously very proud of it. But no. I actually left quite early. I had a nice chat with Anthony and I also met some other people, but the truth is that I'm not exactly a party animal. I'm a vegetarian, so all those pies and sausage rolls did nothing for me, and I'm not really drinking alcohol at the moment either. Anyway, I was expecting an important call at the hotel.'

'Do you know what time you left?' Hawthorne was testing her. He already knew the answer to that.

'As a matter of fact, I can tell you exactly. I asked Kathryn in the hallway – you know, Marc Bellamy's assistant. It was nine twenty-five. That gave me half an hour to get back, which was much more than I needed, and fortunately the minibus was leaving straight away. The driver was standing by the door. He had a beard. I asked him if he was going to the hotel and off we went.'

'Were you alone?'

'There were six or seven other people on the bus, but I'm afraid I can't tell you who they were. It was quite dark and I didn't talk to any of them.'

'What was the call about?'

Anne was becoming increasingly perplexed. 'You don't think I had anything to do with what happened, do you?' she asked. 'I didn't like Mr le Mesurier. I'll admit to that. But I had absolutely no reason to do him harm.'

'Just getting all the facts.' Hawthorne smiled in my direction. 'Tony here may write about all this one day.'

'Well, I hope he'll change my name.' She was clearly reluctant to tell him what he wanted but could see that she had no choice. 'My agent was calling me from Los Angeles.'

'On a Saturday?'

'You obviously don't know Hollywood agents, Mr Hawthorne. My agent doesn't do weekends! And we've had very exciting news, although this is still confidential. Walt

179

Disney are taking an option on the Flashbang stories. They're planning to make a film and it's worth an awful lot of money to me.' She glanced at me. 'That's why I'd prefer you not to write about any of this. Disney have made me sign a morality clause and it's the most extraordinary document, about twelve pages long. If I'm associated with anything that's seedy or illegal, it could actually invalidate the whole thing. Of course, it's not my fault I've got myself involved in a murder, but we haven't signed the contract yet and naturally I'm on tenterhooks.'

'What did your agent say?'

'In the end I just got a text from her. She said there was no news and we'd talk next week.' Anne fumbled in her handbag and took out her mobile. She turned it on and showed Hawthorne the screen. 'There! I suppose it's your job not to believe anything anyone says, but it still feels quite upsetting, to be honest.'

'I don't mean to upset you, Anne.'

'Well …'

'So you didn't hear anything or see anything that might be useful to us?'

'I would have told you if I had. I only knew what had happened when I came down to breakfast and they told me I wouldn't be able to leave. Can I at least walk out of the hotel?'

'It might be best to tell the receptionist where you're going.'

'I really don't want to be cooped up inside all day.' She looked out of the window. 'I heard the weather forecast on the radio and they say it's going to be a hot one, so I might go for a walk. They have such beautiful beaches here. How long will they keep us on the island?'

Hawthorne shrugged. 'It could be a few days.'

'Will they pay for the hotel?' She caught herself. 'I've never had a lot of money. The books were my only income and my husband never made very much from his painting even before he left me. But of course it doesn't matter now, not with Disney. My agent says I'm going to be rich!'

'Does your ex-husband know?'

'I haven't told him, but I suppose he'll find out. Everyone knows everything these days, don't they?'

She finished her tea and got up. Her books had been successful, selling in six languages, and she had just sold an option to Walt Disney. It was everything a writer could hope for. But she still looked sad as she left. Her career was fine. It was life that had let her down.

12

Civil Disobedience

Terry was still waiting for us outside the hotel and quickly folded away a copy of the Alderney *Journal* when he saw us approach. We got in the back of the car and Hawthorne told him where we wanted to go. 'There's something you can do for me,' he added as we pulled away.

'Whatever you want, Mr Hawthorne!' Terry was so excited, I was surprised he was able to stay on the road.

'Do you know the driver of the minibus? The one that picked up guests from the party last night?'

'That's Tom McKinley. Of course I know him.'

'Could you tell him I want to talk to him?'

Hawthorne was right next to me and I glanced at him curiously. 'Is this about Anne Cleary?' I asked.

'It would be interesting to know if she really was on that bus.'

'You're not serious.' It had never occurred to me that she might have lied about her journey home the previous evening.

'Actually, I am. When someone tells me something, I check it out. That's what I do.'

'I can't think of any reason why Anne Cleary would want to kill Charles le Mesurier.'

'So what's new?' Hawthorne didn't speak to me again until we arrived.

Our destination was Beaumont Farm, the home of Dr Queripel and his wife. It was on the east side of the island, where the two coastlines curved in towards each other, between Saye and Longis beaches. Curiously, the house itself had no view of the sea, at least not from the living room. Instead, a double-sized picture window looked out onto an oddly disjointed landscape. Much of it was made up of scrub grassland, the wild mix of grass and bracken that I'd seen all over the island, but it was interrupted by strips of cultivated farmland and allotments. A couple of tropical palm trees sprouted incongruously in the middle of it all, as if planted quite by accident. Further away, there was a scattering of industrial buildings – sheds and warehouses – and in the far distance, under a huge sky, a dead straight line that could have demarcated the end of the world but which was actually the edge of the island, with the English Channel on the other side.

According to Terry, the house had been in the Queripel family for generations and it certainly looked the part: solid and sensible rather than beautiful, but dominating its surroundings with a self-confidence that any new build could only envy. It was white with black beams, two storeys high, with a front door and six perfectly symmetrical windows on one side and the inevitable French windows looking out onto a garden filled with flowers on the other. The roof was red-tiled with a single, central chimney, which I guessed would almost certainly be in working order.

Terry also gave us a full rundown on the occupants. That was the joy of living in Alderney. Everyone knew everyone. More than that. They seemed to know everything about everyone too.

'He's a good stick, Dr Queripel. Everyone likes him. My mum had a cancer scare last year and he looked after her, made sure she got into the University Hospital in Southampton. He inherited the house from his dad. He was also a doctor but he died in a car accident about five years ago in the South of France, his wife with him. Terrible for Dr Queripel, losing both his parents that way. Mrs Queripel's lovely. She teaches at the local school and the kids will do anything for her ... except pass their exams. She's been fighting to keep it open. Spends half her life trying to get funding ... new this, new that. Never stops! People say it's only thanks to her that it's still there. But you can't imagine Alderney without a school. It wouldn't bear thinking about.'

I was relieved when we finally pulled in at the edge of a narrow lane. Hawthorne and I got out. Terry stayed behind the wheel. He was still watching us as we walked up the path to the house.

'Tony, do me a favour, will you?' Hawthorne said abruptly as we reached the front door. 'While I'm talking, try not to give anything away.'

I knew that he was referring to our last two cases. On both occasions, he'd accused me of speaking out of turn. 'That's a little unfair,' I retorted. 'I'd have said I've been very careful so far.'

'Maybe not as careful as you think.'

He rang the bell.

It was opened a few moments later by a strikingly attractive young woman, even if her looks somehow took me back to the 1940s. She had blue eyes and blonde hair tied back in a bun. She had no make-up apart from two very precise strokes of bright red lipstick, accentuated by the paleness of her skin. She was wearing a cardigan and baggy trousers. As she stood there, examining us, I realised that I had seen her before. She was the woman who had been sitting next to George Elkin at my session in the cinema and who had asked the question about teen literacy.

'How can I help you?' She managed to be polite and suspicious at the same time.

'Are you Mrs Queripel?' Hawthorne asked.

'Yes.' Now she was a little puzzled.

'My name is Hawthorne ...'

'I know who you are.'

'I spoke to your husband this morning. Is he in?'

'Yes, he is.' She gave the information reluctantly and she didn't move, still blocking the way.

'I'd like a word with him. Can we come in?'

'Yes. Of course.' Finally, she stepped aside and we went into the homeliest of homes: floral curtains, patterned wallpaper, scattered rugs, furniture that was old without quite being antique, a cat asleep on a rocking chair. 'I'm Susan Queripel. Please come this way.' She led us past the open door of the living room and I glimpsed the picture window, an upright piano and two striped sofas.

'Who is it, darling?' It was Henry Queripel who had called out and a moment later we entered the kitchen, where three people were sitting around a stripped pine table with a kettle steaming gently on an Aga to one side.

Dr Queripel was nearest to the door. He was sitting at the head of the table with his foot dangling, one leg over his knee. I was surprised to see George Elkin, the historian, opposite him. The last person was a woman I had not yet met. She was next to Elkin and my first thought was that she might be his mother. She was twice his size and looked several years older than him. But not that old. On second thoughts, she had to be his wife. She looked cheerful enough, with jet-black hair cut short and a wide smile that dimpled her cheeks, but her massive weight was unnatural and I could see the discomfort in her eyes. She was suffering from some sort of thyroid disease and I even wondered if she was able to walk. Her smile faded as we came in.

'Mr Hawthorne!' Dr Queripel got to his feet. 'I didn't expect to see you again so soon.'

'He said he wanted to talk to you,' Susan Queripel explained, as if she was to blame for letting us in.

All four of them were looking guilty and I could see why. We had interrupted what might have been a war council. There were leaflets and photographs scattered across the table and a great pile of flyers bearing the palindrome I'd seen as I left the airport: BAN NAB. About half a dozen makeshift signs with the same message in bright red letters had been prepared and were leaning against the far wall, waiting to be hammered into place. Elkin had smudges of paint on his fingers; caught, quite literally, red-handed.

'I hope I'm not interrupting anything,' Hawthorne said cheerfully.

'Not at all.' If Dr Queripel had been embarrassed, he was recovering quickly. 'Would you like to sit down? Can we offer you some tea?'

'No, thank you.'

'If you want to speak to me on my own, we can go next door.'

'No. I'm happy to meet everyone.'

'We've already met,' George Elkin said. 'This is my wife, Georgina. This gentleman is a detective,' he told her. 'He's here about the murder.'

George and Georgina. Somehow it suited them.

'And since you ask, yes, you have interrupted us.' Susan Queripel had a self-confidence that was quite steely. She didn't even glance at her husband as she contradicted him. 'We're having a meeting about the Normandy-Alderney-Britain power line.'

Hawthorne turned to Dr Queripel. 'When we met at The Lookout this morning, you told me you weren't involved with those.' He glanced at the painted signs.

'Yes. That was wrong of me and I apologise. Obviously, I was shocked by what had just happened to Charles le Mesurier and I wasn't thinking straight.'

'You lied to me.'

'Actually, that's not the case. You asked me if I was involved in the painting and I don't do any of that. I'm useless with a brush.'

'I do the painting,' Susan Queripel said, with pride.

'We've had to be very careful,' Dr Queripel continued. 'Charles le Mesurier was quite a formidable opponent and he wouldn't have hesitated to bring the full force of the law against us if we'd crossed the line. From the very start, we've restricted ourselves to what you might call acts of civil disobedience. The signs, some graffiti, pamphleteering, demonstrations ...'

'And murder?' Hawthorne suggested.

Susan Queripel laughed. 'That's a ridiculous accusation. If you think any of us would have harmed Charles, then you obviously don't know anything. My husband is a doctor. I teach at the school. George is a well-known historian. None of us has ever committed a crime in our lives. We're merely exercising our democratic right as citizens of this island. We want to stop the power line. It's true that things may change because of what's happened. But that had nothing to do with us. The reason we've met today is to decide how to continue the struggle.'

'It's possible that we may not need to,' George Elkin added. 'Now that le Mesurier's gone, Colin Matheson might explain why he made such a terrible decision to support the line in the first place. My view is that he was running scared. Well, he doesn't need to be scared any more.'

'None of us do!' Georgina exclaimed.

Hawthorne had already returned to Dr Queripel. 'When we spoke this morning, you suggested that le Mesurier had some sort of hold over Colin Matheson.'

'I still believe that.'

'He was firmly against the power line when it was first announced,' Susan Queripel cut in. 'He sat at this very table and told us that it was a terrible idea.'

'So what changed?'

'What changed was that he was appointed by the States to head up the NAB committee. It's funny to think that when we heard that, we were all delighted.'

'It was the best possible news,' Dr Queripel agreed. 'He was our friend. We'd known each other for years. I was the best man at his wedding, for heaven's sake!'

'But then almost overnight he turned against us,' Susan Queripel continued. 'He knew what it meant to us personally, but suddenly that didn't matter any more. He started talking about the financial benefits it might bring to the island.'

'There are no financial benefits,' Georgina scowled.

'Cheaper energy. Faster internet. New jobs. That's what they promised, but none of it is true.'

'I'm surprised Judith went along with it,' Dr Queripel said. 'She's not stupid. And she loves this island. I can't believe she'd just sit back and watch her husband help to wreck it.'

'What can you tell me about Judith Matheson?' Hawthorne asked.

'Colin's nothing without her and everyone here knows it.' It was George Elkin who answered. 'Her family has been in Alderney for generations. They made a fortune out of travel and tourism. Judith set up Colin with his chambers and she got him into the States. It's her house they live in and her wealth that keeps their three children in private school. And God help him if he steps out of line. She's the one who wears the trousers in that relationship.'

I wasn't surprised to hear this. Even from the emails she had sent me, Judith Matheson had struck me as a bit of a control freak and meeting her had only confirmed this. As for Colin, he was unimpressive enough when he was on his own, but on the only occasion when I had seen them together, the 'designated driver' had been almost invisible.

'He's a coward!' Georgina said, solemnly agreeing with her husband.

'I've said it before and I'll say it again. Charles le Mesurier had something on him. It's the only way to explain it.'

'So what happens now – with your protests?' Hawthorne asked.

'We'll wait and see,' Dr Queripel said. 'Nothing's actually been signed and we've written to OLAF—'

'Who are OLAF?' I asked. I'd said nothing up to now, remembering Hawthorne's remarks.

'They're the anti-fraud office working for the EU. They investigate dodgy deals, corruption and the rest of it. We never heard back from them, but we're not giving up.'

'The whole thing could go away now that le Mesurier is dead,' Elkin said. 'Whoever killed him could have done us a huge favour.'

Hawthorne rounded on him. 'You were there that night,' he said. 'At the party.'

'Yes.'

'Did you go into the Snuggery?'

'Why would I have done that?'

'Well, possibly to put a knife into the man who was going to dig up your old grandpa and stick a cable through his grave.'

'How dare you say that to me? Have you no shame?'

But Hawthorne had already moved on. 'What about you, Dr Queripel?'

The doctor's cheeks reddened. 'I already told you. I was here in the house all evening, playing bridge.'

'Who with?'

'My wife and Georgina.'

'Forgive me. I may be wrong. But that only makes three.'

'No. That's right. It was three-handed bridge.' There was an awkward pause. 'We usually play with George, but he felt he had to drive over to The Lookout, even though he didn't want to attend the party.'

For once, I knew exactly what was going through Hawthorne's mind. All four of them had a motive to murder le Mesurier. And they had arranged things so that they were each other's alibis. Could they have all been in it together?

'When were you on the beach?' Hawthorne asked, unexpectedly.

Dr Queripel realised that Hawthorne was talking to him and his cheeks went a shade darker. I had never seen anyone do embarrassment so well. 'What are you talking about?'

'It's a simple enough question. Have you walked on the beach today?'

'No. I've been indoors.'

'It's just that when I came in, I noticed the bottom of your shoe. It's the same shoe you were wearing this morning. It has a distinctive round cap, and more to the point, there are grains of sand caught in the sole.'

193

'Are there?' The doctor had crossed his knee again. He twisted the shoe and examined it. Hawthorne was right. The sand was still there.

'I may have walked on the beach yesterday.'

'Which beach?'

'I don't remember.' Dr Queripel was trying to find a way out of this. But he couldn't lie. It was a small island. He would almost certainly have been seen. 'It might have been Saye Beach.'

'Near le Mesurier's place.'

'The other end, actually. I'd heard there'd been a sighting of a black-winged kite and I was hoping to spot it.'

'You're a birdwatcher?'

'Occasionally.'

'I thought that was his speciality ...' Hawthorne gestured at George Elkin.

'Henry and I often go out together,' Elkin replied, coming to his friend's defence. 'I think it's fair to say that we all have a shared love for this island: its wildlife, its topography, its history, its atmosphere of peace.' He drew a breath. 'It's everything that NAB threatens to destroy.'

'You know, actually, I think I've had enough of this,' Susan Queripel said. 'This is my home. You have absolutely no right to come in here and ask us questions, and certainly not in the way you've been doing. I'd like you to leave. Both of you.'

Well, that was something that had never happened before. I'd seen Hawthorne upset plenty of people, but none of them had ever tried to throw him out. He didn't argue with her. If anything, he seemed amused. 'Whatever you say, Mrs Queripel.' He got to his feet.

It was George Elkin who opened the front door for us and walked with us down the drive as if to make sure we actually got into our car. But once we'd reached the lane, he stopped and looked across the fields that spread out towards the horizon. It was the middle of the day and the sun was directly overhead. I could smell salt in the air. The grass was bowing gently in the breeze.

'It may seem all very stupid to you,' he said. 'But this is what it's all about.' He pointed. 'That's Charles le Mesurier's land. He's sold it to Électricité du Nord, presumably at a massive profit to himself, and that's where they'll build the converter stations, three of them, covering twenty-five acres, with facility areas and new roads attached. Do you know what a converter station looks like? It's concrete and metal with cables and fences. It's probably the ugliest building in the world and that's where it's going to be. No wonder Henry and Susan are thinking of leaving. They've lived in that house all their married life, but it'll be valueless, of course. They'll be ruined.

'But it doesn't end there,' Elkin went on. 'They're putting a transition chamber on Longis Beach, where the sea and the land cables will connect. I don't think we'll be seeing much wildlife after that.' His finger swept across the horizon. 'And they're going to run a 1,400-megawatt link cable across there, through Longis Common. Yes, you're right, Mr Hawthorne. They're going to dig up my old grandpa. But he's not the only one. There are more than a thousand bodies buried there, poor souls who died in the most dreadful way, starved to death, tortured, murdered.'

He stood there, his face expressionless, his eyes far away. It took him a while to return to us.

'I know you're only doing your job, Mr Hawthorne, and you don't really care how you get your results. I was there when you were giving your talk and it struck me then that you have absolutely no heart at all. You don't believe in the law. You don't want to help people or society. You don't seem to have any understanding of morality at all. You're a detective. That's all that matters to you.

'Well, I hope you do find whoever it was who killed Charles le Mesurier. It's wrong that such a person should be at large. But when you arrive at that moment, I hope you'll reflect on this. As the two of you stand face to face, you and the killer, I'm not sure there'll be a great difference between the two of you. I think you live by the same rules.'

As a parting shot, it was a good one. Neither of us spoke as he turned and walked back to the house.

13

Further Information

We didn't say very much on the way back to the hotel either. Even Terry managed to remain unusually quiet until the moment he dropped us off.

'So what time do you want me to pick you up?' he asked. 'I don't mind waiting for you outside if you're going to have a spot of lunch.'

'No thanks, mate,' Hawthorne said. 'I think we're done for today.'

'Tomorrow then?' Terry was like a dog, panting at the leash. 'Best business I've had all year,' he went on. 'You don't know what it's like, driving a taxi in a small place like this. It'll all be mine when Dad retires, but ... I don't know! It's like selling meat to vegetarians. Nobody's got anywhere to go.'

Hawthorne and I had agreed to meet after lunch, but as we walked to the front door we ran into Maïssa Lamar on her way out, in a hurry. The timing couldn't have been worse as far as she was concerned. She would have preferred to leave without being seen, but she was already face to face with Hawthorne and he wasn't stepping out of the way. 'I was hoping to speak to you,' he said.

She looked at him blankly. She hadn't understood what he had said. 'I'm sorry?' She managed to make the two words sound remarkably aggressive.

'I have questions for you.'

'Why?'

'You haven't noticed what's been going on around here?'

'I mean ... why do I speak to you? Who are you? You are not police. You are only invited ... same as me.'

'I'm now working with the police. They've asked me to help them.'

'I speak already with the police. I tell them all I know. I know nothing. Now, please. I am in hurry ...' She pushed past him and continued on her way.

It was the first time I had ever seen anyone refuse to cooperate with Hawthorne. When you think about it, it's something that very rarely happens ... at least, in fiction. When the detective asks questions, the suspects invariably answer them. Nobody ever told Morse or Rebus to mind their own business. It's some sort of peculiar convention that even if the culprits are nervous that they'll slip up and say something that gives them away, they will never hold back.

I thought Hawthorne would be angry that he had just been snubbed by a French performance poet dressed in torn clothes, cheap jewellery and a punk haircut, but he seemed unperturbed. 'Where do you go in a hurry when there's nowhere to actually go?' That was his only remark as we continued into the hotel.

We were about to go up to our separate rooms but as we arrived at the reception desk to pick up our keys, we found Special Constable Jane Whitlock waiting for us. She was sitting in a chair with her hat perched on her knees and looked no happier than she had that morning.

'Deputy Chief Torode asked me to see you,' she said. She produced a thick padded envelope. 'I have some information for you.'

'Let's go in the dining room,' Hawthorne suggested.

The tables had been made up but we were alone in the room, which was long and bright with an archway leading into the bar. Whitlock looked around her. 'This is a nice hotel,' she said.

'It's a shame you couldn't get in,' I said.

'That's what they said. But they were probably thinking about the budget. They've put us up at a place in St Anne.' Wherever she was staying, she clearly didn't like it.

'Have you been to Alderney before?' I asked.

'No.'

She wasn't a great conversationalist, but I persevered. 'What does it mean, exactly? Special constable?'

'I'm not a full-time police officer. I'm a volunteer.'

'So what do you do when you're not with the police?'

'Social work. I'm a community psychiatric nurse.'

'Do you enjoy that?'

She shook her head. 'Not really.'

Meanwhile, Hawthorne had opened the envelope and was removing a handful of photographs taken at the crime scene – the usual black and white horrors. There were also twenty or thirty pages of text and assorted diagrams. He picked up one of them and read it. 'You have the time of death at around ten past ten,' he said.

'That's right. We got witness statements.'

Hawthorne turned the page. 'Two of the guests heard le Mesurier cry out, but neither of them knew what it was at the time,' he told me. 'The jazz band was playing and they couldn't hear above the noise of the music. One of them thought it was a screech owl.' He looked up at Whitlock. 'Are there screech owls in Alderney?'

She shrugged.

'The other one thought it was someone in the garden and went out to see but there was nobody there.' He turned another page. 'The footprint in the Snuggery. Size five shoes.'

'If you say so.'

'That's what it says here. That must be a woman.'

'Could be a child.' Was Whitlock being deliberately difficult? I wondered.

'Is that what Torode thinks?'

'He hasn't told me what he thinks.'

Hawthorne continued browsing until he came to the medical report. '*Death caused by a penetrating stab wound to the neck which severed the common carotid artery, the left internal jugular and both jugular veins.* No surprises there. He bled to death.'

'Can I go?' Whitlock asked.

Hawthorne glanced at her, surprised. 'Aren't you interested in this?'

She shook her head. 'I wanted to help people. Community policing – old people and children. This isn't what I volunteered for ... people putting knives in each other and behaving like animals. It's disgusting.'

'So why did you come to Alderney?'

'Because the DC asked me. If I'd known it was going to be like this I'd have said no.'

'Would you like a drink?' I asked.

'No. I'm on duty.' She stood up and put on her hat as if to prove what she had just said. 'If there's anything more, I'll leave it at the desk.'

She walked out of the room.

Hawthorne went back to the report. 'Cranial blunt force trauma also noted at the back of the head ... no weapon found.' He flicked a page. 'Well, well, well. That's interesting. Cocaine!'

'Charles le Mesurier?'

'Who else? There were traces of it in his blood and on the inside of his nose, and look at this.' He gave me one of the photographs: a view of the drinks cabinet with the door fully open. There was a plastic packet inside – white powder, tightly wrapped – and next to it a chequebook with part of the cover ripped off. A second photograph focused on the surface of the cabinet. It had been taken with a high-resolution camera and revealed an irregular stain. A ruler had been laid beside it to show that it covered an area four centimetres long. 'They found further traces on the surface of the drinks cabinet and on the edge of le Mesurier's American Express credit card. So now we know at least one reason why he went to the Snuggery!'

'Did you notice the chequebook?' I asked.

'I did.'

'He'd torn the cover off to make a tube ... to snort the cocaine.'

'You're right.' Hawthorne handed me a page from the police report. 'They found two rolled-up tubes in his trouser pocket.' He frowned. 'How did you know that?' he asked.

'What?'

'About using a chequebook cover to snort cocaine.'

'I'm a crime writer. I have to know about these things.' I stared at him. 'I hope you're not suggesting ...'

'All right! All right! I was only asking.'

I'd already been arrested once in Hawthorne's company: a shoplifting charge, which, fortunately, had been dropped. It would be nice to think that I could get to the end of a third outing with some of my reputation still intact.

Hawthorne took out the next document, two pages clipped together, and read it quickly. 'Background info on le Mesurier,' he told me. 'No criminal record. Made his fortune in internet gambling and moved into computer games, software development and TV production. Parents retired in the Isle of Wight. He's got a brother who lives there too. No children … we already knew that. He was a nasty bastard, but it all seems fairly straightforward.'

'What about the coin?' I asked. I'd noticed an image of the two-euro coin that Hawthorne had found and left behind.

Hawthorne searched out the relevant information. 'No fingerprints, which is interesting.'

'Why?'

'Because how do you carry a coin, take it out of your pocket and drop it on the floor without leaving a fingerprint?'

'Someone must have wiped it clean.'

'Then why leave it behind? And here's something else to think about. Le Mesurier didn't have any other coins on him and it looks as if he hadn't been in France for months.'

'Maybe the two-euro piece belonged to whoever killed him.'

Hawthorne moved on to another page and read it out word for word: '*According to initial analysis, the tape used to secure the victim's feet and one of his hands was Duck Brand HP260 high-performance packaging tape. It's a fairly common brand, but one not available on the island of Alderney …*'

'Suggesting that the killer brought it with him.'

'Or bought it on Amazon. But, yes. I'd say there's a good chance that he – or she – brought it across.'

'So this was planned,' I said.

Either Hawthorne wasn't listening to me or he'd already worked that out for himself. 'They found the will!' he said, and showed me a photocopy that Torode had included with the other documents. At least he was living up to his promise. He was sharing everything he had. Again, Hawthorne scanned the contents. He gave a low whistle. 'He's left a bit to his mum and dad and big brother, but it looks as if Helen le Mesurier gets the lot: the houses, the businesses, the private jet, all of it!'

I was quite surprised. Helen le Mesurier had said that she loved Charles, but from the sound of it he hadn't been all that close to her, gallivanting around the world and keeping her out of the limelight while she stayed at home. And now she was a multimillionaire! Perhaps it was simply that he didn't have anyone else to leave his wealth to. After all, they had no children. Also, of course, he hadn't been expecting to die.

I watched Hawthorne slide all the pictures and papers back into the envelope. He'd go over them all meticulously when I wasn't there. 'Do you know who killed him?' I asked.

He stopped what he was doing, genuinely surprised. 'Why do you ask that?'

'I'm just wondering. The whole thing is completely unfathomable to me and it doesn't help that there must be half a dozen people who wanted le Mesurier dead, including his wife. But somehow you always work it out and since I'm here, tagging along with you as usual, it would be quite nice to know what's in your head and whether you've solved the mystery yet.'

'Is this for the book?'

'Don't worry. If there is a book, I'll leave the solution until the last chapter. All I'm saying is that there's no earthly reason to keep me in the dark right now. That's all.'

He put the last sheets into the envelope. 'There are an awful lot more than six people who wanted him dead, Tony. I can think of twelve of them and that doesn't include all the lunatics who'd do anything to stop NAB. That's something you can put in your book. It's a line to kill if ever I saw one.'

'So has this got something to do with NAB?'

'You really want to know?' Hawthorne wagged a finger in my direction. 'I'll tell you this, Tony. You need to start with the chair. Charles le Mesurier was tied to a chair by his feet and his left hand. But his right hand was kept free. Why was that? If you can work that out, the rest of it will fall into place.'

'Are you saying that the hand was deliberately left free?'

'I don't think they ran out of tape, if that's what you mean.'

I'd hoped he'd say more but just then we were interrupted by the arrival of Elizabeth Lovell, as ever accompanied by her husband, Sid. It was far too early for dinner, but it turned out that wasn't why they were here. 'There he is!' Sid muttered, as he led Elizabeth towards us. 'Sitting with the writer. Just the two of them.'

Hawthorne got to his feet and pulled back a chair. He was clearly the one they had come to see so I stayed where I was. 'Mrs Lovell ...'

She felt for the chair and sat down. 'Mr Hawthorne! I was hoping I'd find you.' I hadn't seen the medium since the party at The Lookout and we hadn't spoken then. I remembered how upset Anne Cleary had been and part of me recoiled at seeing Elizabeth now. She had used the death of Anne's son as a sort of parlour trick. That was what she did for a living. The fact that she was blind made no difference to me. She and Sid were as bad as each other.

'I was wanting to talk to you too.' Hawthorne plunged straight in. 'I saw you at the party, sitting in the garden.'

'Then you know I have a vice.'

'I smoke too. It's quite handy sometimes. Gets you out of the crowd. It made me wonder if you heard anyone go past. In particular, Charles le Mesurier went to the Snuggery sometime just before ten o'clock. I wonder if there was anyone with him? Was he talking to anyone?'

'Liz wasn't close enough,' Sid said. 'I sat her well away from the other guests. Sometimes she likes to be on her own.'

It was true. I had noticed her some distance away from the main lawn and the path.

'I'm afraid I didn't hear anything,' Elizabeth said.

'Is there anything you can tell me about that evening?' Hawthorne asked. 'Obviously, you have an unusual perspective. But it could be very helpful.'

'There's not very much I can tell you, I'm afraid, Mr Hawthorne. Parties are quite difficult for me, as you might imagine. All the voices tend to blend into each other and there's no room to move around. I didn't stay there very long. What time did we leave, Sid?'

'We got there at about seven fifteen, left just before ten.'

So she hadn't been there when the murder happened.

'How did you get back to the hotel?' Hawthorne asked.

'We took a cab,' Sid replied. 'The driver was a kid with ginger hair. I'm sure he'll remember us.'

'He never stopped talking,' Elizabeth added.

I smiled. That had to be Terry.

Hawthorne didn't have any more questions, so Elizabeth weighed in. 'We want to help, Mr Hawthorne. Or rather, I do. And if you're willing to consider something rather unorthodox, there may be something I can do.'

'And what's that, Mrs Lovell?'

'Elizabeth, please.' She drew a breath. Suddenly, I knew what was coming. 'I have helped the police once or twice in Jersey,' she continued. 'Nothing as serious as murder, but they have called on me and found me useful from time to time.'

'There was that kid that disappeared,' Sid reminded her.

'Yes. We found him. He'd managed to lose himself in the nature reserve at Les Mielles. His parents were extremely grateful.'

'Are you suggesting going to the other side of the mirror?' Hawthorne asked.

He was asking her if she intended to talk with the dead and he was being careful to use her own way of expressing it. I was shocked. It was obvious to me that Elizabeth Lovell was a fraud and that if she did manage to involve herself in the investigation it would only be for the publicity she would gain. Surely he wouldn't accommodate her? But Hawthorne hadn't dismissed her out of hand. On the contrary, he seemed intrigued. I tried to remember what he had said when we came out of the cinema, moments after we had both seen Anne Cleary leave in tears. He had agreed with me. I was sure of it.

But he had thought that the ghosts were real.

'I don't like the word séance,' Elizabeth said. 'It's been used too much in popular culture and it reeks of Harry Houdini and Noel Coward. I don't do table-rapping and I don't turn out the lights and hold hands or anything like that. But if after dinner you would like to meet with me – just the four of us – then it's possible that I'll be able to find a contact, a friend on the other side of the mirror who may agree to help us.'

Get rid of her! I was silently pleading with Hawthorne. I refused to believe that he would take her at her word. He was cleverer than that. He was one of the most cynical people I'd ever met.

'That's very kind of you,' he said. 'Would ten o'clock be too late?'

'Not at all.' She made a gesture and Sid helped her get to her feet. 'They have a private screening room in the hotel. I can ask the reception to reserve it for us.'

'Ten o'clock, then.'

I watched them leave. They were barely out of the room before I turned on Hawthorne. 'Are you serious?' I exclaimed. I wasn't just thinking how stupid the idea was. If he actually went through with it, I'd have to describe it and I wasn't sure how I'd find the words. 'This is all just part of her act! She doesn't call them ghosts or spirits. She calls them reflections. And she doesn't say they're séances – that's too Noel Coward – so she invites us to go to the other side of the mirror, like *Alice in Wonderland*.'

'Actually, that's not *Alice in Wonderland*. That's *Alice Through the Looking-Glass*.'

'Hawthorne ... !'

He raised his hands in a gesture of surrender. 'Let's talk about it at dinner, mate. It's a tricky case. You said it yourself. A dozen people wanted to kill Charles le Mesurier, so maybe we should use any help we can get. You don't have to come if you don't want to. But if you do decide to show up ...'

'Yes?'

Hawthorne beamed at me. 'I wonder if you'd pop into the kitchen and get me a box of cling film?'

14

Some Thoughts

❦

As I reached the door of my hotel room, I heard my telephone ringing. I quickly went in and snatched up the receiver. 'Yes?'

'This is reception.' I had walked past only moments ago. 'We have a call for you. A Mr McKinley.'

The name meant nothing to me. 'Do you know what he wants?'

'He asked to speak to Mr Hawthorne, but he's not in his room so he asked to speak to you.'

Hawthorne must have gone outside for a cigarette. McKinley? Suddenly, it came to me. He was the driver of the minibus that had taken guests from the hotel to the party and back again. 'Put him through,' I said.

There was a click and a moment later a man came onto the line. He had a soft, hesitant voice. 'Hello? Is that Anthony?'

'Yes.'

'I'm Tom McKinley. I'm sorry I can't come round right now, but Terry said you wanted to ask me something so I thought I'd give you a call.'

'That's very kind of you, Tom.' I had already opened a notepad, knowing that Hawthorne would want an accurate account of whatever was said. 'We were wondering if you remembered seeing a particular guest last night.'

'Mrs Cleary? Yes, I did.'

How did he know this was the information we needed? And how had he been able to recognise her?

He explained: 'Terry heard you talking in the back of his cab and he told me you wanted to know about someone called Anne Cleary so I googled her. Dark-haired lady. Late forties. Writes children's books?'

'Yes. That's her. She said she spoke to you.'

'That's right. She was coming out of the house and she asked me when we were leaving. She was nervous about getting back to her room. She said she had something important.'

'Did she say what it was?'

'I don't think so.'

'And the bus wasn't full.'

'It was busy, but not full. I can't tell you how many passengers there were, to be honest with you, because I didn't look and anyway, it was too dark. We can seat eleven. Maybe eight or nine?'

'Is there anything else you can tell me?'

'Not really. I was going back and forth all night, so I was carrying a lot of people. I wouldn't have remembered Mrs Cleary if she hadn't talked to me.'

'Thanks, Tom. You've been very helpful.'

I hung up.

Could Anne Cleary have murdered Charles le Mesurier? I wondered. She had left the party a full forty-five minutes before he had been killed. Kathryn Harris had confirmed the time as nine twenty-five. It was always possible that she could have climbed onto the minibus, made her way along the aisle and jumped out the back, but I was sure the minibus only had one door and anyway, I couldn't think of a single reason why she might have committed the crime. She had never met le Mesurier. She had no connection with Alderney. And she had just signed a major deal with Walt Disney, including a strict morality clause that, almost certainly, prohibited the act of murder. Anyway, could she really have crept in ahead of him, hit him with something and then dragged him onto a chair? Would she even have been strong enough to lift him?

Once I'd started thinking about it, I couldn't stop. My room was too small to have a desk, so I propped up the pillows and sat on the bed with the notepad on my lap. I remembered what Hawthorne had said. *You need to start with the chair.*

All right.

Charles le Mesurier hadn't just been murdered. He'd been tied down and either threatened or humiliated first. I had thought he might have been tortured, but if there had been any marks on him they would have shown up in the police medical report. Why had one hand been left free? According to Hawthorne, if I could work that out, everything else would make sense.

Someone had brought the parcel tape to the island, which indicated that the murder had been planned in advance. Le Mesurier had even been warned. That had to be the meaning of the ace of spades placed on his car. Leaving one hand free had been part of the plan, but what possible reason could there have been? Was it possible that somebody had forced him to write something – or maybe sign something – before they killed him? It could have been a cheque or a codicil to a will or a confession. I jotted all three down on a blank page and drew a box around them. That was a start.

Of course, there was a more obvious reason. Le Mesurier had been wearing a Rolex watch on his right wrist. His wife had valued it at over £20,000. Could someone have killed him simply for the watch? Or was it possible that someone unconnected with the crime had wandered into the Snuggery, found the dead body and cut one hand free to take it? That made sense – but then again, why wouldn't they have left the cut piece of tape behind? We hadn't found it on the floor and surely the police report would have mentioned traces of adhesive on his right wrist if they had been there.

I was sure I was missing something. I examined my own hand and thought about its different uses. Writing, obviously.

Pointing. Getting a manicure. Playing the piano. Was palm reading a possibility? No. Ridiculous. Fingerprints? DNA? Could someone have taken his pulse to make sure he was dead? Unlikely.

I turned to a fresh page and tried to plot out a sequence of events that might make sense of all the clues that Hawthorne had found so far. For the moment, I set aside the two-euro piece. Hawthorne hadn't shown any particular interest in it, perhaps because it was too random. It could have been dropped on the floor a week ago.

What about the footprints? It seemed to me that they told their own story. Someone had been on the beach and that person could have been Dr Henry Queripel, who had claimed he was hoping to catch sight of a black-winged kite. What size were his feet? He or she had climbed up to the Snuggery, knowing that the door had been left open for them by someone at the party. They had killed le Mesurier, but had accidentally stepped in his blood. After that, they had continued into the house and had gone up to the office, where they had left a further bloodstain on the back of le Mesurier's mobile phone. But what had they done once they got there? What had they been looking for?

I'd arrived at a brick wall, so I decided to draw up a list of all the people who might have had a reason to kill le Mesurier, although, as Hawthorne had said, that could easily include half the island – anyone who opposed NAB. It was one of the peculiarities of being involved in a murder investigation. Why should I automatically assume that I had met the killer (or killers)? There had been over a hundred guests at The Lookout last night and not all of them had been connected with the festival. Worse still, I'd only spoken to about a dozen of them. It could have been someone whose name I didn't know: the percussionist with The Channelers, for example, or one of the taxi drivers. This was the biggest risk I faced writing about Hawthorne. There was always a chance that I could write three hundred pages and only encounter the killer in the final paragraphs.

However, he had also told me that he had a dozen suspects in mind. I wrote the name Helen le Mesurier in the middle of the page and drew a circle around it. I saw her sitting in her bedroom, crying her eyes out, surrounded by balled-up tissues. Had it all been an elaborate act?

Certainly, she had a motive – the most obvious in the world. Her husband's death gave her money and freedom. She had said she still loved him, but she was romantically involved with a French land surveyor and maybe she had decided it was time for a change. I had seen her leave the party at about ten past nine, on her way to the bedroom, but I hadn't actually seen her go upstairs. I only had her word for it that she was in bed when Charles le Mesurier was killed, and she had definitely seemed defensive and even nervous when Hawthorne had questioned her about what she had seen out of the bedroom window.

Henry Queripel. Susan Queripel. George and Georgina Elkin. They all had the same motive: the power line. More than that, they were actively working together to prevent NAB from being constructed and all of them believed that without le Mesurier there to guide it, it might not go ahead. If he disliked le Mesurier so much, why had George Elkin even gone to the party? He had vehemently denied entering the Snuggery, but he could easily have slipped across the garden and unbolted the door at the back to allow one of the others to climb up from the beach. The three-handed bridge game was very convenient. It drew them all in together and gave each of them an alibi.

Colin Matheson. I added his name to the list and stared at it on the page. The barrister and States member was also implicated with NAB but in a different way. Everyone believed that Charles le Mesurier had some sort of hold over him and that Colin was acting against his conscience by supporting the line. Could le Mesurier have been blackmailing him? Suppose that was the case and Colin had finally decided that he'd had enough. But then again, why that business with the parcel tape and the single free hand? What would have been the point of that?

From everything that I had been told, Colin Matheson was very much under the control of his wife. George Elkin had said that it went further, that he depended on her for his very livelihood. Was she a possible suspect? It was certainly true that of the two of them, she was far more likely to have had the guts to commit a murder. When Hawthorne and I had arrived at The Lookout after the body had been discovered, she hadn't been shocked or upset. She had been angry. Could it be that she knew her husband had committed the crime? Could they have done it together?

That was eight names so far ... if I included Anne Cleary. To reach the full dozen, I would have to fold in some of the other guests who had been invited to the Alderney Literary Festival and I knew at once which name I had to add to the list.

Kathryn Harris.

I had seen Charles le Mesurier trying to impose himself on her not once but twice. And although she had tried to pretend otherwise, she had been seriously upset when I spoke to her in the kitchen on the night of the party. As its name implied, the Snuggery had been used by le Mesurier as his own den of vice, and his behaviour – tiptoeing there in the darkness, the cocaine use – suggested a sexual assignation. Suppose Kathryn had pretended to accept his offer and had tied him down as some sort of bondage thing? That made sense. She could have killed him and then taken the watch: it would be a year's salary for her. It was true that she looked too ordinary, too vulnerable to be a psychopathic killer, but then, from what I'd read, most psychopathic killers are just like that. It's why they're so hard to catch.

Marc Bellamy.

Her boss struck me, frankly, as too much of a buffoon to be a murderer, but then everything about him – his clothes, his catchphrases – was a construct, a television persona. Who could say what it might conceal? He and Charles le Mesurier had gone to the same school – Westland College – at the same time and he hadn't enjoyed it. If there was one thing that my own experience had taught me it was that the private-education system could create grievances that would stay with you for a lifetime. Good old Flash had been taunting Tea Leaf from the moment the two of them had set eyes on each other at The Divers Inn. Who could say that le Mesurier hadn't accidentally triggered some childhood psychosis, with lethal results?

I would have dismissed Elizabeth Lovell immediately, but my long experience in the world of murder mystery – what I had written and what I had read – had taught me that the killer was often the most unlikely suspect, which actually propelled her, along with Anne Cleary, to the top of the list. There was no love lost between the two of them, but for the moment they shared a page.

Elizabeth was blind. Even with Sid's help she would have found it hard to stab le Mesurier, particularly with such surgical precision. Could Sid have tied him down to allow her to strike the final blow, helping her to get revenge for something that we didn't yet know about? It was a neat idea and one that would have looked good in a television drama-tisation, but even as I wrote it down it seemed extremely unlikely. First of all there was no motive ... not unless le Mesurier knew something about the couple that nobody else did. But secondly, there was a question of timing. I had seen Elizabeth in the garden, on her own, not that long before the murder had taken place. Would she have sat there smoking a cigarette if she was about to take part in a killing?

Derek Abbott. That was the next name I wrote down. I underlined it twice.

I hadn't spoken to him at all so far, and Hawthorne had also done what Deputy Chief Torode had told him and kept away from his old enemy. Even so, Derek Abbott was definitely involved. Quite apart from his own unpleasant background, he had been close to le Mesurier, working as his financial adviser until the two of them had fallen out. It was Anne Cleary who had provided this information and it still had to be corroborated, but for the moment I assumed it was true. There had been a disagreement about money. Derek Abbott was about to be fired. He was an obvious suspect, but even so I really hoped that he had nothing to do with the crime. I had known from the start that he was going to be a major problem for me. It would have been better if I'd never heard of him at all.

Paedophiles are not at all easy to write about because, at the end of the day, what is there to say? They're sick. They're disgusting. They're evil! We all know that and I'd have to be out of my mind to write anything positive about such a man even if he was an accomplished pianist, a great raconteur, a philanthropist. Who would care? The crime is so uniquely unpleasant that it's like a black hole, sucking everything else into it, and as I sat on my bed in my hotel room I was annoyed that when I did write the book he would end up being in it. What Abbott represented was completely at odds with everything I would enjoy writing about: blue telephone boxes, beaches and fortifications, sea-gulls, miniature steak and kidney puddings, ginger-haired taxi drivers.

It was also quite likely that Abbott was the one who had killed le Mesurier. Despite his crippled leg, he was a large man and could easily have stunned him – perhaps with his walking stick – and then forced him into that chair. He had a motive. He'd been there on the night of the crime. But if Derek Abbott was revealed to be the killer at the end of the book, who would actually care? If you read Agatha Christie, you may have noticed that every single one of her killers manages to elicit a modicum of sympathy. You may not approve of what they've done, but you understand it. Derek Abbott was beyond the pale.

I put him out of my head and turned instead to my last suspect: Maïssa (and I enjoyed putting the two dots above the i) Lamar. It wasn't a name I'd come across before. Unfortunately, there wasn't a great deal more I could add. She had refused to speak to Hawthorne and in the brief moment I'd met her, she had denied having a friend here on the island, even though I had seen him at the airport and later in the street. The man in the leather jacket had no name so I represented him with a question mark in a circle. It was impossible to guess their relationship. Friends? Lovers? Accomplices? He hadn't been at the party, but she had. And she had also been up to the first floor – even if this had been before le Mesurier was killed.

Finally, I wasn't convinced by her performance poetry. No poet was as bad as that. I thought back to the haiku she had recited, the one about her ex-boyfriend. On an impulse, I reached for my phone and opened Google Chrome. First I went to Wikipedia.

WIKIPEDIA
The Free Encyclopedia

Maïssa Lamar

Maïssa Lamar is a French spoken-word artist, author and poet.

Contents

1 Early life
2 Career
  2.1 2012 to present
3 Selected works
4 Awards and honours

Early life

Born in Rouen on August 6 1981, Maïssa Lamar has become one of the most powerful new voices in today's poetry scene, with a particular love of Norman culture. Her writing began with a visit to the Seine-Maritime department, where she holidayed as a child.[1][2] She lives in Paris, France.

Career

2012 to present

Lamar has won numerous awards for her poetry, which draws on many inspirations, from the Petrarchan sonnet to the Japanese haiku. Her poems have been published in several countries and she has been a member of the Académie Mallarmé since 2013.

She performs much of her work in Cauchois, a largely forgotten dialect which she learned from her grandfather. *Le Monde* described her as 'a leading light in the revival of Cauchois culture' and in 2011 she was given the Freedom of the City of Lille. Her poems have been published in French, German, Italian and Spanish.

Selected works

- *L'Autostop et autres poèmes* (*Hitchhiking and Other Poems*), Cheyne éditeur, France, 2009, ISBN 978–2-84116–147-8
- *L'École en lames de rasoir* (*The School Made of Razor Blades*), Cheyne éditeur, France, 2006, ISBN 978–2-84116–116-4, republished in 2008[14]
- *Le Livre de feuilles et d'ombres* (*The Book of Leaves and Shadows*), Cheyne éditeur, France, 2004, ISBN 978–2-84116–096-9

Awards and honours

- Prix Louis-Guilloux – 2014
- Prix Mallarmé – 2012
- Grand Prix de poésie de la SGDL – 2009

The entry told me nothing that I didn't already know, but the mention of Japanese haikus reminded me of the final poem she had recited. It had meant something to me, even though, as far as I could see, none of her work had been quoted on the internet and her three books weren't available on Amazon or Kindle, so how could I possibly have known it? I tried to remember how it went.

> I see the light
> And something comes after me.
> Your place or mine?

It wasn't quite that, but I put the words into the search engine anyway. It revealed nothing. I fiddled with the first line, without success, then turned to the third. *Your shadow or mine*. That was it! I entered the words and immediately the entire poem appeared on the screen, all three lines of it.

> I look to the light
> But a dark shape pursues me.
> Your shadow or mine?

There it was – but the author was not Maïssa Lamar. The very mention of a haiku should have taken me back to my not entirely comfortable encounter with Akira Anno, the feminist writer who had actually produced an entire book containing two hundred haikus. One of them had turned out to be a major clue in the murder of the celebrity divorce lawyer Richard Pryce, but while turning the pages, I had happened to notice an earlier haiku written by Akira and this was it.

Maïssa had stolen it!

I stood up with a sense of excitement. In the course of two investigations with Hawthorne, I had worked out precisely nothing. I had written about him, but I had been no help at all and it was quite possible that everything I had written here, all my deductions so far, were completely wrong. But this was, unquestionably, a breakthrough. I had been right at the airport. Maïssa wasn't what she seemed.

I couldn't wait to tell Hawthorne and I was out of my room at twenty-five past seven, on my way to meet him for dinner. In fact, about halfway down the corridor a door opened and Hawthorne emerged. I couldn't help but notice, incidentally, that his room was rather larger than mine and had a sea view.

'Hawthorne—' I began.

He stopped me. I wasn't going to tell him about Maïssa right then. Nor were we going to have dinner together. The séance was going to be cancelled, too, because, it turned out, he'd just had a telephone call from Deputy Chief Torode.

'It's bad news, mate,' he said. 'Helen le Mesurier has disappeared.'

15

The Isle is Full of Noises

It was the housekeeper who had raised the alarm. Deputy Chief Torode was waiting for us in the hallway when we arrived at The Lookout and he explained what had happened.

'Her name is Nora Carlisle,' he said. He hadn't expected to be called back to the house and he didn't look too pleased about it, somehow communicating that first a murder and now a disappearance shouldn't have been allowed to intrude on his quiet Sunday evening. 'She arrived at the house just after the two of you left. Did Whitlock turn up with the information I sent you?'

'Yes. We got it, thanks,' Hawthorne said.

'I'm worried about Whitlock. Why is she so bloody miserable all the time?'

'Nora Carlisle …' Hawthorne reminded him.

'Oh, yes.' He lowered his voice. The housekeeper must have been somewhere near. 'She just came marching in as if nothing had happened and even when we told her what was going on, she didn't seem to care. What did it matter that her employer had just been murdered? She had a house to clean.'

'She works on a Sunday?' Hawthorne asked.

'Not normally. She'd agreed to come in to help clear up after the party. Her husband had brought her over. He's a car mechanic in a local garage, two kids – but she'll tell you all this. It's hard to get her to stop talking, to be honest.'

'You let her in?'

'She didn't give us much choice. She said she wasn't leaving until she'd seen that Mrs le Mesurier was OK, and then Mrs le Mesurier came down and the two of them almost fell into each other's arms. In the end, it seemed easier to let her stay. We'd already moved the body by then and the main crime scene is across the garden, not in the house, so there didn't seem any harm in it. She could look after Mrs le Mesurier and while she was at it I asked if she might be able to rustle up some lunch. Those steak and kidney pies were very good. But they were small.'

'So what happened next?'

'I can't tell you that exactly. I left the house to get that information together and to talk to some of the people who were here last night. I hear you've been doing the rounds, by the way, Hawthorne, making lots of new friends. Have you got anywhere yet?'

'Not yet.'

'Just be sure to tell me when you do. Anyway, according to Mrs Carlisle, the two women had lunch together and then

Mrs le Mesurier announced that she wanted to go out for a walk. She said she needed some fresh air and insisted that she wanted to be on her own, but she'd be back in an hour.'

'And you let her go?' Hawthorne said. There was a note of incredulity in his voice.

'I wasn't here.' Torode was offended. 'She spoke to Wilson and he said yes. He's the forensic coordinator and not bad at his job, but of course it was bloody stupid, letting her leave the house.'

'So where were you?'

'I was over in the Buggery or the Snuggery, or whatever it's called.'

Hawthorne didn't comment on this. 'Did she take a car?' he asked.

'She went on foot. Mrs Carlisle went up and did the bedroom, changed the sheets and all the rest of it, then waited for her to come back. Except she didn't. She went out at two o'clock. Since then, there's been no sign of her.'

'Have you tried calling her?'

'Her mobile's upstairs.'

Hawthorne considered. 'Where is Mrs Carlisle?'

'Through here. But I'm warning you, you'll find it hard to get a word in edgeways.'

Nora Carlisle was sitting in the sun lounge, perched on a wicker chair. The walls had been slid back into their correct positions, creating a much smaller space, hemmed in by potted plants. This was where the band had played the night before.

She was a small, neat, serious woman, aged about fifty. Torode introduced us and we sat down on a sofa opposite her.

'This must be very upsetting for you,' Hawthorne began.

'Of course it is. Of course it is. I've worked for Mrs Lem for twelve years. To come here this morning and find all these police officers here and the house turned upside down, well, I couldn't believe it. And then I heard! Well, I'm telling you, I can't imagine why anyone would want to do Mr Lem any harm. He's done so much for the island ... not that he was ever here that often. He was a very successful business-man, always jetting off all around the world. Mrs Lem was in a real state when I got here. The two of them were a perfect couple and I don't care what people say. He never came home without something special for her. She loved him and he loved her. You can take it from me.'

'So tell me about Mrs le Mesurier's movements today.'

'She was very glad to see me, poor thing. You'd have thought somebody would have been looking after her, but she was all on her own with complete strangers rampaging around the place. I left her in the bedroom while I did the housework and made her some lunch and after we'd eaten she said she wanted to go out. That was two o'clock. I wanted to go with her, but she insisted she'd be all right on her own.'

'She didn't say where she was going.'

'She said she wasn't going far, that she'd be back in an hour or so, but when it got to four o'clock I got worried about her. I mean, after what she'd seen with Mr Lem in the Snuggery, she wasn't herself, poor thing. I blame myself, really. I shouldn't have let her go out without me. I could see she was still upset. And when it got to four fifteen, I knew something was wrong and straight away I called Mr Matheson and Dr Queripel – they'd always been close to her – but they hadn't seen her. I tried some of her other friends … she keeps an address book with their numbers by her bed. None of them had seen her. So then I went and told the police officers that they needed to do something. But would they listen to me? They were far too busy packing up to get home. So that was another hour wasted. Finally, I put my foot down. I said there was obviously someone dangerous on the island – I mean, anyone could have told them that – and that if anything had happened to her it would be down to them. And that was when they called their boss – not that he's been much help.' She scowled at Torode. 'I mean, where is she? She can't just have disappeared.'

'How well do you know Mrs le Mesurier?'

'I told you. I've been with her for twelve years. And although I wouldn't say this to anyone, I'm not just her housekeeper. I like to think of her as a friend. She's always asking after my family and she's generous too. There's always an envelope at Christmas and presents for my girls.' She sniffed. 'People may say bad things about her. Well, of course they would. She's wealthy and she's gorgeous and she has all this. But she's one of the most good-hearted people I've ever met. Look at the school! Both my girls went to St Anne's and she's always helping with books for the library and prizes for sports day. She took twenty of the children to London once – to the Natural History Museum – and it all came out of her own pocket. The coach, the ferry, everything. That's the sort of person she is, and if someone's hurt her ... well, it doesn't bear thinking about.'

I looked out of the window. It wasn't anywhere near dark yet, but the sun had sunk low in the sky and I realised that it was too late to begin a search. Mauve shadows stretched across the lawn, the silent bulk of the Snuggery beyond, and for some reason I found myself thinking of Shakespeare's play *The Tempest*. When I was at school, I'd played Caliban (although I'd auditioned for Ariel) and I recalled the lines:

Be not afeard; the isle is full of noises,
Sounds and sweet airs, that give delight, and hurt not.

But the noises on this isle were all bad. Perhaps it had come with the Nazis when they built their labour camps and had been lurking ever since, but I felt it now: a malign presence that had somehow insinuated itself into Alderney. The macabre death of Charles le Mesurier, the disappearance of his wife, the rancour surrounding the power line, the crimes of Derek Abbott ... they were all part of it.

'You said people say bad things about her,' Hawthorne remarked. He paused. 'What people? What things?'

'Well ...' Mrs Carlisle hesitated. 'Mrs Lem was an actress when they met. She used to appear in his online promotions and when they got married there were people who said she was only in it for the money, that she'd managed to spin the wheel in her own favour, that sort of thing. But that wasn't true. I told you. It may not have been a conventional marriage, but they were happy with it and it worked.'

'Did she ever bring anyone back here?'

Nora Carlisle looked at Hawthorne with disdain. 'How would I know?'

'Well, you made her bed. I'd imagine it would be fairly obvious.'

'That's a wicked thing to say and I can't imagine what gives you the right to make such accusations.' The housekeeper looked to Deputy Chief Torode as if he could put a stop to this line of questioning. 'She would never have behaved that way. She wasn't like that at all.'

'You never met a man called Jean-François Berthold?'

'I've never heard that name.'

'When she went out at two o'clock, did she say she was going to meet someone?'

'Not to me. She just said she wanted a walk.'

Helen had left her car – a Land Rover Discovery – outside the house. It had been parked there when we arrived. So wherever she had gone, it couldn't have been far.

'Is there anything else you want to know?' Mrs Carlisle asked. For the first time she sounded tired, as if all the talking had worn her out.

'No. You've been very helpful.' Hawthorne smiled.

'Well, I'll go home then. There's no point my staying here now.'

She bundled herself out of the chair and left the room.

'I'm sure there's a perfectly simple explanation for all this,' Torode remarked, lazily uncurling himself from the sofa. 'She probably felt uncomfortable sitting here with the police around. And having that woman here all day … that would have done anyone's head in! My guess is she's gone to the pub.'

'Have you rung the pubs?'

'Not yet.'

'Have you even checked that she's still on the island?'

Torode frowned. 'Actually, I hadn't thought of that. We could put a call into the local airline.'

'She had a private jet.'

'Oh. Right. Well, we'll look into it. Anything else?'

'Yes. I'd like to go upstairs.'

'She's not there.'

'No. But her phone is.'

We went back up to the bedroom we had visited only that morning. Everything was very clean and dust-free. Mrs Carlisle had made the bed, puffing up the pillows, arranging silk cushions and placing a small white teddy bear holding a sachet of dried lavender in the middle of it all. I had thought the room, with its elaborate furniture and excessive ornamentation, very much a reflection of its occupant. Without her, it felt empty and strange.

Sure enough, there was a pink iPhone on the dressing table. Torode picked it up. 'I assume this is hers,' he said. 'But I don't know how you're going to break into it without a passcode.'

'I've got someone in London who may be able to help,' Hawthorne muttered. But even as he spoke, he was rifling through the address book that Mrs Carlisle had mentioned. It had been on the bedside table, an expensive thing with gold-edged pages and a padded cover with a Liberty pattern. He turned to the back and smiled. 'No surprises here,' he said. 'Credit cards, computers, mobiles, the lot. Seems that "Mrs Lem" liked to keep all her passwords in one place.'

'Very foolish of her,' Torode said. 'Anyone could have found it.'

'I just did.' Hawthorne took the iPhone from the police officer and entered the code to unlock it. He quickly scrolled through the most recent text messages, reading them intently. When he looked up, he was uneasy. 'You should see this,' he said.

Torode and I moved closer as Hawthorne held out the screen and showed us a chain of communication between Helen le Mesurier and an unknown correspondent, the panels alternating white and blue. This is how it read:

> What happened last night?
> I saw you leave with Charles. Into the sunggery. WTF?

235

I don't know what you're talking about.

I SAW YOU!!!!

Who did you tell?

I didn't tell anyone why are you even asking me that?

We may have problems. We need to talk.
Can I come over?

IDK. I've got police all over the f*ing house. This is crazy.

Can you come to me?

OK. When?

2.30pm

OK. OTW. CUL8R.

'What does that mean? "CUL8R"?' Torode asked.

'See you later,' Hawthorne said.

'Well, it should be easy enough to find out who she was talking to.'

Hawthorne shook his head. 'Not necessarily. There's no name or phone number showing at the top of the screen. Whoever texted her could have been using a burner phone. Or there are plenty of websites he could have logged into to make himself anonymous – Bollywood Motion, SeaSms. com and so on. It depends how careful he was being.'

Hawthorne knew a lot about computers. He had mentioned he had someone who could help him in London and I had actually met him. He was a neighbour, a young man with muscular dystrophy, who sat in a room surrounded by industrial-sized computers and high-tech paraphernalia and helped Hawthorne hack into the police computer system whenever he needed information. Just for fun, he had even hacked into my phone.

'How can you be so sure it's a he?' I asked.

'There's something about her texts that make me think they're addressed to a man.' Hawthorne was still holding the phone in his hand. 'If it was a girlfriend, I think she'd be a bit more personal. Also, unlike her, he doesn't use any abbreviations.'

'Mrs le Mesurier knew who killed her husband,' Torode said. 'She was protecting him.'

'She saw something out of her bedroom window last night,' Hawthorne admitted. He was angry with himself. 'I knew she was lying to me when I spoke to her this morning. She was too bloody insistent. *Even if I had looked out of the window – and I didn't – it would have been too dark* ... But in the next breath she was telling me that there were lights on in the Snuggery, which would have lit up anyone who approached. A double lie.'

'Shame you didn't tell me this sooner,' Torode muttered.

'Shame your people let her leave,' Hawthorne replied.

He was still thumbing through the other messages on the phone. It's interesting how we all carry around with us a complete record of our lives, where we've been, what we've been thinking at any given time. Writing the biography of people born in the twenty-first century will be incredibly easy because the researchers won't have to do any work. It'll all be there, spelled out in minute detail.

Helen le Mesurier had texted Nora Carlisle with shopping lists and cleaning instructions, but it was all quite brisk, with no sign of the fondness that the housekeeper had suggested. She had maintained a brisk, quite business-like relationship with her husband; none of the texts between them were more than half a dozen words. On the other hand, she had sent gushing messages to 'JF' in Paris and I was just glad that she hadn't attached photographs. JF wasn't alone. There was Martin, Bobby, Otto, Sergei ... a long list of men with whom she had been entwined. Hawthorne had to scroll through a string of messages before he found the texts he was looking for. They were spread out over a week. They had been sent six months ago and whoever had received them had replied by phone, as if they didn't want to commit themselves to anything in writing.

> Hi, Colin. No regrets. You warm, funny, kind man. Talk soon. ILU.

Don't blank me, C. What happened happened.
Je ne regrette etc. Let's talk soon.

Colin. Call me!!!

OMG, Colin. That's not possible. OK.
Will call again tonight. No more texts.
Are you sure? What has he got?

Col, I need to see you! We can work this out.
Where/when? LMK. Really worried now.

'Any idea who Colin is?' Torode asked.

'Could be anyone,' Hawthorne said.

It was Colin Matheson — who else could it be? I remembered the barrister in her bedroom only that morning, coming to her defence when Hawthorne had asked her about the power line. I had thought at the time that they were closer than they were pretending and Colin had been the first person Mrs Carlisle had called. But I had never thought they were as close as this. Standing there in the bedroom, I was careful not to say anything, but I was quite surprised that Hawthorne didn't share Colin's identity with Torode. I understood that he wanted to solve the case ahead of the police. That was the only way to be sure of getting paid. But wasn't he actually obstructing their investigation, not giving them such vital information?

'Well, we can give Colin a ring, I suppose,' Torode said. 'I see we've got his number at the top of the screen. Mind you, I doubt it's relevant. This exchange happened a while ago and there's still every chance that Mrs le Mesurier will show up.'

'Let me know if she does,' Hawthorne said, grimly.

Torode took the phone back. 'We'll send you a transcript of whatever else we find on this,' he said. 'I'll get Whitlock to bring it over – if she bothers to show up again.'

'Thank you.'

'We've already made quite a bit of headway. Let's hope you can get a result soon.' He slipped the phone into his pocket. 'What's the food like at your hotel?'

'It's very good,' I said.

'Well, it's terrible at our place. I had a shepherd's pie just before I came out. Dry as a bone. No meat in it. None to speak of.'

Hawthorne nodded and the two of us left. He was deep in thought and didn't say anything on the way back to the hotel and even Terry – who had been waiting outside – picked up on his mood and left him alone. He didn't want dinner so I ordered room service on my own before falling into an uneasy sleep.

I couldn't see the sea from my bedroom, but I could hear the waves breaking in the distance. They reminded me that I was on a tiny island – and so was the killer. We were both trapped.

16

The Search Party

The search for Helen le Mesurier began the next day.

The island of Alderney is tiny; it adds up to no more than three square miles. But it would be hard to imagine anywhere with more places to conceal a dead body. There were beaches and coves, rock faces, pools, caves and tunnels, dozens of fortifications, many of them abandoned and in ruins. If Helen had been killed, she could have been buried inland or weighed down and dumped at sea. There were dozens of isolated farms and houses where she could be held prisoner; dilapidated barns, hangars, warehouses, sheds. We'd managed to establish that Helen hadn't left Alderney, at least not in her private jet or on a scheduled flight. But that might be bad news. Her text messages made it all too clear. It seemed that she had seen the killer and had arranged to meet him. If so, she had made a terrible mistake.

To be fair to Deputy Chief Torode and the Criminal Investigation Department of the Guernsey police, they had wasted no time in pulling together a sizeable force, ferrying about twenty men and women from one island to another at the crack of dawn and recruiting locally too. By eleven o'clock they had spread across a section of the northern side of the island from Fort Albert to Veaux Trembliers Bay, the idea being that they would spread themselves out along the coast and then circle back inwards. It was a sensible strategy, given the position of The Lookout and the fact that Helen had left on foot. According to her text message, the meeting had been arranged for half past two and she had left more or less on the hour. How far could she have gone in thirty minutes?

We saw something of the search under way as we left the hotel, driving to Colin Matheson's house. He lived on the other side of Alderney, just inland from Longis Beach, but we'd taken the long way round so that we could see some of the activity. It was a cloudy day and there was a slightly forlorn quality about the line of people, some in police uniform, others dressed casually, silhouetted against the coastal sky, poking at the grass with long sticks. I saw a couple of dogs straining on leads, but I can't say they exactly filled me with confidence as they were pulling in completely opposite directions. Someone was shouting, but the wind swept the words away and I doubted anyone could hear.

'They haven't got a chance.' That was Terry's view and Hawthorne didn't disagree.

We turned away, cutting through farmland and heading towards the other coast. Of course, in Alderney, whichever way you drove you'd soon reach water.

'I was surprised you didn't tell Torode about Colin Matheson,' I said. I spoke in a low voice, aware that Terry was eavesdropping on everything we said. I had already told Hawthorne about my phone conversation with Tom McKinley.

Hawthorne was less discreet. 'Haven't you got it in your head yet, mate? Torode hasn't got a clue and if he did have one, he wouldn't know what to do with it. You heard what he said! He's not going to solve this case. He's got more chance of finding the meat in his shepherd's pie than he has of working out who killed le Mesurier. And it probably matters more to him too.'

Terry laughed at that. I was right. He was listening to every word.

Judith and Colin Matheson lived with their three children in a converted barn whose true glory should have been the gardens that surrounded it – and in particular an immaculate lawn that sloped gently down from the edge of the building to the road. But as we drew in, we saw that the lawn had been desecrated. Someone had recently taken a spade to it and gouged out six letters, each one about two metres in length, the fresh earth spelling out a familiar message:

BAN NAB

The work had been done quickly, perhaps under the cover of darkness. The first N was twisted on its side and the final B was too big. It was a particularly ugly piece of vandalism, given how much care had been put into the rest of the garden. Hawthorne and I both saw it as we walked up to the front door but neither of us said anything, as if it would be somehow indecent to comment.

Colin Matheson had seen us arrive and opened the door before we rang the bell. He looked utterly worn out. The first time I'd seen him, he'd reminded me of a junior doctor. Now he was more like an undertaker. 'I wondered if I might see you today,' he said – to Hawthorne, not to me. 'Is it true what I'm hearing about Helen?'

'She's disappeared. Yes.'

'They haven't found her yet?'

'They're looking.'

'Please come in.' But Hawthorne stood where he was, examining the garden. He didn't need to ask anything. Matheson volunteered. 'It's horrible, isn't it? Someone did this on Saturday morning while Judith was out with Lucy, our youngest. She has horse-riding lessons every weekend and our other two are at boarding school, so I expect they knew that the house would be empty. When she got back, this is what she found. I was actually with you when she rang.'

So this explained why Judith Matheson hadn't come to hear me and Hawthorne give our talk. *I had some issues at home*. That was what she had said, and Matheson had been deliberately vague about it too.

'I know the point they're making,' he went on. 'Digging up my garden just like those cables George Elkin was going on about. But it all seems so personal, so vindictive. I wish I'd never heard of that bloody power line. I thought it would benefit the island. I thought it would help secure our future. But all it's done is tear us apart. I don't think this place will ever be the same again.'

He turned his back on us and walked into the house. We followed him into a wide hallway that ran all the way to the garden at the back, with a flight of stairs twisting round to the first floor. The house was elegant, classical, with landscapes and horse pictures on the walls, nineteenth-century furniture (real, not repro) and everywhere a sense of neatness and order.

'Who is it?' a voice called out.

'It's Mr Hawthorne, dear.'

'Oh.' A door opened and Judith Matheson strode out of the kitchen, wearing an apron, drying a plate. She saw us. 'You didn't say you were coming,' she said accusingly.

'Well, I'm investigating a murder and now a woman has gone missing, so I wasn't exactly waiting for an invitation,' Hawthorne replied.

Judith processed this. She gave the plate another couple of wipes. 'Take them into the drawing room, Colin,' she said.

You can probably tell a lot about a house by whether it has a drawing room, a living room or a lounge … certainly about the people who live in it. A few minutes later, we found ourselves sitting on high-backed, remarkably uncomfortable sofas that surrounded a coffee table, with gold mirrors and more horse pictures on the walls. A faded grand piano stood to one side and I noticed books of Grade 2 piano music – the first suggestion that there were actually children who also inhabited this house – scattered over the top. The curtains had been drawn across the windows that would have looked out over the front garden, but I could see a greenhouse and vegetable patch round the side.

For a few minutes we chatted aimlessly to Colin, whose role, it seemed, was to keep us occupied without saying anything of any significance. Then Judith reappeared, carrying coffee and biscuits on a tray. We hadn't asked for them. Maybe it was her way of making everything feel normal.

'You've seen the garden,' she said, before she'd even sat down. 'It's a wicked thing to have done. Just wicked!'

'Actually, we're here about the murder, Mrs Matheson,' Hawthorne reminded her.

'Of course. I know exactly why you're here. But although it may not have occurred to you, everything that happens on this island is connected. My grandfather planted that lawn and four generations have been looking after it, keeping it perfect – not just for our pleasure but for everyone who passes.'

'And George Elkin's grandfather is buried at Longis Common, which is going to be dug up too,' Hawthorne said, innocently. 'Is that the sort of connection you mean?'

Judith fell silent, so her husband cut in. 'I think that's a little unfair. The plans for Longis Common allow for the complete restoration of the grasslands. In fact, they insist on it. There will be a few months' disruption, but after that nobody will notice any difference.'

'Is it disruption? Or desecration?'

'Are you taking the side of the protestors, Mr Hawthorne?' Colin Matheson was as close to anger as he could manage. 'Because if so, I think you should leave my house.'

'I'm not taking anyone's side,' Hawthorne replied. 'It was your wife who suggested a connection between what happened here and the death of Charles le Mesurier. I'm just trying to understand the mindset. Anyway, from what I understand, now that le Mesurier is dead, the line may not go ahead.'

He had somehow made that sound like an accusation and Matheson flinched. 'Charles le Mesurier had nothing to do with the decision-making process,' he replied. 'He made his views known, but so did many other people. The committee made its recommendations based on the evidence: the financial and technological benefits weighed against any environmental consequences.'

Hawthorne turned to Judith. 'Did you support the line?' he asked.

She hadn't expected the question. 'Nobody asked me my opinion,' she faltered.

'But ... ?'

'Obviously, I supported my husband.'

'How well did you know Charles le Mesurier?'

She looked to Colin Matheson as if he could somehow prevent this line of questioning, but he couldn't help her. 'Charles le Mesurier was probably the most famous person on the island,' she said. 'Everyone knew him.'

'That's not what I asked you.'

'I met him socially quite a few times. He invited us to dinner once or twice. I wouldn't say we were friends. Of course, I got to know him better through the festival. Once he got involved.'

'The festival was your idea.'

'Yes.'

'How did you get him to finance it?'

'It was a business opportunity,' Judith said. 'I told him sponsoring a literary festival would be good for Spin-the-wheel. And he liked meeting well-known people. Unfortunately, that didn't quite work out. We invited lots of famous authors – Philip Pullman, Val McDermid, Jacqueline Wilson, Alexander McCall Smith – but they all turned us down.'

'What did you think of Charles le Mesurier?' Hawthorne asked. At least he had the decency to avoid my eye.

'I didn't really have an opinion.'

'What about his wife?'

Judith Matheson sat up stiffly. 'I hardly knew her.'

'But everyone's connected on Alderney.'

'I met her a few times. We had nothing in common.'

Colin Matheson leaned forward. 'Actually, Mr Hawthorne, if you don't have any more questions ...'

'I've nothing more to ask your wife,' Hawthorne said. 'But if you don't mind, I'd like to talk to you.' He paused. 'Alone.'

Judith wasn't having any of that. 'Anything you want to say to my husband, you can say in front of me.'

'That's fine by me,' Hawthorne said, not put out at all. He smiled at Matheson. 'Shall I go ahead, then?'

But Matheson wasn't stupid. He was, after all, a barrister and he must have sensed what was in the air. He turned to his wife. 'Actually,' he demurred, 'if this has anything to do with States business, perhaps it might be best if you weren't here, darling. I wouldn't want you to be compromised.'

He was lying, of course. He knew that whatever Hawthorne had in mind had nothing to do with the island's parliament. And Judith was equally disingenuous. She must have guessed that he was lying, but she went along with it. She stood up. 'All right.' She was still indignant. 'I'll be in the kitchen.'

She walked out of the room.

'There's something you have to understand about Judith,' Matheson began as soon as the door had closed. 'She loves this island. In fact, it's very hard to get her to leave it ... even for holidays. She's always believed that everything is perfect here, so why would she want to go anywhere else? But as a result you could say that she is insular in the exact sense of that word. She was very upset by all the arguments about NAB, and as for what happened to le Mesurier ... well, I hardly need tell you, there's never been a murder on Alderney ...'

'You don't,' Hawthorne agreed.

'But I've been married to her for twenty years. I love her very much and I wouldn't want anything to harm her.' He took a breath, waiting for the blow to fall. 'So what do you want to ask me?'

'I think you already know, Mr Matheson. Helen le Mesurier has gone missing, but we've managed to recover certain text messages from her phone that suggest the two of you were ... how shall I put it ... ?'

'We were lovers. Briefly, stupidly, insanely.' The collapse when it came was total. Colin Matheson buried his face in his hands and his whole body shuddered. 'She was the one who drew me in. She was the one who started it. I wish I'd never met her!'

Hawthorne was unforgiving. 'Why are you talking about her in the past tense, Mr Matheson? Do you know she's dead?'

Matheson looked up. 'I'm talking about her in the past tense because my relationship with her is over,' he said. 'It wasn't even a relationship. It was sex. Twice. Never again. I hated myself at the time. I love Judith and I'll never forgive myself for being so stupid.'

'Where did you have sex?'

'In that place at the bottom of the garden. The Snuggery.'

'And she suggested it?'

'Look ... I'm not going to make excuses for myself. It was my decision and God knows I regret it. But, yes, she was the one who made all the running. She threw herself at me.'

'Why were you at the house?'

'I was on States business. We were fund-raising for the school and I was on the committee. She invited me to The Lookout to talk about a possible bequest and then ...' His voice was hoarse and he swallowed a mouthful of lukewarm coffee. 'I'm not going to talk about it. If Judith ever finds out, I'll be finished. I love her. I love my children. This house! I'll lose everything.'

I had never seen anyone quite so lost. Colin Matheson was crying. Every piece of him seemed to be on the point of collapse.

'Do you really believe in this power line?' Hawthorne asked. 'When I spoke to him yesterday, Dr Queripel said you were being forced to support NAB. He was the best man at your wedding, but that doesn't seem to matter to you any more. You've lost a lot of friends. When you were put on the committee, they all thought you'd be on their side. So what happened?'

Matheson fought for control. Still, when he spoke, his voice was hoarse and strangled. 'If I tell you the truth, is there any way you can keep it from Judith?'

'She's going to find out everything if you don't.'

'All right.' He took out a handkerchief and wiped his eyes. It took him another minute to recover. Eventually, he began. 'It was six months ago,' he said. 'Helen took me to the Snuggery, but what she never told me was ... there's a security camera.'

I glanced at Hawthorne. I couldn't remember seeing a camera. But he didn't interrupt.

'What happened between us was recorded. And a few weeks later I got a phone call ...'

I wasn't sure what was going to come next, but it was the last thing I had expected.

'Derek Abbott,' he said, his voice full of hatred.

'He was blackmailing you?' Hawthorne asked.

Matheson nodded. 'I don't know how he got his hands on the footage. He never told me. But he made it quite clear what he wanted – my support for the power line.'

'What was in it for him?'

'He has shares in Électricité du Nord. If NAB goes ahead, the shares are going to surge in value. That's what it all comes down to. He wants to make money! And he doesn't care if he trashes my life to get it. I told you. That man is vile. He should never have come to this island. He's positively evil.'

'Have you paid him money?'

'No. He's cleverer than that. All he wanted was for the line to go ahead. That was what he told me. My job was to sway the committee, to use my influence so the decision would go in his favour. If the vote was passed, he'd destroy the evidence.'

'You were against the line.'

'To begin with I was undecided. On the face of it, there seemed to be benefits. But the more I looked into it, the more I saw the harm that it could do. I have friends. I've known Henry and Susan Queripel most of their lives. Do you think I want to see their beautiful house ruined?'

'But that's exactly what you do want to see,' Hawthorne said. 'You did what Abbott told you. You supported the line. You got it signed off. You've sold all your friends up the river to protect yourself.'

Matheson had no answer to that. He'd been defeated when we walked in. Now he was destroyed.

Hawthorne got up. 'We'll show ourselves out,' he said.

We left the house together but we didn't get back in the car. Hawthorne didn't want to talk where Terry could overhear, and anyway, he needed a cigarette. We stood in the road in front of the house while he smoked.

'I didn't see a security camera,' I said.

Hawthorne looked surprised. 'Well done, Tony. I wondered if you'd notice. That's because it wasn't there.'

'So how … ?'

'How did Derek Abbott get pictures from a camera that didn't exist? Well, there are two possibilities. The first is that he somehow found out what was going to happen and he put it there. The second is that there was a camera six months ago, but for some reason Helen le Mesurier or her husband decided to take it down.'

'How will you find out?'

'Well, I'm not sure Derek Abbott will tell us anything – not when it's going to put him back in jail. So our best chance is Helen le Mesurier.'

'If they ever find her.'

'And if she's still alive.'

They did find her, later that afternoon. She wasn't alive.

A railway line – used only for tourist rides in the summer – ran along the edge of Mannez Quarry, about twenty minutes' walk from The Lookout. The line split into three and continued down to a large shed which housed the diesel engine and carriages that made the journey to Braye Road Station, twice a week on Saturdays (I had seen flyers advertising the trip back at the hotel). My first thought, as Hawthorne and I drew up, was that despite the blue water and an abundance of bright yellow gorse sprouting all around, it was a remarkably desolate, even a grim place. Perhaps it was The Odeon, the naval tower built by the Nazis, that inspired my sense of unease. It stood high above, as sinister a building as I had ever encountered, with its three dark slits dissecting the grey concrete. From the day of its construction it had been a witness to murder and barbarity. It was somehow fitting that this should have continued into the twenty-first century.

Underneath it, there was a cave, presumably man-made and used to transport food supplies or munitions. It would be easy to miss. There was no sign, no indication that it existed apart from a flattening of the grass towards the entrance. I had been unfair to the sniffer dogs. Apparently, one of them had barked to be let free and had then run inside.

Torode had rung us with the news and he was waiting for us when we arrived. 'In there!' He looked tired and ill. He didn't say anything else.

We made our way towards it, passing the rusting skeleton of an old carriage that had been abandoned in the long grass. Old, abandoned machinery can have a certain beauty, but this was different. Maybe it was just the mood I was in, but somehow the broken, twisted metal unnerved me: a ghost train in every sense of those words. I was filled with dread as we reached the mouth of the cave and went in, leaving the light behind.

The roof was high enough for us not to have to bend down. The ground near the entrance was covered with rubbish: old tyres, crates, coils of wire. From there, the cave continued a surprising distance into the cliff and we would have needed torches, except that the police had already rigged up a looping series of electric bulbs, dangling from the walls.

Helen le Mesurier was about halfway to the end. Just as we reached her, there was the flash of a camera and I saw her as if in a photograph, an image frozen in the brilliant light.

She had been struck several times with a rock. It was lying on the ground next to her, smeared with blood. I remembered the woman I had met at the party with her strawberry blonde hair, her designer dress, her diamond necklace. Again, I thought of her sitting in her bedroom, the white teddy bear with the sachet of dried lavender. This brutalised and casually discarded body was not her. The injuries to her head and to her face were vicious. She was almost unrecognisable. But it was more than that. She had been bored, sullen, sexy, distraught, angry, obstinate. Whoever had killed her had taken all that away and there was nothing left behind.

Three police officers were moving around her. One of them was the photographer. The other two were scouring the floor and the walls, examining everything minutely. We hung back, unable and perhaps unwilling to get too close. The air in the cave was cool and clammy. It was a horrible place to die.

'Did she meet her killer here?' I asked. My voice didn't sound like my own, underground, with the rock and the soil pressing down.

'I don't think so,' Hawthorne replied. 'Whoever texted her asked her to come to them.'

'Then why did she come in here?'

'She could have been attacked outside and then carried in.' Hawthorne examined the ground. 'Doesn't look like she was dragged.'

'If she'd told you what she'd seen out of her window on the night of the party, she might have saved her own life.'

Hawthorne nodded. 'Maybe.'

We made our way back into the daylight, squeezing past the stretcher-bearers who had arrived to take the body away. I had never been more glad to feel the sun on my skin.

'She was on her way to a meeting,' I said. 'So whoever it was must live quite close.' I looked around me. 'The lighthouse?'

The lighthouse stood some distance away, a clean, modern-looking building painted black and white. I had already seen it twice: once from the airplane as we approached the island and again, briefly, when I had cycled round the island.

'Not the lighthouse,' Hawthorne said. 'But over there ...'

I followed his eye to a small farmhouse standing on its own in the middle of a field. At the same time, Torode came over and joined us.

'Is that inhabited?' Hawthorne asked him.

'Yes,' he said. 'It's occupied. And guess who by.'

'I never guess,' Hawthorne said, gloomily.

'It's a friend of yours. Derek Abbott. That's where he lives. Maybe it's time the two of you had a chat.'

17

Where the Light Doesn't Shine

We walked together from the railway line, the lighthouse ahead of us, standing guard against a hostile sea. Quesnard Cottage stood nearby, dark and solitary, almost silhouetted against a streak of crimson light that had seared itself across a darkening sky. A breeze had sprung up. The trees were writhing and long, wild grass was licking at my feet.

I could tell that Hawthorne was uneasy. He didn't speak. His eyes were fixed straight ahead. And he smoked – mechanically and apparently without pleasure. He had come to Alderney, he had said, because he wanted to see what had happened to Derek Abbott, but all along there had been much more to it than that and I could see it now. He had the appearance of a man on his way to confront some sort of demon. But was it a demon that he had pushed down a flight of steps in a London police station or one that had entered his life a long time before and which had done him harm in ways that I could not understand? Perhaps I was about to find out.

'Are you all right?' I asked as we crossed the main road and entered a track that would bring us to the house.

'Why shouldn't I be?' he snapped back.

'You just seem very quiet.'

'I'm thinking.' We took a few more steps. 'You know, maybe it would be better if you didn't join me for this one.'

'What are you talking about?' I stopped. 'Of course I've got to be there.'

'I can tell you what happens.'

'No! You can't!' For a brief moment, I was actually quite angry. 'I never get any credit from you,' I said. 'I never do anything right. I think you forget that you were the one who came to me in the first place, and to be honest, there are times when I wish you hadn't. But right now I'm stuck with you. I don't get very much pleasure out of your company, but wherever you go, I'm going too. I'm going to describe what I see and what happens, and assuming you manage to track down whoever killed Charles and Helen le Mesurier, I'm going to describe that too. But it's my book! You don't tell me what happens. That's my job!'

I think that was the most I had ever said to Hawthorne in one breath and he seemed amused. 'What are you going to call it?' he asked.

'The book? I don't know. Not *Hawthorne Investigates*.'

'Well, be careful with this one.' Hawthorne nodded towards the house. 'Don't trust anything he says. Don't let him get under your skin.'

We continued on our way.

On closer inspection, Quesnard Cottage was a solid Georgian farmhouse with three, maybe four bedrooms and a large garden. Sadly, the owner had let it slip into disrepair. There were tiles missing from the roof and tufts of moss had insinuated themselves into the gaps. The glass in the windows was dusty and a couple of the smaller panes were cracked. The garden was full of weeds. I wondered if builders, decorators and gardeners had all refused to come here. As we approached the front gate, I heard classical music – Mozart – playing inside. We had to knock several times before the door opened.

Derek Abbott stood in front of us. He was on his own and at home but he was still wearing a suit, albeit without a tie. It was the first time I had actually been close to him and I was immediately struck by his bad teeth, his receding hairline and the curious sheen of his skin, which gave him the appearance of having had plastic surgery multiple times. He did not have the walking stick. Perhaps he didn't need it when he was in his own house. He was not pleased to see us. No. That's an understatement. He would have slammed the door if Hawthorne hadn't reached out and held it open.

'Get off my land,' Abbott snarled.

'We need to talk to you,' Hawthorne said.

'Give me one good reason why I should give you any of my time.'

'I'll give you two. Charles le Mesurier. Helen le Mesurier.'

Abbott shook his head. 'No. I'm not fucking talking to you, Hawthorne. You're not coming into my house. If you don't leave, I'll call the police.'

'I'm working for the police.' With his one free hand, Hawthorne produced an envelope I hadn't seen before. 'If you don't believe me, read this. I've been officially engaged by Deputy Chief Torode on behalf of the Guernsey police. He knows I'm here now. If you won't talk to me, he'll want to talk to you, and the first question he'll ask you is why you wouldn't talk to me.'

'I won't talk to you because you're a ****.' Swear words bore me. I don't like using them. And he had used one that was unprintable.

'Suit yourself. But right now you're the prime suspect in two murders—'

'Helen's dead?'

'You knew that already.'

'I knew she was missing and an hour ago I saw police cars and an ambulance arrive at the quarry. I'm not stupid.'

'So are you going to cooperate with a double murder investigation or not?'

The Mozart had been playing throughout all this. It was his Requiem Mass. Had Abbott been playing it for Helen le Mesurier? He came to a decision and stepped back, allowing the hall light to reach past him. 'All right. Come in, you bastard, and ask your questions. But I don't want to be in any fucking book, so you can forget that for a lark.' He turned his eyes, behind the steel frames of his glasses, on me. 'I read about myself, I'll sue you to hell. Do you understand?'

I nodded but said nothing.

He stepped back and went into a hallway dominated by a central hexagonal table. A large room led off to one side. Looking through the open door, I saw drawn curtains, a luxurious suite of furniture – three armchairs and a sofa – hundreds of books, a massive TV screen mounted on the wall, stand-alone speakers, a desk with a computer and printer, a stack of DVDs, piles of magazines. We didn't go in. He led us the other way into a kitchen that was similarly over-equipped, with multiple ovens, sinks and saucepans and dozens of storage cupboards. In neither room did I notice any photographs of family or friends. Nor were there any ornaments, souvenirs, curiosities. It was the house of a man who lived entirely alone.

We sat facing him across a pine table with the walking stick lying on the surface. He did not offer us coffee or tea.

'So this is where you ended up,' Hawthorne said. There was no malice in his voice. He sounded politely interested.

'This is where you put me.'

'It looks quite cosy to me. I'd have put you somewhere very different.'

'What is it with you, Hawthorne? What did I ever do to you?' To my surprise, Abbott suddenly turned to me. 'I went to your session.'

'Yes,' I said. 'I saw you.'

'What did he tell you about me?'

'He didn't tell me anything.' That happened to be true ... at least, until we'd arrived in Alderney. I'd found out about Abbott from another detective, a man called Meadows, and he hadn't actually known very much. For example, he'd only described Abbott as a former teacher without saying anything about his business interests in advertising and media.

'He doesn't know anything about me. He never did.' Abbott leaned forward. 'I never laid a finger on any kid, not in my entire life. I was a businessman. That's all. And you might not have liked some of the stuff that I was producing, but it was all one hundred per cent legal. The simple truth is that the police picked on me. They decided to bring me down and once they'd made that decision there was nothing I could do to stop them.'

It was funny. Five seconds ago, Abbott had been snarling at me not to write about him but now he was giving me his entire life story. Speaking in a low voice, fixing me with his malevolent gaze ... he let it all pour out.

'All that stuff the police said about me, it was lies, every word of it. Yes, I travelled in Thailand and Cambodia and the Philippines. That was where the factories were. The printing presses. But when you're making money, you make enemies. Anyone will tell you that. People made up stuff about me and the police swallowed it hook, line and sinker because they wanted to – even though they were never able to prove a single word of it. Two years they investigated me. Oh, yes – and they had their trips to Bangkok and Siem Reap too. They enjoyed those! Do you know how many thousands of pounds of tax payers' money they spent pursuing me? They got nothing! So that's why they planted the evidence against me. They put that stuff on my computer to justify their own incompetence and corruption. Do I look stupid to you? Do I look like the sort of person who'd keep kiddie porn on his hard drive? Of course not! They were wrong to start the investigation and they knew it, and they brought me down because if they hadn't it would have been their own jobs on the line.'

He went on like this for some time and I could write down a whole lot more of it. But after a while I found myself losing focus and I might as well have been listening to the drone of a mosquito. What did I think of Derek Abbott? The truth is that I understood why Hawthorne had been reluctant to let me come into the house and part of me wished I had taken his advice. *Don't let him get under your skin.* That was what he had said – and it was exactly what Abbott had done. I won't say that he was evil, but he was, undoubtedly, one of the most unpleasant people I had ever met and the more he talked, the more I believed the version of events that

Hawthorne had described when we stood below The Lookout on the edge of Saye Beach.

Hawthorne himself was still sitting at the table, his face utterly blank as Abbott continued his monologue.

'Everything I had was taken away from me,' he was saying. 'My business. My savings. My reputation. My life. I was locked up with animals – real animals – for six months and every single day I was threatened and degraded. I will never go back to prison. I don't care what happens to me in my life, but I will never let that happen again. Every minute of that place was like death to me.

'And do you know what it's like to come out again into a world where nobody wants you?' He wasn't asking us for our pity. He was telling us the facts. 'Nobody would see me any more. All my friends had deserted me, of course. Even my family ... I have a sister and my mother was still alive then. They say what happened to me killed her. Collateral damage. Nobody ever recognised that I was the victim in all this.

'I moved to Alderney because I had nowhere else to go. It was an island, small enough and far away enough to let me be anonymous. I bought the most isolated house I could find ... near to the lighthouse.' He half smiled. 'When I first got here, the light used to shine at night, but they shut it down a few weeks after I moved in and now it's pitch-dark. I prefer it like that.

'Of course, most of the people here know who I am and what happened to me. But you know the great thing about this island? Live and let live. People aren't judgemental. When Charles le Mesurier asked me to help him with his finances – particularly the publishing end of his business – it wasn't just a job. It was a lifeline. He believed in me and because of that a lot of other people on this island were prepared to do the same. To see me for what I am, not for what you made me out to be.'

That hadn't been my impression. Nobody had so much as looked his way when he came into the theatre and they hadn't been queuing up to chat to him at the party either. Even the state of his house told me something about him. No Norah Carlisle for him. She wouldn't have come near.

'Why don't you tell me about le Mesurier?' At last Hawthorne broke his silence.

'I didn't kill him.'

'How long did you work for him?'

'With him. Not for him. About five years.'

'But it wasn't going to be much longer, was it? Things were over between you.'

That surprised Abbott ... the fact that Hawthorne knew. 'Who told you that?'

'It doesn't matter who told me. The two of you had a falling-out.'

In fact, we had got the information from Anne Cleary. She had heard it from Charles le Mesurier himself at the party. He had told her that he'd argued with his former friend and was about to fire him.

'He owed me money. That was all it was. Charles never knew what he was saying after he'd had a drink. He would have come to his senses in the morning.'

'So the two of you argued, then? Did he fire you that night?'

Abbott faltered, realising that he had given away more than he intended. 'Of course not,' he snapped. 'He'd never have been able to manage without me.'

'Then what did you mean when you said he'd come to his senses?'

'I meant he might actually apologise. He drank too much, like he always did, and he said some stupid things. If anything, I should have been the one who resigned.'

'How much money were you owed?'

'That's none of your fucking business. It was peanuts. Do you know how rich he was? And thanks to me, thanks to the advice I gave him, he got even richer. As for the job, I didn't need it. I've got savings. And there's nothing to spend money on in this shithole anyway.'

And just a few moments ago he'd been extolling the island of Alderney for its sense of fair play.

'Did you go into the Snuggery?' Hawthorne asked.

'No, I did not go into the Snuggery.'

'You didn't take cocaine with Charles le Mesurier?'

Abbott let out a brief bark of laughter. 'No, I don't do drugs. No, I did not put a knife in him. When are you going to stop making up lies about me?'

'Tell me about Helen le Mesurier.'

'What do you want to know about her?'

'How often did you see her?'

'I saw her when I saw him.'

'Why did you arrange to meet her yesterday?'

'I didn't.' He gave Hawthorne the full gun-barrel eyes. 'That's another lie.'

'She sent you a text. She'd seen you go into the Snuggery with her husband just before he was killed and she wanted to know what was going on. You told her to come here at half past two, but she would have cut across the railway line and you were waiting for her there. You killed Charles le Mesurier because he'd fired you and you killed her because she saw you.'

'I never texted Helen. I didn't kill Charles. She didn't see anything.'

'I've also spoken to Colin Matheson.' It was like some kind of vicious chess game between the two men. Each move was another attack. Hawthorne waited a moment for a response and when it didn't come he went on. 'He's told us that you were blackmailing him.'

'So now it's murder and blackmail?'

'You had compromising photographs of him and Mrs le Mesurier. You coerced him into supporting the Normandy-Alderney-Britain line.'

'And why would I do that?'

'Because you have shares in Électricité du Nord. You wanted to raise their value.'

For the first time, Derek Abbott seemed to relax, finding himself on safe ground. He sneered at Hawthorne. 'That's another lie and this time I can prove it. You can check out the shareholders of Électricité du Nord. It must be on public record. You won't find my name. I don't have any shares in anything any more.'

He reached for his walking stick, as if signalling the end of the interview. I saw that his hand was shaking.

'Colin Matheson is a prat. He never liked me and now he's trying to stir up trouble for me. But whatever he says, it's his word against mine. I never threatened him. I don't have any photographs of him. I never received anything from him and I didn't know he was shagging Helen le Mesurier. But since you've been so kind as to mention it to me, perhaps I'll have a word with his wife. I'm sure she'll be very interested to hear about all this.'

It was his one small victory and in his twisted smile I got a clear picture of the unbridled nastiness of the man. Derek Abbott struggled to his feet, but before he could move away from the table, Hawthorne reached out and grabbed hold of his walking stick, pinning him in place. 'I haven't finished,' he said.

'Yes, you have.' Abbott jerked the stick free. 'You've got absolutely nothing on me, just like the last time. Only the difference is, you're not even a detective any more. You've been thrown out, like me, and now you're on the sidelines, scrubbing around for whatever petty cash you can persuade the police to throw your way and employing a second-rate hack author to write about you because you need the money. That's what you've come to and I'm not afraid of you. *Hawthorne Investigates*? You're pathetic!'

The two of them were standing close together and at that moment something very strange happened. Abbott was staring at Hawthorne. All along he had been confident in his anger and his hostility, but right then I saw a look of puzzlement come into his eyes. Was it recognition? Or even fear? It was as if he had become aware of something that had always been there but which he had only just noticed. For his part, Hawthorne twisted away, turning his back on the other man. 'We don't need to stay here any more,' he said to me.

A minute later we were standing outside and I was desperately searching for something to say. I was certain that I had just witnessed something that mattered but at the same time I knew I couldn't ask Hawthorne what it was. This business between him and Abbott was too convoluted. It ran too deep.

Terry had driven round in the car and neither of us spoke as we walked over to him.

In the background, the recording of Mozart's Requiem had reached the last section and I heard the words of the Communio sung by an alto voice that seemed to cut through the gloom. *Lux aeterna luceat eis, Domine*. 'May eternal light shine on them, O Lord.' And as I listened, it occurred to me

271

that there was some sort of justice in the world and that even if he had escaped a long prison sentence, Derek Abbott had been punished for his past sins. He was utterly alone, not just trapped on a tiny island but further isolated from it in a house to which nobody came. The living room I had seen was exactly that: the room in which he lived his life. Charles le Mesurier might have decided to champion him for his own amusement, but that too was over.

Even the lighthouse had given up on him. That was his fate. To be an outcast, lost and forgotten in a place where the light never shone.

18

The Hercule Programme

If there hadn't been a glitch with the hotel computer, we would never have seen Maïssa Lamar again. She was arguing with the hotel receptionist when we got back, trying to settle her bill.

'Please … I have to leave now.'

'I'm sorry, Ms Lamar. What was your room number again?'

'I already tell you!'

She was not alone. The fair-haired man I'd seen at Southampton Airport and later in the street outside the cinema was standing next to her. They both had suitcases.

'You on your way home?' Hawthorne had already noticed the taxi waiting outside. He closed in on her with relish.

'Mr Hawthorne!' She was annoyed and didn't try to hide it. 'Yes. I wish to return home at once.'

'That's very strange. I thought we'd all been told to stick around.' He examined the other man. 'And you must be the toy boy Tony saw at the airport. It seems he was right after all.'

'Here you are!' The receptionist had won control of the computer. He hit a button and the printer spat out two sheets of paper.

But it was too late for Maïssa. 'You talk to me now or I'll close down your flight,' Hawthorne said. 'Don't believe I can't do it. And maybe you should drop the pantomime French. I know who you are. I know what you're doing here. You've been interfering in what has now become a double murder investigation. You have no idea how much trouble I can make for you.'

She hesitated, but not for very long. 'We will pay the account in a minute,' she told the receptionist and I noticed an immediate improvement in her English. 'Where do you want to talk?' she asked.

'The lounge.'

It was half past six and a few guests had already trickled into the dining room. The four of us made our way to a table in the far corner of the room next door. With everything that had happened – the disappearance of Helen le Mesurier, the discovery of the body, the visit to Derek Abbott – I hadn't had a chance to tell Hawthorne what I had discovered. 'She's not a performance poet!' I blurted out as we sat down.

Hawthorne looked at me a little sadly. 'I know that, mate.'

Even Maïssa looked unimpressed. 'So how do you know about me?' she asked, addressing Hawthorne.

'It was pretty easy, to be honest with you, love. At the airport you said you'd just given a performance at the Red Lion theatre in Camden. There's an Old Red Lion theatre, but it's in Islington. So then I looked you up on Wikipedia.'

'I looked at her entry too!' I said. 'It didn't tell me anything.'

'Well, it told me a lot. For a start, most of it's rubbish. If you cross-reference, I think you'll find most of it's been nicked from another poet, Linda Maria Baros, including her date of birth and the titles of her poems ... although they've made a few changes. She didn't win any of those prizes. It took me about five seconds to check and they went to Hubert Mingarelli, Yves Namur and Jean Orizet. Good luck to them! But the biggest mistake was also the most obvious.'

'What was that?' I asked.

'She's only translated into German, Italian and Spanish, so why would she even have a Wikipedia entry in English? It doesn't make any sense unless it was deliberately put there for anyone at the Alderney Festival who happened to look her up.'

'So who is she?' I asked.

'Well, since she's somehow got permission to shove off while the rest of us are stuck here, and since there are no scheduled flights at this time of night, she must be working with the French authorities. I'd say she's from OLAF.' Hawthorne glanced at her. 'Is that right?'

Dr Queripel had told us about OLAF, the European anti-fraud office. He'd said he had written to them.

Maïssa nodded.

'And while we're all sharing confidences, why don't you tell us your real name?'

'Maïssa Lamar is my actual name. This is my colleague, Emil Odoli.' She was referring to the fair-haired man who had taken a seat, sullenly, next to her.

'You've been sent here to look into the power line. I mean, the idea of going undercover with a bunch of second-class writers at a festival nobody's ever heard of sounds pretty lunatic to me – but then I suppose you are French ...'

'Thanks, Hawthorne,' I growled.

A waitress came over to see if we wanted anything, but Hawthorne waved her away.

'All right,' Maïssa began. It was strange how everything she said, and the way that she said it, was completely at odds with her appearance. I wondered if the haircut and the piercings had been imposed on her as part of her disguise. Surely she didn't always look like that? 'You are absolutely correct. Emil and I are investigators with OLAF, working with the Hercule Programme. This programme is designed to combat embezzlement and misconduct in public procurement, among many other things.' She paused. 'What I am about to tell you is, of course, confidential.'

Hawthorne was losing his patience. 'Come on, please. I think we're a bit past that now.'

'Very well.' She took a breath. 'So ... six months ago we received information which related to the activities of a company called Électricité du Nord, which is based in Rennes and is involved with the construction of the Normandy-Alderney-Britain power line, or NAB, as it is called here. The information suggested that they were making large payments to a person on the island who, in return, had promised to use his influence to make sure that the States gave their support to the project.'

'You're talking about Charles le Mesurier,' I said.

'Exactly. He received several cash payments in his capacity as adviser to the company, but we believe that a much larger sum of money was concealed in the purchase of a land *parcelle* that he owned, which would be used as the site for the converter station. Électricité du Nord agreed to pay five times the actual value of the land once the permission had been granted, and that was how he would make his profit.'

'But you had no proof,' Hawthorne said.

'That is right, Mr Hawthorne. Everything I have told you so far was based on anonymous *avertissements*. How do you say that?'

'Tip-offs,' her partner volunteered.

'Thank you, Emil. Yes. Tip-offs and speculation. We had no actual evidence. We looked. We went deep. But it was not there.

'And then we discovered that there was to be a festival of literature on the island and we had the idea to create a performance poet who could take part and who would be able to get close to Monsieur le Mesurier, even into his house. We were very pleased when we heard that there would be a party actually inside The Lookout. It was the perfect opportunity.'

'How did you make sure you were invited?' I asked.

'That was not difficult. A cultural foundation in Paris made a financial contribution to the festival on the condition that a French poet was included. It was at the same time that a fake entry in Wikipedia was constructed. We thought it unlikely that anyone would take interest in an obscure poet working in a language that was almost unknown, but in the event that anyone looked, it was there.

'And so I came to Alderney. I will admit that I was concerned to encounter you at the airport, Mr Hawthorne. It was foolish of me not to have studied the programme more carefully and I was alarmed when you mentioned that you had investigated financial crime. I did not want my enquiry to become entangled. It was important for me to be acting independently of the British police.'

'You should have told me who you were,' Hawthorne said.

'We did discuss exactly that. Emil was in favour of joining together with you and maybe it would have been for the best. I apologise, but it was the decision that I made.'

'Go on.'

'I stayed with the other writers and tried to be part of the *esprit de corps*, although it did not help that your friend had happened to see Emil talking with me when we were at Southampton. I gave the talk. I had learned a number of poems which I hoped nobody would recognise.'

'You stole a haiku from Akira Anno.' It was the one thing I'd managed to guess. I wanted them to know.

She didn't respond. 'And so we arrived at the party on the Saturday night. I will tell you now my plan as it had been conceived. The most important thing for me was to get access to le Mesurier's computer. Emil was here to provide me with technical support and he would find it a simple matter to bypass the security and access the database. We knew already that the office was on the first floor. The question only was how to get into the house without being seen and I found the answer to that almost at once.'

'The Snuggery,' Hawthorne said.

Marc Bellamy had seen Maïssa in the garden – but that had been several hours before the murder, at half past seven.

'Exactly. I found this strange little construction at the end of the garden where le Mesurier liked to hide and at the back there was a door which opened onto the path that led up from the beach. I drew back the bolt so that the door remained unlocked and this would allow me to return later in the night. Then I went back to the party and joined in with everybody else. There were just two other things that I did before I left.'

'You fixed the kitchen door.'

'Yes. I placed a little ball of paper into the lock to ensure that it could not close properly …'

I remembered now that the newspaper print had been in French. That should have told me something.

'This was my route back into the house. I also went upstairs. I needed to know the exact location of the office so that Emil and I could easily find it. We would return at three o'clock. Le Mesurier and his wife would be sound asleep. We would take the information that we needed and we would leave.'

'But that's not how things worked out,' Hawthorne said.

'It was a nightmare,' Emil muttered in a low voice.

'It was exactly that. We returned to the beach at three o'clock the next morning and climbed back up to the Snuggery. Of course, the intention was only to pass through, to continue through the garden and into the kitchen, using the door that I had prepared. But instead, when we entered the Snuggery – we locked the door behind us – we were confronted by a scene of the worst horror. Le Mesurier was sitting in a chair. He had been tied down. There was a knife coming out of his throat. It was evident that he had been dead for many hours.'

'But you didn't raise the alarm,' Hawthorne said. There was something in his voice that sounded almost like admiration. 'You didn't even hesitate. You weren't going to let something trivial like a violent murder get in your way.'

The two investigators glanced at each other uncomfortably. 'Of course we considered every possibility,' Maïssa admitted. 'It was not an easy decision to make. But in the end we realised that, no matter what had occurred, we had been given an opportunity and it would be foolish not to exploit it. Le Mesurier had a mobile phone. We could see the outline quite clearly in his trouser pocket.'

'So you took it out. And you used the fingerprint of his right hand to unlock it.'

She cast her eyes down. 'You think we are disgusting.'

'I don't think of you at all, Ms Lamar. Just tell me this. You needed his print to open the phone. So did you cut the tape that was holding him down?'

'No. We already noticed that one hand was free. We remarked on it. But we were aware that it was a crime scene. We disturbed nothing.'

'That's not quite true. You managed to step in his blood, leaving a footprint. You left another footprint on the beach. Whoever killed le Mesurier was actually a lot more careful than you.'

Maïssa ignored this. 'We left as quickly as possible. We took the mobile and proceeded across the garden. We entered the house through the kitchen door and went upstairs. We used the passwords contained in the mobile to open the computer in le Mesurier's office and Emil downloaded all his files, including his emails and accounts, to a memory stick.

This took very little time. The house was silent. His wife was asleep. We made no sound.

'Our work was finished. We left the phone in the office. To return to the Snuggery was not an option to be considered and fortunately we had locked the door behind us. We left the house through the front door and returned to our separate hotels. Unfortunately, it was impossible to leave the island immediately, which is what I wished to do, but now our director of operations has been in contact with the Guernsey police department and we go tonight.'

Her story made complete sense, at least in the context of the facts that we had been able to establish. There had been the footprint on the beach and the second footprint in the dead man's blood, but the door at the back of the Snuggery had definitely been locked from the inside when we examined it on Sunday morning. Le Mesurier's body had been saturated in blood, which explained the stain that Hawthorne had found on the back of his phone in the study, and indeed why the phone was there at all. And I had seen Maïssa coming back downstairs when she had made her initial recce, checking where the study was for later.

Even so, it occurred to me that there was a piece missing from the jigsaw. 'Can I ask something?' I said. I didn't want to annoy Hawthorne.

'Go ahead, mate.'

'Did either of you drop a coin inside the Snuggery? A two-euro piece?'

When she was pretending to be a poet, Maïssa had treated me with disdain and I hoped it had been part of her performance. But even though she had now been revealed as an undercover investigator, her attitude remained the same. 'Why would we do that?' she snapped. 'Do you think we are idiots?'

I didn't know how to reply, but for once Hawthorne came to my defence. 'Actually, I'd say that both of you are fucking idiots, if you want the truth,' he began. 'You come over here like Batman and Robin and you get yourselves involved in a murder investigation. But you don't help anyone because you've got bigger fish to fry. In fact, you were obstructive. You say you made no difference to the crime scene, but that's not true. You took the mobile phone even though it was covered in blood and you left it in the office. You opened and you locked a door. You didn't even report the crime! You let him sit there all bloody night while the trail went cold. Who knows – but for your meddling, Mrs le Mesurier might be alive right now. You left her to find her husband's body, but if we could have got there sooner, if we could have questioned her before she'd had time to think, she might have told us what she knew.

'So you two can piss off back to OLAF and I hope you find what you're looking for on your memory stick, although it looks to me as if the whole thing is going to be a complete waste of time anyway because the line is dead – as are Helen and Charles le Mesurier – and you've got nothing left to investigate except for some French company that will probably walk rings around you. What time is your flight?'

'The plane is waiting now.'

'Well, I won't say *bon voyage*. Just, get lost.'

Maïssa Lamar and her assistant made no reply. They picked themselves up and Emil collected the suitcases. They were heading for the door when Maïssa stopped and turned round. 'There is one thing,' she said. 'When I came to the party at The Lookout, I carried with me a purse which I left in the hall. I thought it would be safe. But when I left the house, I discovered that it had been opened. A fifty-euro note had been taken and some of the coins had spilled out.'

'Do you have any idea who took it?'

'No. Perhaps the girl who was serving ... I don't know. But it is possible also that a coin may have gone.'

'Thank you.' Hawthorne watched them leave and I think we were both in full accord. We were glad to see them gone.

19

The Simple Answer

After Maïssa had gone, I called the waitress over and ordered a double gin and tonic. Hawthorne asked for a glass of water, which arrived with a slice of lemon. 'Don't you ever drink anything except water?' I asked him.

He seemed surprised by the question. 'Not really.'

'Have you ever drunk alcohol?'

'No.'

It was time for dinner and I wondered if we might eat together, not that I had much appetite after everything that had happened that day. The drinks came and we sipped them in a silence that might, I suppose, have been called companionable. The argument we'd had just before we'd visited Derek Abbott had been forgotten and it seemed to me as good a moment as any to press him for some of the information that always seemed to be just out of my grasp.

'When we were doing our event together, you said that you didn't have any brothers or sisters,' I began. 'But when we were in London, you mentioned that you had a half-brother who was an estate agent.' I waited for him to comment. He said nothing. 'Did one of your parents remarry?' I asked.

'No.'

'Are they still alive?'

'No.' The monosyllables were in stark contrast to his performance in front of an audience. They also made no sense. How was it possible to have a half-brother if his parents had never remarried?

'What did your father do?' I tried again. 'Was he a police officer?'

'No.' Hawthorne had lost patience. 'I don't really like talking about myself.'

'You did well enough when you were on the stage.'

'Well, that was different – and it's not going to happen again.' He paused. 'You can do the next one on your own.'

'I think people are more interested in you than they are in me.'

He looked at me in surprise. 'That's not true.'

'It is. Even Colin Matheson got it right when he introduced you. He said you were the real thing. Why do you think there are so many detective stories? People are fascinated by detectives, by what you do. I am too. It's one of the reasons why I agreed to follow you around.' I picked up my drink.

'I'm sorry I got angry with you when we went to visit Derek Abbott. We've just got to try to be more of a team.'

Hawthorne considered what I'd just said, but before he had time to reply, the door opened and Torode and Whitlock came in. They came straight over to us and sat down.

'I was hoping to find you here,' Torode said. He looked as if he was off duty, wearing a jersey that was one size too big for him. It hung off his chest in softly undulating folds. Whitlock was in uniform. Perhaps she had forgotten to pack anything else.

Torode eyed our drinks. 'Who's buying?'

'You are,' Hawthorne said.

'Well, that's not very friendly – but never mind.' He called out to the bar. 'A pint of best, please. And what will you have, Whitlock?'

'A tomato juice, please, sir.'

The barman acknowledged him and Torode turned back to us. 'I've got a few things to tell you, starting with Maïssa Lamar.'

'We already know about OLAF,' Hawthorne said.

'Yes. That was a bit of a turn-up for the books, don't you think? Or for the book!' He smiled at me. 'I had her boss on the phone just now and he didn't give me any choice. I had to let her leave. Anyway, it's one suspect less, so I suppose that's something to be grateful for. And while we're on the subject of suspects, Hawthorne ... You're not going to like this, but we're going to have to let all the other writers go too.'

Hawthorne didn't look particularly put out. 'Is that a good idea?' he asked. 'One of them might have committed two murders – Helen le Mesurier just a few hours ago.'

'That's true. But we can't keep them locked up on Alderney for ever and I can't see any of them committing a double murder. Mr Pastry, perhaps, with his steak and kidney puddings? Or Mrs Fizzbang? Whitlock here can't wait to get home.'

'I wish I'd never come,' Whitlock said, looking as miserable as ever.

'I know! I know!' Torode shook his head. 'As for the others, I imagine you've had a chance to talk to the whole lot of them by now. Any thoughts?' The barman brought over the drinks. 'Put them on his room.' Torode pointed at me and lifted his glass. 'Cheers!'

Whitlock stared at her tomato juice but didn't touch it.

'I'll make sure you've got all their addresses and contact numbers,' Torode went on. 'But if your reputation's anything to go by, you've probably worked it out by now anyway. If not, this might help.' He produced a second envelope, just like the one Whitlock had given us the evening before. 'Mrs le Mesurier's medical report. No surprises there. Blunt trauma. Three blows more or less caved in the skull, leading to massive haemorrhaging. There was enough blood swilling around in there to fill a coconut.'

Whitlock looked up from the tomato juice. Her face had gone pale. 'Excuse me, sir ...' She hurried out of the room.

Torode watched her leave. 'Sorry about that. She's done nothing but complain since I brought her here. I won't make that mistake again.'

'What happens to the money?' Hawthorne asked.

'What money? Oh – you mean the will. That's a good question, considering that Mrs le Mesurier just became a wealthy woman ... not that she had any time to enjoy it. I've spoken to her solicitor. No children of her own, of course, but she has a brother and a sister and it's their lucky day. They get everything. But there's no chance that either of them had anything to do with it, if that's what you're thinking. One works for Goldman Sachs in London and the other's a teacher in Wales. There was one little thing that surprised me. She left a hundred thousand to the school here in St Anne. Wouldn't have thought she'd have cared.'

I knew better. Colin Matheson had told us that he had first got close to Helen when he was on an education committee. *She invited me to The Lookout to talk about a possible bequest.* I'd never heard of anyone being murdered to benefit a school library, but it still made me wonder who on the island might have known about the money.

'What else?' Hawthorne asked.

'Derek Abbott,' Torode replied. He knew the effect the words would have. He let them hang in the air. 'You went to see him,' he added.

'Yes.'

'And?'

'He didn't fall down any stairs if that's what you're asking.'

Torode wasn't amused by that. 'Come off it, Hawthorne. You know what I mean.' He waited. 'Did he kill her? Did he kill both of them?'

Hawthorne blinked. 'What makes you think that, Deputy Chief?'

'I think you're forgetting something.' Everything about Torode was lazy: his smile, his dress sense, his work ethic. It was also true of the menace that he was now directing at Hawthorne. 'The only reason you have any authority on this island is because of me. And I thought we had an agreement. I help you; you help me. What do you know?'

'I know it's a mistake letting everyone leave the island.'

'About Derek Abbott!' Hawthorne said nothing, so Torode went on, keeping his voice low. 'All right. Let me tell you where I am with this, just so you don't think I've been sitting on my arse all day while you've been gallivanting around. First of all, I know that Abbott was working for le Mesurier as some sort of business adviser, but the two of them had fallen out. Anne Cleary told me that, just like she told you. She also said that there was money involved, and maybe I can tell you something you don't know.'

'There's a first time for everything,' Hawthorne said.

'Take a look at this.' Torode reached into the envelope and took out a sheet of paper. He slid it across the table. It was a photocopy of a cheque for £20,000, made out to Derek Abbott and signed by Charles le Mesurier.

'Abbott personally presented this to the cash desk in Lloyds Bank in Victoria Street this morning. The date is the Saturday of the murder and the number of the cheque accords with the last one torn out of the chequebook we found in the Snuggery. I didn't know people were still making payments this way – not that it made any difference. The bank can't honour it, pending probate, but they were smart enough to take a copy, which they passed to me. Makes you think, doesn't it.'

'He told me that he was owed money,' Hawthorne said.

'I bet he didn't mention he'd been paid – and I'll tell you why not. It's very simple, really. Sometime on the night of the party, the two of them have a falling-out over money that results in Abbott getting the chop. He's not happy about it, so he follows le Mesurier into the Snuggery—'

'Nobody saw them go in together.'

'We'll come to that. You know the weird thing about this whole business? It's Charles le Mesurier tied to that chair but one hand left free.' Torode pointed at the photocopy. 'That's the simple answer. At first, it was all friendly. Maybe they took a few lines of cocaine together. But then Abbott got the better of him. He could have used that walking stick of his to hit le Mesurier on the head. He tied him to the chair, but he left one hand free – his right hand – because he needed him to sign something. A cheque! He must have threatened him with something nasty to get him to cooperate, but when le Mesurier signed this piece of paper he wasn't thinking straight. It was his death warrant. Of course Abbott couldn't keep him alive, because if he did, the next day le Mesurier would simply ring the bank and cancel the cheque. So he killed him.'

'For twenty thousand quid?'

'And the Rolex watch. That doubles it.'

'Have you spoken to Abbott yet?'

'I'm speaking to you first.' Torode was enjoying himself, knowing that he had Hawthorne at a disadvantage. 'Now, let's go back to what you said about nobody seeing the two of them go in together. That's not true, of course.'

'Helen le Mesurier ...'

'That's right. Nice of you to show me those texts. Put them together and they make complete sense.' He took out a notebook and read from it. '*What happened last night? I saw you leave with Charles.*' He looked up triumphantly. 'She was a witness. She saw someone cross the garden from her bedroom window.'

'But we don't know who.'

'No. But we know it was someone who lived less than thirty minutes away from her home on foot. She left at two o'clock for a two-thirty meeting and I got Whitlock to time it for me. You can easily walk from The Lookout to Quesnard Cottage in half an hour – and her route would have taken her right next to the Mannez Quarry. Easy enough for Abbott to wait for her, talk her into going into that cave for a bit of privacy and then do her in with a rock.' He frowned. 'Maybe I shouldn't have made that remark about the coconut. Whitlock's very highly strung.'

'She's also a volunteer,' I reminded him.

'Was. She's handed in her notice.' He drank some of the beer. 'Then there's that other text to consider. Bit sneaky of you not to tell me that Colin was Colin Matheson, but I suppose you were trying to earn your fee. Anyway, it didn't take me long to work it out for myself. There are thirty-eight Colins living on the island of Alderney, but only one of them was at the party that night so it wasn't too hard.'

'Great detective work,' Hawthorne muttered.

'Sarcasm won't get you very far with me, Hawthorne. So what does the text tell us? Colin Matheson and Helen le Mesurier were having an affair and they both came to regret it. What had happened? I went round to Mr Matheson – and his wife – and we had a little chat. I can't say Mrs Matheson was too pleased to hear what hubby had been getting up to, but that's his problem. He told me he'd already spoken to you and that you know the rest of it – that Derek Abbott was blackmailing him about this stupid power line. Something to do with shares in a company called Electricity de Nord. So whatever happens, I think we can be confident that Mr Abbott is going right back where a pervert like him belongs.'

'Blackmail?' Hawthorne looked doubtful. 'You'll have to prove it and there's no evidence. It's Matheson's word against his.'

Torode ignored this. 'Blackmail's only the start of it. It would only get Abbott five years in jail, if we were lucky. I'm not going to let him slip through our fingers a second time, the way you did. I want him put away for life.'

'So why haven't you arrested him?'

Torode drank half his beer and wiped his lips with the back of his hand. He looked annoyed and it didn't take me long to work out why. Despite everything, he still needed Hawthorne. 'I haven't arrested him because you're right,' he explained. 'At the moment, most of the evidence is circumstantial. I haven't found anyone yet who can put him in that cave with Mrs le Mesurier or, for that matter, in the Snuggery with her husband. I was rather hoping that you might have come up with something.'

'You're one step ahead of me, Deputy Chief.'

'Well, I suppose I should take that as a compliment,' Torode remarked, but I knew differently. He wasn't one step ahead of anyone. There wasn't a single thing he had said that Hawthorne hadn't already worked out for himself long before. 'Anyway, perhaps you'll understand now why I'm letting the other writers go. No point hanging on to them when we've got our prime suspect sitting right here on the island.'

'When are they leaving?'

'There's a flight at eleven tomorrow morning. I imagine you'll be going with them.'

Hawthorne considered. 'There doesn't seem much more for me to do here.'

'No. That's right. Of course, I'm afraid that puts an end to that little agreement we talked about at the start of all this. It turns out that I've done all the work for you, so I don't think I can justify any ex officio payments. You do understand?'

'I'd say I've put in the hours.'

'That may be true, but we only pay for results.' He drained his beer and glanced at me. 'Thanks for that, Andrew. Very nice.' He stood up. 'I suppose I'd better go and find Whitlock. She never even touched her tomato juice.'

He left.

Hawthorne picked up the piece of lemon and dropped it back into his glass. He had finished his water.

'Are we really going to leave tomorrow?' I asked.

'You heard what he said. It looks like he's got it all wrapped up.'

'You think Derek Abbott committed the murders?'

'What do you think, mate?'

I'm not sure Hawthorne had ever asked my opinion before.

'I don't know,' I began. 'Listening to what he said, it does all sound fairly straightforward. Abbott had a motive for both the murders. He was close to le Mesurier and he lives right next to the quarry. There's that business with the cheque.' I stopped. 'Please tell me I'm wrong.'

'Why?'

'Because if Derek Abbott turns out to be the killer, I'm not sure there'll be a book in it.' Quickly, I explained what I'd already been thinking when I was in my hotel room – my fear that if he turned out to be the killer, nobody would care. 'Actually, it's even worse than that,' I concluded. 'If I write about what's happened here, I'm going to have to say that Torode solved it. He got there before you.'

'Are you sure?' Hawthorne looked genuinely puzzled. 'You're the author. You can say I worked it all out and he didn't know anything. You don't even have to mention he was here.'

'I can't do that!' I exclaimed. 'That's a complete fiction.'

'I thought that's what you wrote.'

'Even when I'm writing fiction I try to write the truth.' Suddenly, I was depressed. 'Tell me you're keeping something to yourself. Tell me he didn't do it.'

'I'm sorry, mate. I can't help you.' Hawthorne shook his head sorrowfully. 'If Abbott didn't do it, I've got no idea who did.'

20

Is There Anybody There?

Hawthorne and I did have dinner together, but it wasn't exactly a joyous affair. The cooking at the Braye Beach Hotel was fine but he was distracted and I wasn't too happy myself. I was still thinking about our conversation in the bar and the distinct possibility that after everything that had happened on the island, I wouldn't actually have a book that I could write.

In fact, Alderney had been a complete washout. I had been sidelined during our session, there had been no books to sell and there had been none of the camaraderie that usually made festivals such fun. How could there have been when every other writer I'd met had been a suspect in two violent murders? I felt particularly sorry for Judith Matheson. She'd put so much work into organising the weekend and what had she got out of it? A dead sponsor, a cut-up lawn and a divorce.

I was hoping that Anne Cleary or even Marc Bellamy might turn up and join us, but the room was almost empty. This was a Monday night and anyone who had come for the weekend had long since checked out. Maybe the other writers had found somewhere cheaper to eat in town now that the festival was no longer picking up the tab. But just as we were finishing the main course, Hawthorne looked up, and turning round, I saw two people I knew approaching the table. One of them was Elizabeth Lovell. The other, guiding her by the arm, was her husband, Sid.

'They're here,' I heard him say. 'Just finished eating. Fish, by the look of it. Mr Hawthorne facing us. His friend on the other side.'

They came over to our table and stopped, hovering over us a little awkwardly. I wondered if I should invite them to sit down, but the truth was, I didn't want their company. 'Are you going home tomorrow?' Elizabeth asked.

'That's right,' Hawthorne said. 'And yourself?'

'We have a flight to Southampton and then back to Jersey. We're leaving very early.' She stared over the table. 'That only leaves tonight, if you still want to take me up on my offer.'

She was referring to the séance that she had suggested the night before and Hawthorne didn't hesitate. 'I'd like that very much,' he said.

I was less keen. 'Actually, I was just going to bed,' I said.

'No, Tony. I think you should join us. Four feels like a better number and Elizabeth here has got form. She helped the police in Jersey.' Was he being sarcastic? He sounded completely straightforward.

'Well, all right ...'

'I'm so glad.' Elizabeth Lovell smiled, an action that stretched the tendons on either side of her neck. It was perhaps unfair to be judgemental, but with her hunched-up body and the dark glasses masking so much of her face, I found her rather alarming. 'Shall we say the screening room at ten o'clock, then? Sid can ask at the reception desk, but the hotel seems to be half empty so I'm sure it will be free.'

The two of them walked away and as soon as they were out of the room, I turned to Hawthorne. 'What are you playing at?' I demanded. 'You've already told me you don't believe in this stuff!'

'She may be able to help us,' Hawthorne replied, simply.

'What? By chatting to Charles le Mesurier? Maybe she can get Helen along too ...'

'What else have you got to do tonight, mate? Wash your hair? Watch TV?' I had no answer to that, so he went on. 'You said it yourself. We're out of here tomorrow. So let's use what time we've got.' He took out a packet of cigarettes and stood up. 'I'll see you there.'

I knew he was heading outside. For my part, I went back to my room and actually I did watch TV for half an hour; anything to get my mind off the events of the day. I was half tempted to ignore Hawthorne and give the whole thing a miss. I was convinced it would be a waste of time. But if there was one thing I'd learned in our time together, it was never to second-guess Hawthorne. If he believed something was worth doing, he would probably be right, even if it wasn't for the reason you thought.

So at ten o'clock, I made my way down to the hotel's screening room, which was certainly not the sort of place Noel Coward would have chosen to set a séance. It was relentlessly functional, windowless, of course, with chunky leather chairs on a modern black and white striped carpet and recessed lights. Presumably it had been put in for the hotel's corporate guests. Certainly it was nothing like the antiquated cinema just up the road.

Sid had arranged for a table and four seats to be brought in. These had been placed on a raised platform in front of the screen. Elizabeth Lovell was already sitting down. Sid was fussing over her, pouring her coffee, making sure she was comfortable.

Hawthorne had arrived just ahead of me. To my surprise, he was holding a glass of red wine that he must have brought from the bar. It made no sense. That very same evening he'd told me that he never drank alcohol. Maybe it was for me. He sat down at the table and placed the glass beside him, on the floor. I took the last place, next to him. If anyone had come in, they might have thought that we were about to play bridge, but, foolishly, had forgotten to bring the cards.

Sid was the first to speak. He was so short, he had slipped down behind the table and, like a child, peered across the top. 'They're both here,' he told his wife unnecessarily, as she must have heard us. 'Let me explain a few things,' he continued. 'This is very hard for Liz. It's not usually what she does and she's only doing it because she wants to help you.' He grimaced. 'Personally, I advised against it. When she deliberately makes the journey to the other side of the mirror, she has no idea who she may come up against. You were there when she gave her talk on Saturday. They're not ghosts. They're not spirits. They're not always friends. What she's doing tonight is the difference between wandering into someone's private property by accident and deliberately trespassing. There can be repercussions. Whatever happens, do not get out of your seats. Do not touch her. Do not interrupt. Do you both understand? If she needs help, that's what I'm here for. I know what to do. You just stay where you are.'

It was well rehearsed and smoothly delivered. But it was still mumbo-jumbo. It might have convinced the Jersey police when they were searching for a lost kid in a nature reserve, but I didn't believe a word of it and nor – I was sure – did Hawthorne. He was sitting silently with his hands folded in front of him. I tried to catch his eye, but he avoided me.

'Are you ready, love?' Sid asked.

Elizabeth nodded.

'I'm right next to you. I'm with you all the way.'

'Thank you, Sid.' She took a deep breath, her chest rising and falling, her hands resting on the arms of the chair. She didn't go into a trance. There were no exhalations, no rolling of the eyes. If anything, she might simply have dozed off. I had thought Sid would lower the lights, but they were still on at full strength. Despite that, I was aware of the shadows in the corners of the room. The four of us were very still.

'Is there anybody there?' Elizabeth asked. I was surprised that she had started with such a cliché. Surely she could do better than that?

Nothing. Just the sound of her breathing.

'Phyllis? Consuela? Alessandro?'

'These are reflections who have appeared to her before,' Sid explained, in a whisper. 'With a bit of luck, one of them might come forward.'

Consuela was a Spanish name and Alessandro an Italian one. I wondered if Elizabeth would be able to speak to them in their own language. Or did everyone speak the same language when they died, trapped in some sort of eternal Google Translate?

Three or four minutes passed. Elizabeth seemed to be searching with her unseeing eyes while Sid waited nervously. Hawthorne was showing no emotion at all. The séance was about as action-packed as the empty screen behind us and I was beginning to think that the main feature might have been cancelled when Elizabeth suddenly tensed. Her head jerked, first one way, then the other.

'There is someone ...' she announced.

'Who?' Sid whispered.

'I can't see. I can't see. They're getting closer. They're coming towards me now.' Her voice wavered, on the edge of fear. 'I don't want to hurt you! I just need your help!' She was addressing whatever presence was gliding towards her and I was annoyed with myself: I was almost unnerved. 'It's Marlon!' she exclaimed.

Sid visibly relaxed. 'Marlon is a friend,' he whispered. 'He's helped us before.'

'Dear Marlon! Please forgive me for disturbing your rest, but I need help. Can you help me? Can you tell me anything about a man who has recently crossed to the other side? His name is Charles le Mesurier and he was taken before his time, violently. He must be in great pain and we only want to give him comfort.'

We waited in silence. Did Elizabeth know that Helen le Mesurier had also been killed? It was quite possible that she hadn't been told ... especially if she'd spent the whole day in the hotel. Her focus was only on Charles.

She cried out, her voice catching in her throat. 'Marlon is calling him!' she told us. There was another long wait. 'He's there!' She called out to him: 'Charles? Can you hear me? I want to help you.'

A long silence, broken only by the sound of Elizabeth's breathing.

'Charles isn't sure,' she explained. 'He's very confused. But I think he's going to talk to me.' She shivered. 'Sid, I'm terribly cold.'

Sid slipped off his jacket and placed it over her shoulders. 'Charles is here!' she whispered.

The strange thing was that I was unsure how much time had actually passed. Maybe it was down to all the theatrics or simply because we were in an enclosed space, in a basement, with no connection to the outside world. I still didn't believe any of it, but I would be doing Elizabeth Lovell an injustice if I didn't admit that I was captivated by her performance.

'He's talking but I can't hear what he's saying,' she continued. She lowered her head. 'Charles, do you remember me? We met at your house ... your home on this side of the mirror. The Lookout. Do you remember?' We had no way of knowing if he did or didn't. Elizabeth cried out and writhed in her chair. 'No! We want to help you! We want to find the person who hurt you. Can you tell us who it was?'

'They always hate talking about the moment of their passing,' Sid explained quietly. 'It's too traumatic.'

'You were at the party. You drank champagne. But then you went into the garden.' Elizabeth said all this as if she was merely repeating what she was being told. Then she asked: 'What time was it? Who was with you?'

We all waited for the answer.

'A friend. He was close to you. You trusted him.' Elizabeth was breathing more and more heavily. 'He worked for you. Can you tell me who he was?'

Hawthorne was leaning forward, listening intently. Sid rested his hand on Elizabeth's arm.

'It was just before ten o'clock,' Elizabeth said. She wasn't reminding him. Again, she was repeating what he was telling her. 'He went with you across the garden, to the Snuggery. He had a walking stick.'

Derek Abbott! Who else could it be? And of all the people she could have chosen, why had Elizabeth decided to light on his name? So many different thoughts were going through my head, but first and foremost I realised that she had given Hawthorne the final piece of the jigsaw that Torode had been asking for, even though it was completely useless. How could he hope to arrest Abbott using a witness statement that had come from 'the other side of the mirror'?

'You went in together and then, and then—'

Elizabeth cried out. She jerked in her seat as if she had just been electrocuted.

Sid sprang to his feet and put his arms around her, his head against hers. 'It's all right, love,' he muttered. 'It's all right. You're back with us.'

'So much pain!' Elizabeth moaned. Her shoulders were rising and falling. Her hands were writhing. Sid rubbed her shoulders and slowly she recovered. She turned to him and asked weakly: 'Can I have a glass of water?'

'I've got some wine,' Hawthorne said.

'No, no …'

But he was already reaching down. Before anyone could stop him, he picked up the glass of wine he had brought with him. I thought he was going to pass it to her, but to my horror he suddenly hurled the contents in her face. Elizabeth cried out and raised a hand in self-defence. Sid reacted with shock. I couldn't believe what I had just seen. What was Hawthorne doing?

And then I saw that the wine was still in the glass. It was like a magic trick. Not a single drop of it had reached Elizabeth.

What had just happened? I looked back at the glass and saw the thin sheet of plastic wrapped across the top. I remembered Hawthorne asking me to get him some cling film from the kitchen. I'd never actually done it. He must have gone in himself. Now I understood why he'd needed it.

And Elizabeth had reacted! She had held up a hand to protect herself.

She had seen!

'That was a great performance, love,' he said to Elizabeth. 'But you can take off those stupid glasses. We know you can see.'

'What?' I couldn't believe what he had just said. 'She's faking being blind?' It was one of the most disgusting things I'd ever heard.

'I told you she was a fraud,' Hawthorne said. 'She did it very well on stage. A complete pro. But outside that, she made so many bloody mistakes.' He peeled off the cling film and slid the glass of wine across the table. 'Why don't you drink this, love? You look like you need it.'

'You bastard!' Sid exclaimed.

'Now, now!' Hawthorne warned him. 'If you're going to get nasty, the whole world's going to know about this. I'm not sure what your fans will think when they find out you've been ripping them off, but I've got a feeling it's not exactly going to catapult you into the best-seller lists. At the moment, there's just the four of us who know that your wife is a cold-hearted, manipulative bitch. Maybe it would be a good idea to keep it that way. What do you think?'

There was a silence even more dramatic than the one that had opened the séance.

Elizabeth Lovell was the first to recover. 'Let me explain something to you,' she said. She picked up the wine and downed it in one. When she continued, she sounded desperate – and genuine, for perhaps the first time. 'It wasn't a lie,' she insisted. 'Not completely. Everything I have written about in my books is true, I swear to you, and I've been an inspiration to many, many people. I *do* have diabetes, and in my twenties this resulted in serious damage to my eyesight – proliferative retinopathy. I can show you the certificates. For a while I suffered almost total vision loss. This happened at the same time that I realised I had the abilities which I discussed in my talk—'

'So how come the miracle recovery?' Hawthorne interrupted.

'I had eye surgery to remove scar tissue from the back of my retina and although it was still damaged, some of my sight returned.'

'Enough to see Derek Abbott and Charles le Mesurier walk to the Snuggery together just before ten o'clock on Saturday night?'

She nodded.

'But why all this pretence?' I demanded. I knew Hawthorne didn't like it when I interrupted, but I couldn't stop myself.

'It was Sid's idea,' Elizabeth said. 'The whole thing with Blind Sight.'

'That's not true!' Sid snarled. 'Don't you bloody say that.'

'You suggested it.'

'All right! All right!' Sid drew a breath, then turned to us. 'There are psychics up and down the country,' he grumbled. 'Half of them are fake. Not like Liz. She's the real thing. But that's not good enough, not these days, when everyone's looking for something more. How were we going to get her on *Good Morning Britain*? I told her she needed something special, a trademark. We weren't telling a lie. We were just embroidering the truth.'

'But all that rubbish just now ...'

I understood exactly what had happened. Elizabeth had been sitting outside The Lookout on the night of the party, smoking a cigarette. She had clearly seen Derek Abbott and Charles le Mesurier walk past her, crossing the garden, but she couldn't say anything without giving herself away. At the same time, Derek hadn't realised he'd been spotted. That was why he had been able to deny entering the Snuggery with such confidence. He thought she was blind! As for the charade we had just sat through, Elizabeth could have sent Hawthorne an anonymous message, but she and her husband must have been thinking about the publicity value. A psychic helping the police to solve a double murder! How many books would that sell?

'What time did you see them leave the house?' Hawthorne asked.

Elizabeth had no choice. 'About ten to ten.'

Le Mesurier had been killed about twenty minutes later. Two guests had heard him cry out.

'Were they talking?'

'Yes. I couldn't hear what they were saying.'

That was probably true. Elizabeth had been sitting over to one side of the house.

'But you must have been able to tell something from their body language.'

'I don't know what you mean.'

'Come on, love!' Hawthorne was irritated. Elizabeth Lovell's entire act was based on her ability to 'read' a room, to pick up innocent cues from people and to turn them into a narrative of her own making. 'Were they friendly?'

'I can't tell you what you want to know, Mr Hawthorne. It was dark. They were a distance away. They had their backs to me. But if it's any help, they were quite close together, side by side. They weren't unfriendly. Charles le Mesurier was doing most of the talking. I saw them for less than a minute. Then they went into the building.'

'Did you see Abbott come out again?'

'No. Sid came for me a few minutes later. That would have been ten o'clock. We went back into the house and then we took a taxi to the hotel.'

'Derek Abbott was the last person to see le Mesurier alive,' Sid said. 'That's useful information. Maybe he was the killer and it's thanks to her that you'll have cracked the case.'

'What are you suggesting, Mr Lovell?'

Sid licked his lips nervously. 'Look, I know we got off to the wrong start, but we can put all that behind us. And maybe we could come to some sort of arrangement. I mean, it would be very useful to us if you could see your way to acknowledging her contribution publicly.'

'I'll tell you what I'll do,' Hawthorne countered. 'I'll have a good think about it and it's just possible that I might not tell the police that you withheld vital information for forty-eight hours or recommend that you're both arrested. And when my mate Tony writes his book about what happened here on Alderney, which is what he's going to do, I might persuade him to moderate his language and not point out that the two of you are lying scumbags who feed on people's grief to line your own pockets and that what you did to a friend of ours – Anne Cleary – in front of a paying audience was about as low as it's possible to get. Apart from that, what I'd suggest is that you both fuck off out of here before I really lose my temper.' He smiled. 'How does that sound?'

The two of them got stiffly to their feet. Sid held out a hand to help guide Elizabeth out of the room, but she shrugged it off. I waited until the two of them had gone. 'What were the mistakes?' I asked.

'I'm sorry?'

'How did you know she wasn't blind?'

'The first time I met her, at the theatre, you introduced me to her and she held out a hand ... sort of in my direction. But since I hadn't said anything, how could she have had any idea where I was? When she first came to see us in the dining room to suggest this séance, I held out a chair for her and she felt for it. But again, I hadn't made a sound. There were lots of things like that. The truth is, the two of them were so amateur that I'm surprised more people didn't notice what they were up to.'

'But you said the ghosts were real!'

'The lady who drowned in the bath and Anne Cleary's son? They might have been wandering around the room with chains on their ankles, holding their heads in their hands. But that doesn't mean she was able to see them.'

'So what now?' I asked. 'Will you tell Torode about Derek Abbott going into the Snuggery?' It was exactly the piece of evidence that the deputy chief had been waiting for.

Hawthorne shrugged. 'I wouldn't have said I had much choice. What do you think?'

'No,' I admitted. 'I don't think you do.'

*

That might have been the end of it, except that the night still had one other small surprise waiting for me.

I went up to my room, but I wasn't in any mood to go to bed. I was really shocked by what Sid and Elizabeth Lovell had done, the double deception, the way they had hurt Anne Cleary and many others like her. I needed to get some fresh air, so I went back downstairs and strolled out onto the terrace where breakfast would be served. It was a lovely night. Half the stars in the universe seemed to have crowded together above the sea. I could taste the salt in the air.

And then I saw him. Hawthorne was walking along the edge of the beach, heading in the direction of The Lookout. This wasn't a late-night stroll. I could tell from the way he walked. He was on his way somewhere.

He came off the sand and continued along the road. I wanted to call out to him, but I didn't. I watched him until he disappeared into the dark.

21

The Full English

Elizabeth Lovell and her husband were the first to leave the next morning. They were actually going through the front door as I came downstairs and I hung back, not wanting to have to talk to them again. Sid had his arm around his wife, guiding her, even though he knew she could see perfectly well, and I wondered how much longer they would continue to keep that up now that Hawthorne and I had latched on to their secret. As far as I can tell, they haven't appeared in public again since Alderney.

I noticed Anne Cleary paying her bill and went over to her. 'Are you on the eleven o'clock flight?' I asked her.

She shook her head. 'I just couldn't wait that long, I'm afraid.'

I was sorry to hear it. Maïssa Lamar and Elizabeth Lovell had both turned out to be frauds. I'd barely spoken to Marc Bellamy or George Elkin. Anne was the only writer I'd actually connected with during my long weekend in Alderney and I'd thought that at least we'd travel back together.

'I suppose this has been all right for you,' she went on. 'You like murders and all that sort of thing.'

'Not really.'

'Well, I've had enough of it. I'd have taken the first flight this morning except that it was sold out.' She glanced out of the door. The Alderney Tours bus was parked on the other side of the street with the driver, Tom McKinley, loading up the cases. 'Do you know who did it yet?' she asked.

'No.' I didn't want to tell her about Derek Abbott.

'Well, I hope you find out. Charles le Mesurier may not have been a very nice man, but nobody deserves to die in that way. And as for his wife, I don't understand that at all. It seems to me, the only thing she ever did wrong was marrying him.'

The sound of hooting came from outside.

'I'd better be on my way.' She picked up her suitcase. 'Do come and see me if you happen to be in Oxford.'

'I'd like that.' We kissed and she went on her way.

She had no sooner gone than the lift doors opened and Kathryn Harris came out, struggling under the weight of two bags, her glasses slipping off her face. There was a third case behind her in the lift. I went over to her. 'Can I give you a hand?'

'Thank you.' She let me take them. They were just as heavy as they had been when they came off the plane. 'They're both Marc's,' she explained. 'I'm afraid we didn't sell as many books as we'd hoped.'

'Where are you heading to?' I asked.

'Back to London. Marc's filming a guest spot on the Christmas edition of *Celebrity Storage Hunters*.' She pulled a face. 'Don't tell him I told you! It's meant to be a secret.'

I left Kathryn's cases by the front door, then went to the reception desk to pay my bill (the last two nights had not been included). The same young receptionist who had checked us in was behind the desk and she looked at me sadly. 'We're going to miss you,' she said. 'We're not used to this sort of excitement in Alderney. We've never had a murder here before.'

'You're not the first person to tell me that,' I said.

Finally, Hawthorne came down, carrying his suitcase, his coat neatly folded over his arm. 'Are you OK?' I asked.

He looked surprised. 'I'm fine.'

'I couldn't sleep at all,' I said. 'After what happened, I had to go out and get some air.'

I wanted him to tell me where he had gone after our session with the Lovells, but he wasn't playing. 'I slept fine,' he said. He looked past me at Kathryn, who was waiting to take the lift back up. 'Have you seen Marc Bellamy?'

The receptionist overheard him. 'Mr Bellamy is having breakfast on the terrace,' she said.

We went out and found him.

He was sitting on his own at the far end, tucking into the sort of breakfast that he would have promoted on his television programme: eggs, bacon, sausage, beans, fried bread, mushrooms. He was wearing a tweed jacket and a cravat. It was as if he had already dressed up for his appearance on *Celebrity Storage Hunters*.

'How do!' he exclaimed. 'Are you on your way out of here?'

'The same flight as you,' Hawthorne said. Without asking, he sat down at Marc's table. 'You enjoying that?'

'There's nothing to beat the full English,' Marc exclaimed. 'And don't you give me any of that continental rubbish. Yoghurt and croissant and that horrible concoction they call muesli. If you ask me, that's the best thing about getting out of the EU, and there's a long list where that's concerned. Bring back the great British breakfast!' He poked his sausage with his fork. 'Mind you, this is a poor excuse for a decent banger. The skin's synthetic and it's got way too much rusk and water. You can tell from the way it's shrunk.' He was enjoying himself, playing to invisible cameras.

'There was something I wanted to ask you,' Hawthorne said.

'Ask away. But you don't mind if I eat while we talk, do you? I've got a car coming at ten and I don't want this to get cold.'

'I was wondering if you'd let me have the pen back.'

'What pen is that?'

'The pen that was taken from Anne Cleary's room. She said it was a Sakura, made in Japan.'

Marc had just pronged a piece of bacon, but he didn't lift it off the plate. 'I don't know what you're talking about,' he said, without looking up.

'I'm talking about the pen that you stole.'

'I didn't steal anything. And I think you should watch what you say to me, Mr Hawthorne. I've been threatened by experts.'

'I'm not threatening you,' Hawthorne said, reasonably. 'And we can do this two ways. You can give me what I want or I can call Deputy Chief Torode and he'll arrest you and take a look in your luggage. What else will we find in there, I wonder? My guess is that there'll be a gold Rolex watch and also a fifty-euro note.'

'Did he also take my £5?' I asked.

Hawthorne nodded. 'Probably.'

'I didn't take anything!' Marc exploded, his face darkening. 'And I'm warning you—'

'Charles le Mesurier didn't call you Tea Leaf because you drank lots of tea,' Hawthorne interrupted. 'Do you think I'm an idiot? It's cockney rhyming slang. Tea leaf ... thief. And every time he spoke to you, he was rubbing it in. He had a way of doing that, sneering at people. That first night at The Divers Inn: *You always did like to get your hands on a steak pie.* And a minute later: *I always remember you being the quiet type, stealing up into the dorm* and *knocking off the snacks.* Then, at the party: *I'm going to lift one of those, if you don't mind.* Every time he spoke to you, he was hinting at what he knew about you and my guess is, when he said, *You left so suddenly!* he was reminding you that you didn't leave Westland College, you were kicked out.'

'I was unhappy there.'

'You were expelled.'

Marc Bellamy's collapse, when it came, was remarkable. It was as if a plane crossing the sun had cast its shadow over him. In that single moment, the bombast, the jokiness, the sense of authority, the self-confidence were all wiped away. The celebrity was gone and in his place sat a frightened schoolboy with a plate filled with too much food, wondering what was going to happen next.

He pushed the plate to one side.

'It's not my fault,' he muttered in a voice that was suddenly husky. He looked across the terrace to make sure nobody could hear what was being said. But we were alone. 'I don't take these things because I want them,' he went on. 'I can't stop myself. I've had treatment. I've been to shrinks and I've been to doctors. What I have is an addictive disorder—'

'There are a lot of people in jail with addictive disorders,' Hawthorne reminded him.

'You don't know what it's like. I hate it. I hate myself for doing it. It's not as if I've ever taken anything valuable.'

'Like a twenty-thousand-quid gold-plated Rolex, for example?'

Marc's eyes blazed. 'That was different. I took that because it was his and I wanted to hurt him.'

'Did you take it off his wrist?'

'No! He left it in the kitchen. Just before he went out into the garden.'

'He left through the kitchen door?'

'Yes.'

'When was that?'

'Just after nine forty-five. Maybe ten to ten.'

'Was he alone?'

'There was someone waiting for him outside. I didn't see who it was. He took the watch off and put it on a shelf and I thought, you know what? There are still plenty enough people in the house. He'll know it was me, but he'll never be able to prove it. And it really made me smile to think of him losing it, his precious Rolex. I didn't keep it, by the way. I threw it in the sea.' He pointed. 'It's out there.'

'You really hated him that much?'

'You have no idea what that man did to me – at Westland College. How much he hurt me.'

'So tell me.'

'I can't.'

Hawthorne was pitiless. 'You have to, Marc. We only have your word for it that he left that watch on a kitchen shelf. You could have taken it off his wrist after you'd killed him.'

Charles le Mesurier had worn his watch on his right hand, the same hand that had been left untied.

'I didn't kill anyone!' Marc rasped. 'What sort of person do you think I am?'

'That's what I'm trying to find out.' Hawthorne paused. 'Tell me about Westland College.'

'I've never talked about it. Not in my entire adult life.'

'Charles le Mesurier can't hurt you any more.'

'There's nothing left to hurt.' Marc Bellamy had begun to cry. I was shocked. It wasn't just the demolition of the man, in this bright morning sunlight. It was the fact that Hawthorne and I had been the cause.

We waited in uncomfortable silence until he had contained himself.

'Westland was a minor independent school outside Chichester,' he began. 'I told you. I was sent there in 1983, when my dad got posted to the south coast. I was eight years old. Do you have any idea what those places were like back then? It was a bloody bear pit. I'd been perfectly happy up in Halifax. Ordinary school, ordinary friends. I never knew what was going to hit me when I walked in. Boarding school, dormitories, tuck shop. Even the uniform made me feel like a pillock. The teachers were ignorant bastards. The food was fucking horrible.

'But the worst of it was the other boys. If you were going to survive with that lot, you had to be one of them and if you weren't, they knew it in seconds. They'd come from the right homes – rich parents, nannies – and it was like their whole life they were prepared for that sort of place. There was a pack mentality and I felt it the moment I arrived, like some bloody sacrificial lamb. I was small for my age. I could have had the word PREY tattooed on my forehead.

'Well, it started soon enough ... the bullying. Apple-pie bed the first night. Tie cut in half. Letters from my mum stolen and read out so that everyone could have a good laugh. That was the end of the first week. Then there was the name-calling. About six weeks in, I got caught stealing a postal order. Remember those? A £2 postal order. Well, I was up in front of the housemaster for that and three strokes of the cane, but it was the other kids who were worse. After that I was Tea Leaf. Always Tea Leaf. They never let me forget it.

'Charles le Mesurier was the ringleader. I never understood how he got the power because he wasn't stronger or smarter than any of the others. I remember him as a scrawny little kid and there was always this gleam in his eyes as he worked out what sort of cruelty he might get up to next. You know, when you describe all these things later they sound small and petty and you wonder what all the fuss was about. But at the time ... it hollows you out. It makes you feel worthless. I saw it when I met him again here. It was exactly the same. Flash. He loved being called that. His nickname wasn't an insult to him. He loved it. He revelled in it.

'Every night he'd pick on another new bug, which is what they called the first-years. He was two years ahead of us and he was part of a gang, four or five of them, that used to prowl the corridors after prep. They'd pick you up and throw you in the laundry basket with everyone's dirty clothes and then tie down the lid. You might be there for an hour before someone let you out. Or he'd do the same thing in your study ... tie you to a chair with parcel tape so you'd be late for chapel and get a bollocking from the housemaster. One day, I came into my study and he'd vandalised all my photographs ... my mum, my dad, my dog. He'd drawn things with a Magic Marker. I don't need to tell you what sort of things. He was sick, I really believe that.'

He drew a breath.

'I went on stealing. And when I got caught the third time and was thrown out of Westland, it was the happiest day of my life. My dad never forgave me, though. He was a lieutenant commander on a frigate – *Broadsword*. And having a son who'd been caught pilfering, he thought it reflected on him. He never really spoke to me very much after that. I tried to explain, but he wouldn't listen.'

Marc Bellamy reached into his inside pocket and took out a slim silver pen. He placed it on the table. 'Here you are,' he said. 'That's Mrs Cleary's pen, and when you return it to her, you can tell her I never went into her room. She lent it to Kathryn, and Kathryn left it in the bar.'

'You took fifty euros from Maïssa Lamar's purse.'

'I can give you that back too ...' He fumbled for his wallet.

Hawthorne stopped him. 'There's no need. She's gone. Did you take any coins?'

'No. Nothing else.'

'Yeah. Well. Thank you for being so frank with us.' Hawthorne stood up and I wondered if he might be a little bit ashamed about what had just happened. As for myself, I felt nothing but pity for Marc Bellamy. I'd been through the private-education system myself – another version of the full English – and knew only too well how the casual cruelty and the pack mentality that he had described could stay with you for the rest of your life.

We left him sitting there and went back into the hotel. I'd lost any appetite for breakfast, but Hawthorne poured himself a black coffee.

'That story he told,' I said as we sat at another table. 'Charles le Mesurier tying him down with parcel tape.' Suddenly it was obvious to me. 'Bellamy killed him!'

But Hawthorne shook his head. 'We haven't told anyone the full details of how le Mesurier was killed,' he said. 'So if Bellamy had decided to re-enact some sort of revenge, do you think he'd have told us what was done to him back in his schooldays? It would have been the same as confessing to the crime.'

'Maybe that's what he just did.'

Hawthorne didn't reply, but it only allowed my thoughts to race ahead of me. Was it possible that someone else had been to Westland College at the same time as Charles le Mesurier? Colin Matheson, perhaps, or Dr Queripel? They were both about the right age. Could it be that despite all the evidence, Derek Abbott wasn't the true killer?

Everything had changed. I might have a book after all.

22

Gannet Rock

I was looking forward to leaving Alderney. As we drove past Fort Tourgis, making our way back towards the airport, it was hard to believe that I had only been on the island for five days. So much had happened – two deaths! At the same time, Hawthorne and I had left a wake of destruction behind us. Anne Cleary had been trashed by Elizabeth Lovell, who had then been exposed as a cheat and a liar. Marc Bellamy had been forced to relive his own childhood trauma and had admitted to being a thief. Judith and Colin Matheson might divorce. Derek Abbott was heading to jail for blackmail, if not murder. There are victims in every murder story, and not just the ones who are killed.

Terry was sad to see us go, although I couldn't say I'd miss him very much: he had presented me with an enormous bill in return for his services. As usual, he filled the journey with his chatter.

'So, you don't know who did it!' he exclaimed, casting an eye at Hawthorne, bouncing it off his driving mirror.

Hawthorne was in no mood to reply.

'There are plenty of people on the island who will be glad to see the back of him. My dad for one! We were talking about it only last night. I told you Mr le Mesurier was planning to start his own car service, as if he needed any more business in Alderney. Not that I'm saying my old man had anything to do with it, mind you. Did you talk to that French lady? I took her to the airport and she said she was a poet, but what sort of poet would have a private jet waiting for her? There was something going on there.'

We reached the top of the hill. I could see the airport in the distance.

But Terry hadn't finished. 'I still don't believe I was actually parked outside the house when Charles le Mesurier was done in. And I saw his wife – his widow, sorry – the day she died too!'

That interested Hawthorne. 'When was that?' he asked.

'About two o'clock. I drove past her just as she came out of the house. She turned left, heading up towards the quarry.'

'Was she alone?'

'I didn't see anyone else. I thought about offering her a lift, but I was going the other way, and anyway, that slightly defeats the point of being a taxi driver – giving people lifts for free!'

As we turned into the approach road that led to the airport, we were overtaken by another car and I saw Special Constable

Whitlock driving with Deputy Chief Torode in the back seat. He was sitting with his head against the window, part of his face pressed flat by the glass. He hadn't noticed us and I thought he might be asleep, but when we finally drew up in the car park, he got out and came over to us.

'Hawthorne …'

'Have you come to say goodbye, Deputy Chief?'

'I wish. But actually, it seems I may need your help after all.'

We were standing in the car park with the entrance to the airport in front of us. I noticed the minibus that had met us when we'd arrived. Marc Bellamy was just getting out, followed by Kathryn Harris. As usual, she was carrying all the luggage. The aircraft that would take us all to Southampton was waiting beside the runway.

'We went to arrest Derek Abbott this morning,' Torode continued.

'And?'

'He's not at home. He's not answering his phone.'

'You think he's done a runner?' Hawthorne was amused.

'I would have thought that unlikely. This is an island.'

'I hadn't noticed that.'

Torode frowned. 'Look here, Hawthorne. You talked to him. You know him better than any of us. I thought you might want to come along because you might see something that could help us find him. Or you can get on a plane and piss off home and we can forget we ever met. It's entirely up to you.'

There were actually a few things that Torode was forgetting, starting with the fact that it was Hawthorne who had supplied him with the information that had enabled him to arrest Abbott in the first place. Also, Torode had reneged on his agreement and had told Hawthorne that he wasn't going to be paid.

Despite all this, I wasn't at all surprised when Hawthorne turned to me and asked: 'What do you think, Tony? Do you mind getting a later plane?'

I was fine with that. I was uncomfortable about running into Marc Bellamy again and I was curious to see more of Abbott's home. 'Sure,' I said.

So off we went, in the back seat of Torode's car with our luggage in the boot, Torode silent, Whitlock grim, Hawthorne thoughtful. It wasn't the most pleasant journey across the island, passing the sites of not one but two murders, and I was glad when we finally arrived at Quesnard Cottage and got out. There was a uniformed policeman standing at the door; from Alderney or Guernsey, I had no idea. Whitlock stayed in the car, her hands still gripping the steering wheel as if she was afraid someone would drag her out.

The front door was unlocked. Either Torode had found it that way or he had forced his way in. There was no sign of any damage. It was strange what a difference it made, arriving in the bright midday sunlight without Mozart's Requiem playing in the background. I'd had a sense of unease when I had approached it the first time — less than twenty-four hours ago. I'd allowed my knowledge of the man who lived there to influence the way I described the place and it was interesting how little impact his home made on me now. Every writer knows about the pathetic fallacy, where the weather, the light and even music can be used to manipulate a reader's mood. But it seemed that I'd done quite the opposite, allowing my own mood to influence the weather.

We passed into the hallway and I remembered Abbott standing there, ugly and defensive, swearing at Hawthorne before we were allowed in. This time, Torode led us into the living room, Abbott's 'safe space' and the very heart of the house. As well as the chairs and the sofas, the TV and the sound system, there was a large desk with a computer, indicating that this was where Abbott worked as well as relaxed. If there were any clues to his current whereabouts, they would be found here.

Hawthorne quickly checked the surface of the desk. There was a diary open at yesterday's date, but the page was blank. A selection of postcards with views of Alderney were lying on top of an in tray that also contained various household bills. A single rollerball pen lay to one side, the lid missing. 'Have you searched the place?' he asked.

'Not yet.' That surprised me, but Torode explained: 'I'm not even sure what I'm looking for. That's why I thought you might help. The computer's locked, by the way, and there's no convenient password this time. Anyway, it's probably full of porn. To be honest with you, I haven't got the stomach for it. Maybe Whitlock's right. I can't wait to get back to Guernsey.'

'Does Abbott have any friends on the island? Anyone he might have contacted?'

Torode shrugged. 'I doubt it. Most of the people on the island knew who he was and didn't want anything to do with him. I'd guess that Charles le Mesurier was probably the only person who let him come anywhere near – and we all know how that ended.'

'Have you examined his phone records?'

'Do me a favour, Hawthorne. We only found out he was missing half an hour ago.'

I looked around, working out the sequence of events that had led to Abbott's disappearance and wondering where he might have gone. Hawthorne had fired a warning shot with his first visit, but Abbott hadn't been afraid. *When are you going to stop making up lies about me?* He had denied everything, past and present, and then there had been that strange moment of recognition between them – if that's what it was. After that, Abbott had been confident enough to throw him out.

Since then, Hawthorne had discovered one more vital piece of information. Contrary to what he had said, Abbott had been seen accompanying le Mesurier to the Snuggery on the night of the murder. This added opportunity to motive ... Abbott must have been the last person to see him alive. Hawthorne had told Torode, and Torode had moved in to make the arrest.

Could Abbott have known he was coming? Had he seen uniformed policemen approach and made a fast exit out of a back door? Nothing about the room suggested that. There were no half-open drawers or incriminating documents burned in the fireplace. Was it even possible that he had disappeared in the same way as Helen le Mesurier? He had claimed to be a victim when Hawthorne was interrogating him. Could it be that a third murder had taken place on the island of Alderney in almost as many days?

Hawthorne had started with the desk, rifling through various documents and files. I wandered over to the side of the room and cast my eye over the long lines of books arranged on sagging wooden shelves that covered an entire wall. I'm afraid to say that old habits die hard and I was half looking for any sign of my own books. Worse still, I was quite gratified to find a hardback edition of *Moriarty* next to a complete collection of Sherlock Holmes. I didn't allow it to change my opinion of Derek Abbott in any way, of course.

Meanwhile, Torode was examining the different malt whiskies displayed on a trolley. I wouldn't have put it past him to help himself to one. I had seen very little of him during the investigation, but he had come across as venal and self-interested. Even now, after dismissing him only the night before, he had effectively brought Hawthorne here to do his work for him. But then as far as he was concerned, the case was over. He just wanted to find Abbott so that he could go home.

'Take a look at this ...'

Hawthorne had found something in one of the drawers. He was holding a camera, the sort used by sports enthusiasts, a GoPro Hero. It was remarkably small, no more than a couple of inches in height and depth. He was turning it over in his hands, working out how to activate it, and at that moment I realised its significance. Abbott had been blackmailing Colin Matheson about his affair with Helen le Mesurier. Colin had thought that there was a security camera recording what had taken place in the Snuggery, but Hawthorne and I both knew that wasn't true. Was it possible that the footage had been recorded with this tiny device?

Hawthorne found the On button and pressed it. The answer to my question was apparent straight away. The little screen on the back flickered into life and there was the inside of the Snuggery in full colour, empty to begin with but almost at once Colin Matheson appeared. The camera had been concealed above the door. I saw his head and the back of his shoulders as he moved into the room and briefly disappeared out of shot. Helen le Mesurier, wearing a bright red dress that showed more flesh than it concealed, followed, carrying a bottle of champagne. She went the other way and sat down on one of the leather banquettes I had noticed when I had first gone in there. She placed the champagne on the table in front of her. Colin Matheson came back into view as he crossed over and sat next to her.

The bottle was already open. Helen filled two glasses that had been standing on the table. They talked, but there was no sound and because of the high angle it wasn't even possible to read their lips. They kissed. The image was so small and the camera so far away that I couldn't see the expression on Colin's face, whether he was reluctant, embarrassed or passionate, unable to control himself. Paradoxically, the GoPro only gave me the bigger picture. The kiss became more intense. His hands slid under her dress, pulling it off her shoulder. She reached for his belt.

Hawthorne froze the image. He had seen enough.

'So you were right,' Torode said. 'Derek Abbott was blackmailing them.'

'No,' Hawthorne said. 'I was wrong.'

'What are you talking about? You were the one who found the text that Helen le Mesurier sent Colin Matheson. *OMG, Colin ... What has he got?* And Matheson told us—'

'Matheson was wrong too.'

'Well, if he wasn't blackmailing them, what do you think he was doing? Revenge porn? Putting this out on the internet just to annoy them?'

'It wasn't Abbott,' Hawthorne said.

'Then how did this camera end up in his desk?'

Hawthorne put the camera back where he had found it. Slowly, he explained. 'Helen le Mesurier wasn't being blackmailed. She was part of it. And Derek Abbott wasn't the blackmailer.'

'Then who was?'

'Charles le Mesurier.'

I ran that through my head. 'Hawthorne, are you saying—'

'The whole thing was a set-up.' Hawthorne took out a cigarette and lit it. With Abbott absent and quite possibly on the run, there was no need to ask for permission.

'I'll have one of those, if you don't mind,' Torode said.

'Sorry, mate. Last one.' Hawthorne slid the pack back into his pocket.

'What do you mean, it was a set-up?' I asked.

'When we talked to Derek Abbott in the kitchen, he was shit-scared half the time. Of course he denied everything. That's what he's done all his life. But he was also on the defensive. He insisted he hadn't been fired. He didn't want us to know how much money he'd been paid. He said it was peanuts when actually it was twenty thousand quid. He also lied about texting Helen le Mesurier. Of course it was him. She was five minutes from his house when she was killed.

'The only time he relaxed was when I accused him of having shares in Électricité du Nord. That was when he got cocky. He told me to check out the list of shareholders and then he threw me out of the house. Well, I checked the shareholders and he was actually telling the truth. He's got nothing.

'That part of the story was wrong – but where had it come from? It was what Abbott had told Colin Matheson and what Matheson had then told us. So why did he lie? Don't forget, he never took any money from Matheson. All he wanted was for him to influence his stupid committee and get the power line up and running. And who actually had the most to gain from that?'

'Charles le Mesurier.' Suddenly, it was crystal clear.

'That's right. Charles was getting cash payments as an adviser, but we also know that he'd sold a piece of land to the company for five times its true value. That was what was at stake. If he was going to hit pay dirt, le Mesurier needed someone inside the States to get the electricity line off the ground and so he used his own wife as bait. She seduced Colin in front of the camera. And his dirty little friend, Derek Abbott, was the one who put the squeeze on him.'

'And that was why he was paid £20,000!' I exclaimed.

'Exactly. Le Mesurier earned millions, but Abbott got a commission.'

'Wait a minute!' Torode cut in. He pointed at the camera in disgust. 'Are you saying she knew she was being filmed?'

'She was only doing it for the camera,' Hawthorne said. 'Didn't you see it for yourself? Helen le Mesurier was carrying the champagne, but the glasses were already laid out on the table. There was nothing spontaneous about what happened in the Snuggery, no moment of madness. She'd planned it all. And when they came in, Colin turned left, but she turned right. Why? Because she knew she had to be in the shot!'

'But that's disgusting,' Torode said. 'Le Mesurier used his own wife ...'

'They had an open marriage. Sex was no big deal. I wouldn't be surprised if Charles didn't get off watching this. The two of them were as bad as each other.'

The three of us stood facing each other in the empty room. 'So where is Abbott now?' Torode asked.

'That's the question,' Hawthorne said. 'Let's take a look around.'

We went back into the hall and then upstairs. The house had three bedrooms. Two of them hadn't been used for a long time. They weren't just unoccupied, they felt musty and redundant, permanently empty. The master bedroom was cosier, with a king-sized bed and half a dozen pillows that must have mocked Derek Abbott every time he went up there, alone. A bathroom led off it. He had a lot of expensive toiletries.

There was no sign of the man himself and although I noticed a hatch leading up to the attic, Hawthorne wasn't inclined to search there. I supposed it was unlikely that Abbott was intending to hide away in the house until this was all over. I wondered if he had actually gone on the run. Was it possible that he was simply shopping in St Anne?

Hawthorne stopped. Something had occurred to him. 'Downstairs,' he said.

We followed our steps back into the hall. Hawthorne went straight over to the hexagonal table that stood in the centre. I saw now that there was a postcard propped up against the vase of flowers. It showed a view of Gannet Rock, the towering sea stacks and plunging cliffs on the far western side of the island that I had visited on my first day. Why should it mean anything to him? Then I remembered the other postcards and the rollerball pen I had seen on the desk.

Hawthorne turned the card over. There was a handwritten message on the other side.

I can't go back to prison. I'm not doing that. I can't.

He showed the card to Torode. 'Do you know where this is?' he asked.

'Les Etacs. Yes. I know.'

'I think we should go there.'

We went in Torode's car with Whitlock behind the wheel, back across the island and up Tourgis Hill, passing close to the airport. A narrow lane, more like a track, led from the main road through swathes of the strange, pale grass that characterised so much of the island. We pulled up in front of yet another gun emplacement, or the remains of one, a heptagon of grey concrete lying on the ground like an over-sized coin. There were two more of them further up the hill. Dozens of gannets, each one a ball of brilliant white feathers, were soaring high overhead, providing a commentary on the scene with their eerie, sawing cries.

Even before we got out of the car, we could tell something was wrong. A small crowd had gathered on the very edge of the grass, all of them looking out to sea, and there was something about their body language, the way they stood, that warned us that although they might be birdwatchers, they were not now watching birds. We went over and joined them.

I saw the two rock towers rising up out of a steel-blue sea, providing an astonishing breeding ground for twelve thousand gannets. To one side, the land sloped down and there were paths that you could follow all the way to the water's edge, but in front of us the island simply stopped, like a map torn in half, with a sheer drop on the other side of the jagged line.

'He's down there,' someone said, inviting me to join them in this spectacle of death. And sure enough, he was.

Derek Abbott was too far away to be recognisable, but who else could it have been, lying there on the shingle, his body disjointed, exactly like one of those chalk outlines in a bad police drama? The water was lapping at him, but he wasn't moving. I wondered how anyone would reach him. They'd have to send a boat. There was no other way to bring him up to the top.

A man was standing next to me, dressed in an anorak with a heavy pair of binoculars on a cord around his neck. 'Did you see what happened?' I asked.

'He jumped,' the man told me.

I turned away. I'd seen more than enough death on Alderney. Hawthorne was standing right behind me, impassive. I looked him straight in the eye. 'You did this,' I said.

'I didn't do anything,' Hawthorne replied.

But I knew he was lying. Someone had told Abbott that the police were coming to arrest him and I had seen Hawthorne walking out of the hotel late at night.

Now I knew where he had gone.

23

Keep Reading

Two days after I got back to London, I went to see my agent, Hilda Starke. I walked over to Greek Street in Soho, where her office was located on the fourth floor of a narrow building hemmed in between an Italian restaurant and an off-licence. There was no lift and the stairs creaked menacingly under my weight, as if warning me that I was not really welcome here. I think it's true to say that Hilda preferred books to authors. In the three years I had been with her, I'd only gone to her office half a dozen times.

I arrived at a dusty landing where a door opened into a tiny reception area, made tinier by the floor-to-ceiling bookshelves crammed with books. A single window allowed a little daylight to seep through, but it was a room that devoured daylight. I gave my name to the receptionist and told him I had an appointment with Hilda.

'What's this about?' he asked vaguely.

'I'm one of her clients.'

'Oh.'

Ten minutes later, I had squeezed into Hilda's office. There was so little space in the building, all the furniture seemed to be in the way. She was behind her desk, holding a Sharpie and covering a manuscript with black markings. I wondered if she did the same with my work when she received it.

'Have you been offered coffee?' she asked.

'No,' I said. 'Your receptionist didn't even know you represented me.'

She wasn't troubled. 'He hasn't been here long.'

'How are you?' I asked.

She looked at me, puzzled. 'I'm fine. Why do you ask?'

According to Hawthorne, she had been on her way to the doctor, worrying about tests, when I'd met her seven weeks before. Could he have been wrong? The trouble was, if I told her what I knew, it would look as if I'd been prying. 'I just thought you seemed a bit down when we last met,' I said, trying to sound casual.

'No. I'm perfectly well. How was Alderney?'

She was obviously keen to change the subject and I just hoped that whatever the problem was, it had sorted itself out. 'That's why I'm here,' I said. Quickly, I described the festival and the two murders that had followed. 'I don't think I'm going to be able to write the third book in the series,' I concluded.

'Why ever not?'

'I've just explained. Derek Abbott was the killer and he committed suicide rather than go back to prison.'

'What's the problem with that?'

'Well, it's just not a very satisfying ending. He was always the most obvious suspect, so it's not much of a surprise, and he was a thoroughly unpleasant man, so who's going to care? Worse than that, Hawthorne didn't really solve the murder. I mean, he did – but most of the information was handed to him on a plate.'

'What do you want me to do?'

'I thought you might have a word with Random House. Maybe I can write something else.'

She sighed. 'I did warn you against starting this series of books,' she said. 'I always said it was bad idea.'

'It wasn't my idea!'

'And you've got a problem now. Everyone at Random House loved meeting Hawthorne. Graham sent me a note to say how impressed he was. If you don't want to write the third book, I'm afraid they'll look for someone else who will.'

'They can't do that, can they?'

'You don't own Hawthorne, Anthony. If anything, he owns you.'

I sat there gloomily while she let this sink in.

'Anyway, you shouldn't be worrying about the third book,' she continued, eventually. 'You haven't finished the second one yet. Have you got a title, by the way?'

'Yes. I want to call it *Another Word for Murder*.' She made no response so I added: 'After all, it is a sequel to *The Word is Murder*.'

She nodded. 'That's the problem,' she said. 'It sounds like a sequel. People will think they have to read the first one. If I were you, I'd think of something else.'

'But I like it,' I protested.

'I don't.'

A few minutes later, I was back in the street. It hadn't been a brilliant meeting. I'd been told my publishers preferred my main character to me. I'd lost the title of my second book. And Hilda wasn't going to offer me any help with the third one.

My telephone rang. I looked at the screen. It was Hawthorne.

'Yes?'

'Tony, are you around?'

'I'm in town.'

'Do you fancy coming to Oxford? I'm taking that pen back to Anne Cleary and she's invited me to lunch.'

'Did she invite me?'

'No. But she likes you. She'll be glad to see you.'

'What time are you leaving?'

'There's a train at eleven fifteen.'

It was ten fifteen now – but that was typical of Hawthorne. He had a sort of myopia that possibly extended to the entire world, but certainly to me. I would be available when he needed me, although of course it didn't work the other way round. I was tempted to say no, to tell him I was busy – but what was the point? I was only twenty minutes from Paddington Station and I had nothing much to do.

'I'll meet you on the train,' I said.

In fact, Hawthorne was waiting for me at the platform and we travelled together in silence. He was still reading *The Little Stranger*, the book he had brought with him to Southampton, and I noticed that he wasn't many pages further in, but then I could imagine him being not just a slow reader but a methodical one, going over every sentence and every paragraph so that he would be up to scratch when he met with his book club.

It was only in the taxi, driving through Oxford, that I asked him: 'Did you tell Anne I was coming?'

'No. I'm sure she won't mind.'

'But if she's making lunch—'

'You can have mine!'

Anne Cleary lived in exactly the sort of house I would have imagined for her, part of a curving terrace in a quiet area of Oxford with lots of trees. It was Victorian, red brick, with sash windows and a flight of steps leading up to the front door, the kitchen and dining room below street level. Even before we went in, I knew it would have the original cornicing, stripped wooden floors and high ceilings. There's something about Oxford that has always appealed to authors and it seems to me that it has somehow seeped into their work. Think of Tolkien, C.S. Lewis, Iris Murdoch and, more recently, Philip Pullman. It's hard to imagine them living anywhere else.

Anne was surprised, but seemed pleased to see me and led us both into a comfortable front room. She collected Wedgwood porcelain figurines – milkmaids, ballet dancers, Little Bo Peep. They were displayed on shelves along with books, photographs, an ornamental clock, piles of letters and perfumed candles. The room managed to be simple and cluttered at the same time. Anne looked very much at home here. She was the sort of woman who liked to be comfortable, who would wear clothes that were sensible, never expensive. I suspected she had lived there for most of her adult life.

As soon as we sat down, Hawthorne produced the Sakura fountain pen that he had retrieved from Marc Bellamy. Anne snatched it up with delight. 'I can't tell you how glad I am to have this back,' she said. 'I've got other pens, but this one writes so beautifully. Are you going to tell me where you found it?'

'I can't,' Hawthorne said.

'Had someone taken it?'

'Let's just say that I persuaded them to give it back.'

'Well, I'm very grateful to you, Mr Hawthorne.' She placed it on an ornamental table in front of her. 'And I hear you managed to solve what happened in Alderney.'

'You know about Derek Abbott?' I asked.

'I heard he took his own life.' She shook her head. 'I know I shouldn't feel sorry for him, but in a way I do. If he killed two people, then he deserved to be punished, but I don't think it's ever anything to be celebrated, someone taking their own life.'

'Did you actually speak to him in Alderney?' Hawthorne asked.

'No. I told you. I saw him at the party, but we didn't exchange any words.' Anne clapped her hands together. 'I'm so sorry! I haven't offered you tea or coffee. Or perhaps you'd like a glass of sherry? I've made a salade niçoise for lunch and there's plenty enough for three ...'

'I'm all right, thank you,' Hawthorne said. He smiled. 'You know, thinking back, there is something I never understood and it does relate to that evening at The Lookout.' He paused and Anne waited politely for him to continue. 'Charles le Mesurier talked to you about Derek Abbott. He said that the two of them had had an argument and that he was thinking about firing him. It was certainly true that the two of them had fallen out quite badly. Derek Abbott admitted as much when we spoke to him.'

'So what's the problem?' Anne asked.

'Only this. You left the party at nine twenty-five. We know the exact time because you asked the girl at the door. What was her name?'

'Isn't that awful of me? I'm afraid I've forgotten.'

'It doesn't matter. The argument must have happened before then. But here's the thing. Elizabeth Lovell saw the two of them – Abbott and le Mesurier – crossing the garden just half an hour later, at ten to ten, and according to her the

345

two of them seemed to be on perfectly friendly terms. Once they got to the Snuggery, they actually took cocaine together. Abbott denied it, but we found two cardboard tubes in le Mesurier's pocket, so unless he was using one for each nostril, it looks as if both of them had a quick snort.' Hawthorne looked genuinely perplexed. 'It just doesn't sound like the behaviour of two men who have recently had a falling-out.'

Anne had no answer, but she could see that Hawthorne was waiting for her to speak. 'Well, I told you what he said to me,' she said. 'Derek Abbott wanted money and Charles le Mesurier wasn't prepared to pay it. I assumed that was the reason why he killed him.'

'It's a good reason,' Hawthorne agreed. 'But it still doesn't explain why they were so chummy when they walked over to the Snuggery.'

'Did you say that Elizabeth Lovell *saw* them?' It had taken Anne a few moments to work that out.

'Oh yes. She was only pretending to be unsighted.'

'But that's wicked ...'

'There was a lot of wickedness going on that night, Anne,' Hawthorne agreed. 'That wasn't the worst of it.'

The three of us fell silent. Anne picked up her pen. 'You shouldn't have come all this way to give it back to me,' she said cheerfully. 'Shall we go down to the kitchen and have some lunch?'

'There's something else I wanted to ask you,' Hawthorne said.

'You know, really, Mr Hawthorne ... I'm not sure I've got anything to add.'

'It's just that I like to have everything nice and tidy and if Tony here is going to write about this, he needs to know it all too. It's about the girl at the door.'

'I don't know anything about her.'

'You asked her the time.'

'Yes.' Anne was beginning to sound exasperated.

'Why did you do that?'

'I already told you. I had an important phone call.'

'I know. You had to be back at the hotel at ten. But that doesn't make any sense to me. I'd understand it if you had to leave at a certain time, if you asked someone the time and then hurried to get back to the hotel. But you were already on your way out when you asked. So there was no need to. If you didn't know what time it was, you wouldn't have been leaving.'

'I don't know what you're getting at, Mr Hawthorne. My agent in Los Angeles had told me she was going to ring ...'

'Although in the end she didn't.'

'I wasn't to know that. I checked my watch and then I double-checked at the door. I also asked the bus driver when the bus was going to leave.'

'It's almost as if you wanted everyone to know what time you left the house.'

'It may seem that way to you, but nothing could have been further from my mind.' I had no idea where this was going

347

and Anne was beginning to look uncomfortable. She shifted in her chair. 'It's almost as if you're accusing me of killing Mr le Mesurier myself,' she said. 'But that's ridiculous. I hadn't even met him until last Friday.'

'You're absolutely right, Anne. You had no reason at all to kill Charles le Mesurier.'

'Exactly.'

The clock on the mantelpiece pinged as the minute hand passed the twelve. It was an ugly thing, bronze and white marble with an angel holding a spear in one hand and leaning against the casing with the other. Every hour it would draw attention to itself. It was now one o'clock.

'Except, perhaps, the death of your son.' Hawthorne paused. 'I was there when Elizabeth Lovell talked about him at the cinema.'

Anne scowled. 'That woman was hateful. And everything about her was fake. You just said so yourself.'

'She knew about Mary Carrington, the woman who had slipped and drowned in the bath. And she knew about you. She'd done her research.'

'Mr Hawthorne, this is really—'

'She knew that your son had committed suicide at university.'

'My son was an addict. I don't know why you have to bring this up now. It's really very cruel of you. I was forced to explain myself in front of a hundred complete strangers. He took an overdose and he died.'

'Was he a drug addict?' Hawthorne asked.

Anne didn't reply.

'That was the natural inference and I think it's what you wanted us to believe. A drug addict takes a drug overdose and he dies. But there are other sorts of addicts.'

I will never forget the pause that followed. It seemed to stitch itself into the very air.

'Gambling addicts, for example.'

That was when Anne Cleary knew it was all over.

'Internet gambling is a horrible thing,' Hawthorne went on, and for once he sounded genuinely sympathetic. 'Your son was one of around three hundred thousand addicts in the country. There are about five hundred deaths a year and most of them are young men, university students, kids living alone. And the big online gambling companies ... they know what they're doing with those bright lights and flashing colours, the personalised texts and emails, the free bets. You must have been sickened when you got an invitation to a literary festival sponsored by Spin-the-wheel.com. I assume they were the same people who killed William.'

Everything in the room had changed. It was like an image on a computer screen that had suddenly frozen. It all looked the same, but I was aware that something had gone terribly wrong.

'He never told me,' Anne said. 'William had always been such a happy boy and of course I knew something was wrong. He'd changed. But I thought it was down to the pressure of starting at university. He'd never lived away from home before. And of course he'd had to borrow the money to pay the tuition fees and that was preying on his mind. It was only after he died that the police found all the evidence on his computer. He'd gone through his savings and he'd maxed out all his credit cards. And he'd sold things.' Until now, Anne had been strangely dispassionate, explaining her past history as if it was unconnected to her. But for the first time her voice cracked. 'He'd sold the watch we'd given him for his eighteenth birthday and the laptop when he'd started university. He'd sold his clothes. All the time, he was getting more and more desperate, but he kept on playing, spinning the wheel in the hope that he would make everything right. And when it got to be too much, he took an overdose of paracetamol. That was the drug that killed him.'

Hawthorne was accusing Anne Cleary of murder, and I had been witness to two shocking deaths. But I felt only pity for her. 'I'm so sorry,' I said.

She stared at me. 'I don't want your pity. I made the decision to commit a crime. It was a dreadful thing to do and I always expected to pay the full price.' Anne turned back to Hawthorne.

'Two crimes,' Hawthorne said. 'You also killed Helen le Mesurier.'

'Yes.'

Anne Cleary hadn't even tried to deny it. She was sitting very still. I was aware of the hollow ticking of the clock on the mantelpiece. I wanted to get up and silence the wretched thing.

'When I heard about Derek Abbott, I thought that might be the end of it as far as I was concerned,' she said. 'But if you've come here to judge me, you're too late. My judgement has already been made.'

'It's not just you, Anne. You weren't alone.'

That jolted her. 'Yes, I was.'

'Do you really think you can lie to me? Even now? You couldn't have tied Charles le Mesurier to that chair without help, even if you had whacked him with a rock first. You also needed someone to persuade Helen le Mesurier to walk into that cave where you were waiting for her. All of this was carefully planned. And not just by you.'

'I killed both those people. I will pay for it.' She looked at him with a growing desperation. 'What more do you want, Mr Hawthorne?'

'Colin Matheson asked me that when I was doing my talk in Alderney,' Hawthorne replied. 'I told him I wanted the truth, and I suppose that's close enough. But actually, it's more than that. I want you to face up to what you did because here you are sitting in this nice house, surrounded by nice things, but you're not nice, are you? You're a killer.'

'You don't think he deserved it? Charles le Mesurier destroyed my son and made money out of his pain – and the pain of hundreds like him! Go on the website. Look at it.'

'I've been on their website. I've seen what you saw and I'm sorry about your boy. I really am. But nobody deserves to die, Anne. You know that, even if you've persuaded yourself otherwise. That was the mistake you made.'

Silence. The clock ticking. Then ...

'Why don't you ask your daughter to come down?'

Anne stiffened. 'She's not here.'

'Her car's parked outside. I've had a friend of mine watching the house since you got back. I thought you would have got that by now. You can't lie to me.'

The door opened and a young woman came in. 'Mum,' she said.

'Don't—' Anne began.

'It's all right, Mum. He knows.'

Kathryn Harris was wearing jeans and a shirt knotted at the waist. She had taken off the overlarge spectacles that she had used to disguise her face and as she sat down I thought how similar the two women were. But then, from the very start I had said that Anne Cleary reminded me of someone's mother. I just hadn't realised whose.

'How did you know?' Kathryn asked Hawthorne.

'That you were related? Well, we could start with your mum's books. I really did love those books, by the way. Me and my son couldn't get enough of them. Bill and Kitty Flashbang.' He glanced at Anne. 'You told Tony that you'd named the two characters after your own kids. Bill was William, obviously. And Kitty ...'

' … Kathryn,' I said.

'Harris is your married name, is that right?'

'Yes.' Kathryn nodded, suddenly fearful. I guessed that her husband knew nothing of all this.

'There were plenty of clues. You look like each other. You've got the same-coloured eyes. You've obviously lived together for a long time, so you talk in the same way. *It's going to be a hot one*. That's how Kathryn described the summer weather when we met her at breakfast. And Anne, you used exactly the same phrase when you asked if you could leave the hotel. *They say it's going to be a hot one, so I might go for a walk*.

'There were other things, too.' Hawthorne was still addressing Anne. 'Marc Bellamy told me that you'd lent Kathryn your pen. That struck me as strange, if it was so precious to you. Right now you were pretending you couldn't even remember her name. And finally, you're both vegetarians.'

Anne had told us she was a vegetarian when we interviewed her at the hotel, but I was sure that Kathryn hadn't provided us with the same information. I thought back. At Southampton Airport she had ordered a cheese salad. At The Divers Inn she had been nibbling a stick of celery. Her breakfast at the hotel had been muesli and yoghurt. Even at The Lookout, after serving steak and kidney puddings, she had helped herself only to a cheese pastry. Never once had I seen her eat any meat or fish.

'Kathryn never did anything!' Anne insisted.

'Let me tell you what you both did,' Hawthorne cut in. His voice was cold. 'My guess is that this all started with you, Anne. You were invited to a literary festival in Alderney, probably at the end of last year, and you noticed that it was being sponsored by Spin-the-wheel.com. I can imagine how angry you must have felt, though probably your first instinct was to forget the whole thing. But then you started thinking. Maybe you could use it to your advantage. Maybe it was a chance to get close to the people who were responsible for the death of your son.

'At about the same time, Kathryn moved in on Marc Bellamy. She happened to be sharing a room with his assistant, who'd just been offered a job on another cookery show. It was a perfect opportunity. Kathryn was a vegetarian; she didn't like meat. But she persuaded Bellamy to take her on and he was delighted because she was asking for so little money. As soon as she was in there, she contacted Judith Matheson and got Marc invited.' He looked at Kathryn for the first time. 'Is that right?'

'I spoke to his publishers,' Kathryn said. 'He had a new book coming out and they thought it was a great idea.'

'The end result was that you both turned up on the island, but as far as everyone was concerned, you were complete strangers. You'd planned what you were going to do down to the last detail, even bringing the parcel tape with you. You can buy Duck Brand in one shop in Oxford, by the way, just down the road from here. I'm sure the owner will remember you – you being a famous author. If not, there are always credit-card slips.'

'I think you've made your point,' Anne said.

'Gambling.' Hawthorne smiled a little sadly. 'That's what this was all about right from the start. I'm surprised you didn't see that, Tony. What was it you found on Charles le Mesurier's Mercedes?'

'A playing card,' I said.

'That's right. And there was another clue on the floor of the Snuggery, after he was killed.'

'A coin.'

'Cards and coins. They could have left a bloody roulette wheel if they'd wanted to make it any more obvious. So here's what was in their heads.' He was talking directly to me now, ignoring Anne and Kathryn. 'They'd come to Alderney. Somehow, they'd get le Mesurier on his own. They'd tie him down and they'd make him pay for what he'd done to William. And as it happened, le Mesurier played right into their hands. He took a fancy to Kathryn, which made the whole thing a lot easier. But here's something else you've got to understand, Tony. When they came to Alderney, they only had one target: le Mesurier. We were both there when that changed and – I hate to say this, mate – once again you sort of talked out of turn.'

My heart sank. 'What did I say this time?'

'The three of us – you, me and Anne – arrived at The Lookout at about the same time. Anne stopped in the hallway. She'd seen something that had shocked her.'

I remembered. 'It was Derek Abbott talking to Helen le Mesurier.'

'That's right. But it wasn't Derek that she recognised. It was Helen! You've got to remember that Helen wasn't seen out with her husband very often. They had separate lives. At the same time, she was "the face that launched a thousand chips". She'd been an actress and he'd employed her to work on his website. If you check it out, you can still see her now. She's the one spinning the wheel. She's the one pouting and giving the boys the come-on. All very sexy and sultry, and she was probably William's pin-up. Anne recognised her at once. And she was shocked.'

'But she said she'd met Derek in prison!'

'No, mate. You suggested that she might have met him in prison and she grabbed at that to explain why she was so surprised. *I think you're right. That's exactly where I met him.* Of course, later on, she had to say that maybe, after all, he hadn't been in one of her reading groups ... just in case we asked him and he denied it.

'Meanwhile, Kathryn had seen what had happened. She had arrived at the house earlier and she had also recognised Helen. That's why she came rushing over with the drinks and burbled on about the food. She hadn't been able to warn Anne that Helen would be there. So she came over to rescue her before she gave herself away.'

Mother and daughter were listening to all this in silence. They weren't looking at each other. They were barely breathing.

'Anyway, that was when one murder became two murders,' Hawthorne went on. 'And let's see how the rest of the evening plays out.

'At nine twenty-five, Anne leaves the party. She has a fake conversation with Kathryn which establishes the exact time and also makes it clear that she leaves long before the murder takes place. She does the same thing with the minibus driver, Tom McKinley. She tells him that she's in a hurry to get back to the hotel. She's nervous. But that's ridiculous! The hotel's only ten minutes away and she's got thirty-five minutes to get there. She wants him to remember her. She knows that we'll talk to him.'

'She said he was standing by the door,' I said.

'Yes – but not the door of the minibus. McKinley told you he met her coming out of the house ... so it must have been the front door, which gives her a bit more room for manoeuvre. It was too dark to see who was actually on the bus. So all she did was nip out, wait a moment and then slip back into the house again. If anyone had seen her, she could just say that she'd forgotten something. But there were still a hundred people at the party. Who was going to notice one person moving in a crowd?'

It was true. I'd been in the hallway myself at that time. But I'd had my head buried in Marc Bellamy's cookbook and then I'd been talking to Maïssa Lamar. I hadn't seen her.

'Anne Cleary has two people who will swear she's left the house,' Hawthorne went on. 'She tracks back through the kitchen and straight out along the edge of the garden and across to the Snuggery. She knows that Charles le Mesurier is going to be coming there because he's already arranged a meeting with Kathryn and she's agreed.'

'But I spoke to her!' I said. 'I went into the kitchen. She was almost in tears.'

'I think what you saw was an act, Tony. In fact, she couldn't have been happier. Le Mesurier had played right into her hands.

'At ten to ten, le Mesurier goes to the Snuggery and Derek Abbott goes with him. They're still friends. They're going to take cocaine together. Maybe they notice Elizabeth Lovell in the garden, but neither of them is aware that she can actually see them. It's only when they're inside the Snuggery, and perhaps after they've had a couple of lines, that Derek demands the £20,000 that he's owed for his part in blackmailing Colin Matheson. He'd had to pretend to be the bad guy. He was the one with the hidden camera. He was the one who would tell Charles le Mesurier that Colin was having an affair with Helen. Of course, as we now know, all three of them – Charles, Helen and Derek – were in it together.

'Anyway, Derek wants his £20,000, which is actually going to be his pay-off. Le Mesurier fires him, and Anne hears the entire conversation, hiding behind one of those velvet curtains. Why would Charles le Mesurier have told her anything about Abbott at the party? That never made any sense. But it's a gift as far as she's concerned. When she tells us that le Mesurier complained about Abbott earlier in the evening, it's as if she's looking into the future, using her knowledge of what happened at ten o'clock to point the finger at a known criminal and a man who's hated across the whole island.

'In fact, le Mesurier is very much alive when Derek leaves the Snuggery. At that moment, Helen le Mesurier looks out of her bedroom window and later on she'll assume that since he was there just before her husband died, he must be the one who killed him. That's why she sends Derek a text. And that's what will eventually get her killed.

'So now everything is set up. Charles le Mesurier is on his own in the Snuggery, high on cocaine, waiting for his new girlfriend to arrive. But the moment Kathryn appears, Anne steps out from her hiding place and stuns him with a rock or a brick or whatever she's picked up from the garden. Together, the two women drag him into the chair and tie him down with the parcel tape. But they leave one hand free.'

'Why?' I couldn't help myself. 'Why did they do that?'

'I've told you, mate. This is all about gambling. So what they did at the very end was give Charles le Mesurier a taste of his own medicine. Think about it! He's tied to a chair. His head's been cracked open. He's frightened and in pain and worse than that, he's got two loony women facing him and one of them has got the paperknife that she's nicked from his study. Kathryn could have done that any time during the day. But they want the punishment to fit the crime, so they give him one chance. Just like William Cleary, they're going to let him gamble for his life.'

Suddenly I saw it. 'Heads or tails,' I said.

'They'd nicked a coin from Maïssa's handbag in the hall. It's got a tree on one side and a map of Europe on the other, so it's not exactly heads or tails, but it makes sense to use a foreign coin, one that can't be connected to them, and they also wipe it clean to make sure it didn't have their finger-prints.' For the first time in a while, he looked at Anne. 'Am I right?'

'I wanted him to know what it felt like ... to gamble for his life,' Anne said. 'I left his hand free so that he could toss the coin. I told him to call and that if he got it right, I would let him go.'

'And would you have?'

'Of course not. But it didn't matter anyway. He couldn't do it.'

Right then, I saw the whole dreadful scene. Charles le Mesurier, tied to the chair, sitting in his Snuggery, still half stunned from the blow he had received. Kathryn with the knife at his throat. Anne balancing the two-euro coin on his thumb, forcing him to toss it and call. Screaming at him: 'Heads or tails? Heads or tails?' Terrified. But Charles finally doing what he was told, trying to get the coin to spin, hoping to save his own life.

'He dropped it,' Anne said. 'He tried to toss the coin but it fell onto the carpet and we couldn't find it.'

'And then you killed him.'

'Yes, Mr Hawthorne. I killed him. Not Kathryn. She had left by then.'

'We'll get back to that later, shall we?' Hawthorne continued his explanation. 'It was Helen's turn next. Luck was still with you because Helen had seen Derek Abbott out of the bedroom window and arranged to meet him. You'd never have been able to get back into the house with all the police around, but you decided to watch the house in the hope that she'd step out for a breath of fresh air. When she set off for Quesnard Cottage, you followed her.'

'How did they get her into the cave?' I asked.

'That's a good question,' Hawthorne said.

'You've got this part of it wrong, Mr Hawthorne,' Anne replied, quite calmly. 'Kathryn wasn't with me on the Sunday. You're right that I followed Mrs le Mesurier. I caught up with her before she reached the quarry and the railway line and we walked together, chatting quite normally. She mentioned the cave and I asked her to show it to me. It was a little out of her way, but I said I was nervous to go in on my own, so she took me to the entrance. That was where I hit her. I then carried her inside and finished the job inside.'

Was she telling the truth? I'm not sure that Anne Cleary would have been strong enough to carry Helen le Mesurier all the way down the dark passage that led into the rock face. But Hawthorne didn't challenge her. 'Did she deserve to die too?' he asked.

361

'She was just as guilty as him,' Anne said. But I thought she sounded less sure.

'She was an actress, playing a part.'

'My son died. It destroyed my marriage. I have never had a moment's peace ever since.'

'They were horrible people,' Kathryn agreed.

'I don't want you to say anything, Kitty! It's very important that you understand that, now and moving forward.' Her mother had drawn herself up in her seat. She knew exactly what she was going to say. Even as Hawthorne had been speaking, she had rehearsed it. 'Could you please get the letter off the sideboard?' she asked.

'Mum ...'

'Please, dear.'

Kathryn wasn't happy, but she got up and did as she was told. She handed her mother an envelope.

'This may not make a great deal of difference to what you decide to do, Mr Hawthorne,' Anne said. 'For what it's worth, I accept your conclusion. What I did was wrong and I expect to pay. Except that it seems I am paying already.'

She held out the letter. Hawthorne took it, a single typed page. I saw the NHS logo at the top.

'You have heart disease,' he said.

'Left ventricular systolic dysfunction, to be precise,' Anne told him. 'I'm taking various medications ... enzyme inhibitors and angiotensin receptor blockers. But my prognosis is not good. I have weeks, maybe months. It could just be days.'

I knew she was telling the truth. I remembered her breath-lessness and the so-called antibiotics she had mentioned. On the morning after the murder, she'd said she had to leave the island for a doctor's appointment and that was probably true.

'This isn't a payment,' Hawthorne said.

'I'm sorry?'

'If you're suggesting to me that you were sent this heart condition as a punishment for what you intended to do, that makes as much sense as Elizabeth Lovell and her stupid ghosts.'

'Does it matter what I call it? The point I am making, and the only point that should be of interest to you, is that I am going to die very soon.' She half smiled. 'Funnily enough, what I told you about my deal with Disney was true. It just arrived a little too late to be of any use to me.'

'Go on.'

'I won't stand trial. I certainly won't go to prison. I knew that long before I went to Alderney.'

'It was part of the reason *why* you went.'

'Yes. When the doctor told me that my time was limited, I thought a lot about William and how I might make amends. And then, when I was asked to come to Alderney and I saw Spin-the-wheel on the invitation, it felt like it was meant. I had been given an opportunity, in the last days of my life, to take some sort of action ... Punishment, retribution. Call it what you like.'

Hawthorne briefly considered what he had just been told. 'So what are you suggesting, Anne?'

'I killed Charles le Mesurier. I also killed Helen le Mesurier. Kathryn wasn't even there when the second crime took place.'

'You say ...'

'I will confess to both murders. That was always my intention.'

'Until Derek Abbott threw himself off a cliff.'

'Well, can you really blame me for allowing that to change my mind?'

'I don't blame you for that, Anne. I blame you for the vicious, premeditated murders of two people.'

'You're right. I planned them. I arranged them. I took the knife and the coin. It was all exactly as you described. But Kathryn—'

'—was an accessory to murder. That still carries a life sentence.'

'You don't need to tell anyone about her. Kathryn lost a brother she loved. She hardly sees her father and she's about to lose her mother. Hasn't she suffered enough? She's married to a good man, a GP. She wants to start a family. What good will it do, putting her behind bars? Please. I'm begging you. Show a little mercy. As far as I can tell, the police have closed the file following the death of Derek Abbott.' She reached out and took her daughter's hand. 'Why can't you just leave us alone?'

Hawthorne didn't need to think about what she had just said, not even for a minute. He stood up.

'I'm sorry,' he said. 'I can't do that. You're asking me to judge you, but that's not my job. My job was to find the truth and that's what I've done. What happens next isn't up to me.' He looked around him one last time. 'You have to go to the police and tell them what you did. Maybe you'll be able to persuade them that Kathryn had nothing – or very little – to do with it. I'll be honest and tell you I don't really care what happens. But it's like I've said. It's not my decision.'

Anne nodded slowly. 'I understand. How long can you give me?'

'The sooner you do it, the easier it will be.'

'Yes. That's probably true.'

'There is one last thing …'

'What's that, Mr Hawthorne?'

Hawthorne smiled. 'My son couldn't believe I was seeing you today. He's grown out of your books now, but he's still a big fan.'

I couldn't believe what I was seeing. Hawthorne had taken a book out of his inside pocket. It had a brightly coloured picture of two children and a pirate ship on the cover. A one-eyed pirate was waving a sword. The book was called *Flashbang Trouble*, the book that he had mentioned at Southampton and which had made his son laugh out loud. He also had a pen.

'Could you sign it for him?' he asked.

Anne stared for a moment, then took the book and the pen. 'Of course,' she said. 'What's his name?'

'As a matter of fact, he's called William too.'

'Oh.'

I saw her write a message. *To William, with love. Keep reading! Anne Cleary*. She handed it back.

'Thank you,' Hawthorne said.

'It's a pleasure, Mr Hawthorne.'

We left.

24

A Postcard from Alderney

I have to make a confession. All along I'd thought that the real killer of Charles and Helen le Mesurier was Terry, our taxi driver. It was a thought that I'd never articulated – it lurked somewhere in the back of my mind – but he did actually have a motive: he'd mentioned that Charles le Mesurier had been planning to start a new taxi service that would have been enough to put him out of business. And it seemed more than coincidental that he had been present at the times of both murders. He had been outside The Lookout when Charles was killed and, by his own admission, he had driven past when Helen left the next day. I was just glad that I had never mentioned any of this to Hawthorne. I would have looked ridiculous.

In the days that followed our visit to Summertown, I found myself thinking about Anne Cleary a great deal. I've often wondered why people become murderers and I was shocked that I had met her years before, when she had been as ordinary as me, before she had allowed her son's death to destroy her own life. I couldn't get her out of my head: the ticking clock, the porcelain figures, the candles. She was gentler – and more genteel – than anyone I'd ever met. And yet, in Alderney, she had let loose a torrent of blood.

Was Hawthorne right to make the decision he had made?

He could have remained silent. Charles and Helen le Mesurier, two not very pleasant people, were dead and nothing was going to bring them back to life again. They were responsible for the suicide of Anne's son and had probably harmed the lives of countless others – not that I'd thought twice before accepting an invitation to a literary festival sponsored by Spin-the-wheel.com. They had conspired to compromise Colin Matheson. A husband selling his wife, a wife cheerfully prostituting herself for her husband. They had blackmailed Colin and probably destroyed his marriage. They would have been happy to see war graves desecrated and an island torn apart – figuratively and literally – by a power line if it made money for them.

As far as the police were concerned, the case was closed. Derek Abbott, another unpleasant man, had been wrongly identified as the killer and he wasn't going to complain about it any time soon. Anne Cleary was terminally ill. What exactly was there to be gained by dragging her daughter through the courts and putting her in jail?

Hawthorne had chosen to take the moral high ground, which was all very well, but I couldn't forget the part he had played in all this. Although I hadn't challenged him, I was almost certain that he had visited Derek Abbott and told him that the police had all the evidence they needed to make an arrest. Abbott had already spent six months in jail and he had told us that he would never go back. I remembered what he had said. He had used almost exactly the same words as he had written on his suicide note. *I will never go back to prison. I don't care what happens to me in my life, but I will never let that happen again.* Had Hawthorne actually encouraged him to throw himself off the cliff at Gannet Rock? Whatever had passed between them, he had been complicit in the other man's death and he was surely in no position to pass judgement on either Anne Cleary or her daughter.

And yet perhaps he was vindicated by what happened next.

I'm writing this a whole year after the events I have described and I can tell you that Anne Cleary did indeed go to the police and made a full confession to both the murders. As a result, both she and her daughter were arrested.

Anne did not stand trial. She suffered a massive heart attack while she was still in remand and died just a month after we had visited her at her Summertown home. That left Kathryn Harris to face justice alone and she duly went on trial, charged with being an accessory to murder. I saw photographs of her outside the courthouse with her husband, Dr Michael Harris. They looked like any other young couple, very much in love, clutching each other as they faced the press pack.

Kathryn Harris was found not guilty. I can't say I followed the entire case, but I understand it turned on a single issue. In the end, the prosecution was unable to prove that Anne Cleary had informed her daughter that she actually intended to kill Charles and Helen le Mesurier. Kathryn insisted that she had thought her mother had planned only to confront Charles le Mesurier for his part in her brother's death, but at the last minute (after Kathryn had left the Snuggery) she must have lost control and taken her bloody revenge. Kathryn broke down in court. She said she had been shocked to hear what her mother had done and that she was ashamed to have been a part of it.

I know it sounds improbable as I write it here, but then the law is often hard to fathom. The jury was sympathetic and, most significantly, the main witnesses were dead so in the end they believed her. I thought Hawthorne might have been called to give evidence. Deputy Chief Torode certainly turned up, although by then he was plain Mr Torode. He had been quietly sacked for incompetence.

Kathryn might have been charged with various lesser offences, such as lying to the police or obstructing the course of justice. But there was no real appetite to go after her. The press and the public were also on her side ('GP'S WIFE TRAPPED BY A MOTHER'S MADNESS'), and anyway, thanks to Hawthorne, she had voluntarily turned herself in just two days after she had left Alderney. The authorities must have decided that pursuing her would only have been seen as vindictive.

Did she get away with murder?

I'm fairly sure that Kathryn was there when Charles le Mesurier died. Maybe she was laughing as the knife went in. Maybe she was the one holding it. And I still don't fully believe Anne's account of the murder of Helen le Mesurier. Helen was on her way to an important meeting. She believed that Derek Abbott had been involved in her husband's death. Would she really have taken a diversion down a disused railway to show Anne the entrance to the cave? It was much more likely that, once again, mother and daughter were working in tandem. Anne could have told Helen that her daughter was inside the cave, that she had taken a fall and was lying there, injured. They could have waylaid her and led her in at knifepoint. They could even have knocked her out and carried her between them.

I think Anne lied to us because she was aware of the difference between the two crimes. The murder of Charles le Mesurier was wicked enough, but the death of his wife was somehow worse. Hawthorne had got it exactly right. Helen was an actress playing a part. Her only crime was that she had never considered the consequences.

But all of this is irrelevant. The point is that Hawthorne had no choice as to whether Kathryn should face trial or not. It was not his decision to make and in the end he achieved exactly the outcome he might have wanted without having to compromise himself. Kathryn was acquitted. Hawthorne was far from straightforward, but he was always honest and I was glad that things worked out the way they did.

I was particularly busy when I got back from Alderney. It was always the same. If I took a few days off, I would need a whole week to catch up, and to make matters worse, I now knew that I would have to write a third book about Hawthorne, which only added to the pressure to finish the second. I had decided to call it *The Sentence is Death*, although I was already beginning to worry that quite soon I would run out of titles with grammatical allusions.

I was working in my office one morning when my wife popped in with the mail – the usual bills, bank statements and circulars. (I used to look forward to the mail when I was young, but nowadays it's nearly all dreary.)

Rifling through them, I noticed a postcard with a picture of Fort Clonque on the western tip of Alderney. I thought at first it might be fan mail and reached for it straight away. I turned it over and even before I read the brief message, I recognised Derek Abbott's handwriting. He had sent the card to my publishers at Penguin Random House and someone had forwarded it to me. There were just four words. It read:

Ask Hawthorne about Reeth.

Sitting at my desk, I felt a chill in the pit of my stomach. I remembered the postcards that had been sitting on the desk in Derek Abbott's living room. He had written his suicide note on the back of one of them, but then he must have decided to write a second card to me. He knew I was planning several books about Hawthorne. Even as he had left this world, he had wanted to leave some small measure of pain behind.

Reeth.

I have already mentioned the evening at the Station Inn in the Yorkshire village of Ribblehead, when Hawthorne and I were investigating the murder of Richard Pryce. We had travelled there to find out more about a potholing accident that had taken place a few years before and we were having dinner together when a man had come up to us and introduced himself as Mike Carlyle. He had addressed Hawthorne as 'Billy' – which wasn't his name, but was, now I thought about it, the name of his son. And what had the man said? I opened the notebook that I always kept on my desk and found the page.

'You weren't in Reeth?'

'No,' Hawthorne had replied. *'I don't know what you're talking about. I'm just up from London. I've never been to anywhere called Reeth.'*

At the time, I'd assumed that Mike Carlyle had mistaken Hawthorne for someone else and had put the whole thing out of my mind.

But now this.

Ask Hawthorne about Reeth.

It was clear to me that Hawthorne hadn't pushed Derek Abbott down a flight of stairs because he disliked what he represented. The two men had known each other before. I remembered what had happened in Abbott's house just before we left. Abbott had recognised him. I had seen it for myself, the moment when he had realised that he and Hawthorne had a shared history that went all the way back to Reeth. How extraordinary that in the last moments of his life, just before he left to throw himself off Gannet Rock, he should have decided to take this one, final shot at revenge.

I wasn't sure that I wanted to know any more, but I couldn't stop myself. I clicked on my laptop and went to yorkshirevillages.org.

Tucked away in the corner of Arkengarthdale and Swaledale, the village of Reeth is an attractive tourist centre with a popular market every Friday. It has been described as a heaven for cyclists ... The description went on like that for about half a page, with a couple of pictures: a handsome church, a high street, the surrounding Dales. Other websites talked about hiking trails, campsites, the Black Bull pub. I widened my search on Google but nothing of any interest seemed to have happened there. It was not mentioned in any newspaper stories. Nobody famous had lived or died there. It seemed to be a village completely at peace with itself.

What could I do? I had no way of finding Mike Carlyle and I obviously wasn't going to ask Hawthorne. I thought for a moment, turning the postcard over in my hands.

Then I slid it into my notebook, closed it and went back to work.

Writers often feel isolated and alone but the truth is that producing a book is a huge team effort.

It's my pleasure to acknowledge the fantastic support I've been given in the long journey from idea to manuscript to finished publication.

PUBLISHER
Selina Walker

EDITORIAL
Joanna Taylor
Caroline Johnson

DESIGN
Glenn O'Neill

PRODUCTION
Linda Hodgson
Helen Wynn-Smith

UK SALES
Mat Watterson
Claire Simmonds
Olivia Allen
Rachel Campbell

INTERNATIONAL SALES
Cara Conquest
Barbora Sabolova
Laura Ricchetti

PUBLICITY
Charlotte Bush
Anna Gibson

MARKETING
Rebecca Ikin
Sam Rees-Williams

AUDIO
James Keyte
Roy Macmillan

The next thrilling Hawthorne mystery

THE TWIST OF A KNIFE

PRE-ORDER
YOUR COPY NOW

Out 18 August 2022

Stay tuned for updates with
@AnthonyHorowitz and @centurybooksuk